MISTRESS BRIDGET

and Other Tales

MISTRESS BRIDGET

and Other Tales

E. YOLLAND

Edited and with an introduction by

Gina R. Collia

Published by Nezu Press
Queensgate House,
48 Queen Street,
Exeter, Devon,
EX4 3SR,
United Kingdom.

This edition published 2023.
Editorial material and introduction © Gina R. Collia 2023.
Mistress Bridget first published by F. V. White & Co., 1898.
Short stories: 'The Miser's Secret', *Belgravia*, December 1892;
'Only a Smudge!', *Belgravia*, August 1893; 'Impostors?',
Belgravia, April 1894; 'The Secret of the Dead', *Belgravia*,
August 1895; 'Autumn Clouds', *Belgravia*, October 1895; 'On
the Spur of the Moment', *Heart and Hand,* April 1896; 'In
the Days of the Cagots', *Belgravia,* November 1896.

ISBN-13: 978-1-7393921-2-3

In the interest of preserving the original texts, they have not been altered. Fonts used have been chosen to emulate those of the original publications. The punctuation and spelling of the originals have been maintained, and the original formatting has been used wherever possible. Only very minor publisher errors in the original texts have been corrected.

CONTENTS

In Search of E. Yolland

by Gina R. Collia

It is a sad fact that countless books—possibly exceptional ones at that—have been lost to the passage of time; it is equally sad that many authors have suffered the same fate, even if their books have managed somehow, albeit in extremely small numbers in many cases, to survive. When I began looking for information about the author of *Mistress Bridget*, I discovered that not a single fact, not even the tiniest tidbit of information, had been discovered to shed light on E. Yolland's actual identity. There was no clue to the writer's full name or sex, let alone anything more substantial. After reading *Mistress Bridget*, I read all of the author's short stories, and I came to the conclusion that the only thing to do—the only *polite* thing, really, as I'd enjoyed reading her work so much—was to begin my own personal quest to find out who E. Yolland was—to reunite the writing with its writer.

If the publication notices and book reviews that appeared in contemporary newspapers are anything to go by, at the time *Mistress Bridget* first appeared readers were as much in the dark about the identity of E. Yolland as we have been until now; the author's various novels and short stories were attributed to both Mr and Miss Yolland at one time or another. But there was one organisation that did, at the time, appear to know who E. Yolland was. The Society of Authors was founded in 1884, and in 1890 it began producing a quarterly journal: *The Author*. Amongst other things, in its early days the journal began to include lists of its subscribers, and it was amongst the names in these lists that I found the first mentions of Miss E.

Yolland. Our author was an author*ess*, and she was an annual donor to the society's pension fund between 1908 and 1921.

E. Yolland's first published works were short stories, the earliest of which, 'The Miser's Secret', appeared in *Belgravia*, the illustrated monthly magazine, in December 1892. Her last published work was the novel *The Struggle for the Crown: A Romance of the Seventeenth Century*, which was published by Lynwood & Co., Ltd. in 1912. In all, between 1892 and 1912 she produced seven short stories and seven novels, and she appears to have remained active in, or at least connected to, the writing world until 1921, after which time her name disappeared from The Society of Authors' donor lists.

As to the author's background, while reading *Mistress Bridget* I became convinced that she wrote with the knowledge of a resident of Somerset or the neighbouring counties rather than a visitor to the area; I say this as one who lived in and just outside Somerset for more than two decades. Several real locations feature in the book, in some cases with their names only slightly altered, including Withycombe (Rithycombe in the book), Weston (Watson), Dunster (Dunstar), Lyng, Bridgewater and Bristol. In addition to her knowledge of these towns and villages, she appeared to have had a keen interest in English history, and she was obviously educated. Also, the religious references in some of her writing, especially her short story 'Autumn Clouds', published in *Belgravia* in October 1895, suggested that she was also a devout Christian with a firm belief in the survival of the human soul.

So, working on the basis that E. Yolland was old enough to produce a short story in 1892, ceased writing in 1921, was educated, lived at some point in or near Somerset, and may have been active in the church, I headed off to the various registers of births, deaths and marriages, the census returns and the newspaper archives.

I first encountered Mrs Ehretia Yolland at the point where her personal story came to an end, in the pages of the *England & Wales National Probate Calendar*.[1] When she died, on 9 March 1922, she was a widow living in Gloucestershire in the village of Bitton, which is around seven miles from the centre of Bristol, half way between there and Bath. She had reached the ripe old age of eighty-two.[2] Her estate (valued at £3,099 13s and 7d, which would be around £90,000 now) was left to her niece and nephew, Kathleen and George Carwardine Francis. A search of the various registers revealed that Kathleen and George were the children of George and Ann Francis, and the latter had had a younger sister: Ehretia Carwardine.

Ehretia Carwardine was born on 13 April 1839.[3] She was the sixth child of Anne Carwardine (née Rogers) and Reverend John Bryan Carwardine,[4] rector of St. Lawrence, in the Maldon district of Essex. Ehretia's paternal grandmother, Anne Carwardine (1752-1817), had had her portrait painted by George Romney (1734-1802), at one time the most fashionable portrait painter of the day; the artist was a close friend of Anne's husband, Rev. Thomas Carwardine (1734-1824), who was a descendant of Sir Thomas Carwardine, Master of the Revels to King Henry VIII.[5] Apparently, at one time the family also claimed a distant connection to Oliver Cromwell,[6] which might explain Ehretia's interest in the English Civil War.

Ehretia's childhood was spent at the rectory of St. Lawrence, south of the Blackwater Estuary, until, in 1850, at the age of eleven, she and her younger sister Mary were sent away to boarding school. Osborne House School, at 119 New London Road in Chelmsford, was run by Sarah Anne Matson, with the assistance of her younger sisters Caroline and Frances Octavia.[7] The young ladies enrolled at the school received 'a solid English education', combining 'the Continental with the English mode of education'; they were taught

French, German, Italian and drawing.[8] Sarah Anne Matson was an author herself; *An Extract for Every Day in the Year* was published by J. F. Shaw in 1850, the year her school opened, and in 1859 Longman published *Three Hundred Questions and Answers on Various Subjects*, the contents of which had originally been selected for the use of her own pupils.

Bartholomew Stephen Yolland was born on 4 July 1834 in Anderby in Lincolnshire.[9] His father, Rev. John Yolland, was curate of Huxham and Poltimore in Devon,[10] and his mother, Elizabeth Yolland (née Goe), was the daughter of Rev. Bartholomew Goe, vicar of Boston in Lincolnshire.[11] Bartholomew became a student of Lincoln College, Oxford, in 1852, receiving his bachelor's degree in 1857 and his masters in 1859.[12] And in March 1860, he became curate of Earls Colne in Essex,[13] which is where he met Ehretia Carwardine, his future wife.

Ehretia's family had long been connected with the village of Earls Colne; her grandfather Rev. Thomas Carwardine was vicar of Earls Colne from 1786 until his death in 1824, and her uncle Henry Holgate Carwardine became Lord of the Manor in 1825,[14] rebuilt the Priory and practised as a surgeon there until his death in 1867.[15] Apparently, he was also a poet and a good friend of Samuel Taylor Coleridge, with whom he exchanged poetry tips.[16]

Ehretia and Bartholomew were married on 9 April 1861 at St Nicolas' Church, Witham.[17] Later that year, they moved to Thornton le Moor in Lincolnshire, and their first child, John, was born on Christmas Day 1861 at Thornton Rectory.[18] Bartholomew became curate of that parish the following February,[19] and the Yollands remained in Lincolnshire until 1865, adding two daughters, Elizabeth and Alice, to their family while they were there, in January 1863 and July 1864 respectively.

Ehretia was pregnant with the couple's fourth child when Bartholomew was appointed to the curacy of Great Waltham in Essex, and Frances was born there in January 1866.[20] The following January, his brother Field was born,[21] and two years later William joined the little family.[22] A Victorian clergyman's life was a busy one, as was his wife's. In addition to bringing up young children (admittedly, with the assistance of a nursemaid), there were church duties to carry out, various charitable works to perform and good causes to support, and the Yollands were regular attendees at the local musical and literary events, amateur theatricals and Great Waltham Penny Readings; the latter took place at the National Schoolroom and were extremely popular, always attracting large audiences. Bartholomew often took part in the various local entertainments, giving readings of humorous stories or poetry, including selections from Wordsworth. Apparently, his readings of 'The Wonderful History of Master Mouse' and 'An Old Sailor's Yarn' created 'much merriment, calling into action the risible powers of the audience.'[23]

In May 1870, the foundation stone of St. John's was laid at Ford End, Great Waltham, with much ceremony; it was consecrated by the Lord Bishop of Rochester and witnessed by a large crowd, including 'the *elite* of the neighbourhood'.[24] Apparently, during the previous two years church services had been carried out in a barn.[25] In June the following year, Bartholomew was appointed vicar of the new church,[26] and the Yollands moved to the new vicarage. In the October of the same year, the couple's seventh child, named Ehretia after her mother, was born.[27] It must have been a time of great celebration, but the Yollands' happiness was to be short-lived. On 15 November 1871, Ehretia's father died, and just four months later, on 14 February, six-year-old Frances Yolland passed away at the vicarage 'of malignant sore throat'.[28]

By the beginning of 1880, the Yollands had three more children: Stephen, Beatrice and Henry, born in July 1874, November 1876 and February 1878 respectively.[29] And in the August of that year another daughter, Mary, was born.[30] As was customary for a clerical family, all of the Yollands were active in the church. And by the end of 1880, the efforts of Bartholomew, Ehretia, their children and all of the good reverend's parishioners were focused on raising £100 for the purchase of two new church bells for St. John's. By July the following year, the church bells had increased in number to five; on 14 July, to celebrate the occasion, the Essex Association of Change Ringers rang the bells for two and a half hours, with brief intermissions. The lessons were read by the Yolland's oldest son, John, who also played the organ.[31]

In January 1882, John, who was twenty years old by then and under articles with Mr Edwin Walter (of Wade, Wix and Wade, Solicitors, Great Dunmow), sat the intermediate examination of the Law Society; one month later he received the news that he had passed.[32] And by the end of that year, the church at Ford End had another bell, due mainly to John's effort in raising the necessary funds; the inauguration took place on 23 December, when all six bells were heard together for the first time.[33]

In 1884, life at the vicarage took a turn for the worse. On the afternoon of 21 July, Bartholomew was driving to Chelmsford with two of his daughters and his groom when he encountered a bicyclist travelling at speed. The reverend managed to overtake safely, but the bicyclist began ringing his bell, which startled the horse and set it off at a gallop towards a five-foot-deep, water-filled ditch.[34] Bartholomew, his daughters, the groom, the horse and the party's luggage were submerged in slimy, black water. Nobody was seriously injured, and the horse received only a few small leg wounds, but poor Alice Yolland, already in delicate health, was terrified and exhausted by the time she was rescued. And the carriage they had been riding in was left an utter wreck. Less than four months later, on 8 October, John Yolland, the son who had shown so much promise, died at just twenty-two years of age.[35] The following year, Alice Yolland, who had been so effected by the road accident, passed away at the age of twenty-one on 18 July.[36]

In September 1885, a public argument took place, within the pages of the local newspapers, between Bartholomew and Rev. J. C. Cox concerning a political meeting that took place on the 16th of that month in Felsted in Essex. Bartholomew and Ehretia had been invited to attend the meeting by one of its promoters, but on arriving were asked to leave in an unpleasant manner by Rev. Cox.[37] The Yollands weren't the only attendees who were put out by the poor behaviour of Rev. Cox, who appears to have paid particular attention to evicting ladies from the meeting,[38] and Bartholomew's wasn't the only letter of complaint that appeared in the local newspapers. In Cox's public response, he claimed to have 'expressed the surprise [he] felt at seeing Mrs. Yolland at an evening political meeting,'[39] and insisted that he would do exactly the same thing again tomorrow if necessary. Here, I am including a short excerpt from a letter sent by Bartholomew to the *Chelmsford Chronicle,* as it gives us quite an insight into Ehretia's husband's views on the status of women:

'I did not hear you "express surprise at seeing Mrs. Yolland at an evening political meeting," and I think if I had I should have regarded it rather as an impertinence. I feel somewhat surprised that you did not advise certain ladies of your own parish to retire, as you are so decidedly of the opinion that the attendance of ladies on such occasions is a matter of questionable propriety.

There was, indeed, much confusion and disturbance at Felsted, which made the meeting uncomfortable both to ladies and gentlemen also."[40]

Ehretia's husband was active politically and regularly attended political meetings, and he encouraged his wife to be equally active, despite the fact that she was at that time denied the vote. As one of the correspondents involved in the argument at the time pointed out, if women were eventually to be called on to vote, they would not know what to do with that vote if they were denied access to political meetings.

On 30 August 1886, the Yolland's daughter Ehretia died; she was two months shy of her fifteenth birthday.[41] Two months later, Bartholomew was offered the rectory of Proston, Suffolk. After taking medical advice, he turned down the living on account of the delicate state of his family's health.[42] The following year, however, he accepted the position of vicar of Doynton, near Bath.[43] On 10 April 1887, as Ehretia and Bartholomew were preparing for the family's departure to the new parish, their eldest daughter, Elizabeth, passed away; she was twenty-four years old.[44]

On 15 May 1887, Bartholomew gave his farewell address at a special evening service attended by around four hundred people.[45] Then, after sixteen years at the rectory at Ford End, the Yollands left friends and everything they knew behind and travelled across the country to begin anew, arriving at the Royal Station Hotel in Bath during the last week of May.[46] Just over two months later, on 8 August, William Yolland died at the age of eighteen.[47]

In December 1888, Field Yolland became a student at Lichfield Theological College, in preparation for taking holy orders.[48] He was supposed to remain at the college for two years, but in 1889 he left England for British Colombia, Canada. Two years later, he became curate of St. James' in Vancouver.[49] A year after Field's departure, on 26 Aug 1890, his brother Stephen died at the age of twenty-six.[50] By the end of 1890, Ehretia and Bartholomew had lost all but four of their children, and their oldest living son was now residing overseas, never to return to England.

Bartholomew Stephen Yolland died on 13 October 1891; he was 57 years old.[51] Of course, Ehretia and her family could not continue to live at the rectory after her husband's death; that was needed for the new vicar. So, on 24 November an auction was held to dispose of furniture and other possessions that the remaining Yollands could not take with them to their new home, including a pony, gig and harness,[52] and the rectory at Doynton was left empty by Christmas that year.

One year later, short stories by E. Yolland began to appear in the illustrated monthly periodical *Belgravia*; the first, 'The Miser's Secret', a tale of murderous wreckers, religious persecution and a hidden inheritance, was published in the December edition and includes a slight supernatural element. The following year, 'Only a Smudge!', another tale with supernatural undertones, in which an inheritance is again the central theme, appeared in the August edition. And in April 1894, 'Impostors?' was published; it contains no hint of the supernatural but again focuses on an inheritance, this time the lengths that three young sisters are forced to go to in order to inherit their deceased Aunt Maria's fortune.

In 1895, two stories were published in *Belgravia*: 'The Secret of the Dead' in August and 'Autumn Clouds' in October. In the former, the narrator is on a walking holiday in Derbyshire when he comes across a quaint old church nestled in a hillside. Tired from the day's trudging, he goes inside to rest and is startled when a figure from a carved stone tomb appears to come to life before him:

'The kneeling lady rose swiftly from beside the coffer, and fell almost prostrate at my feet with thin hands raised in piteous prayer, and heavy tears trickling down the saddest face I ever saw. I rubbed my eyes to clear my vision, and with a start jumped up from what I suppose you will call a *doze*. I think otherwise, but that matters not.'

'Autumn Clouds' is a tale of pure fancy, in which rainclouds are worked by means of internal reservoirs and syringes. In it, a young cloud, going out into the sky during a storm for the first time, is horrified by the scenes of human suffering he sees below him. He sees a world filled with inequality, where, during a drought, 'the poor and the feeble had suffered greatly' while 'the rich could still buy their water.' It is an overtly religious story and, whilst inventive—thunder and lightning are created by a thunder-car and the clouds drench the earth with their 'great squirts'—it is Ehretia's least successful.

Two stories appeared in 1896: 'On the Spur of the Moment' in the April issue of *Heart and Hand* and 'In the Days of the Cagots' in the November edition of *Belgravia*. *Heart and Hand*, founded by Rev. Charles Bullock in 1876, was one of the Church of England 'penny newspapers'. Its advertising claimed that it was a 'wholesome' publication; it contained no police news, no sensational reports of murders and other violent crimes, it didn't attack anyone's character and wasn't a vehicle for slander and defamation. It prided itself on the fact that there was 'nothing in its pages to pander to the worst passions of young or old.'[53] Interestingly, the tale that Ehretia chose to submit to this Christian magazine isn't even slightly religious in tone. 'On the Spur of the Moment' is the tale of a brother and sister who, robbed of their inheritance when a speculating banker causes The Spindle Bank to crash, attempt to improve their financial situation by entering a competition to produce a mechanical clock for the town hall of Niedrichstein. There is no supernatural element to the story, but the sister's ordeal in it is slightly horrific if you suffer from claustrophobia.

'In the Days of the Cagots' was Ehretia's final published story. It is set in the French mountains and tells the tale of young Marie Duclos, who is kidnapped by a violent Cagot leader and taken away to his hideout.[54] While her fiancé, François, leads a search party to attempt to locate and rescue her, Marie remains imprisoned in her murderous captor's stronghold, trying to fend off his advances. There is no supernatural element, and the ending is religious in nature.

Aside from these two short stories, 1896 saw the publication of Ehretia's first novel, *In Days of Strife: Fragments of Fact and Fiction from a Refugee's History in France, 1666 to 1685*, a tale of adventure, mishap and religious persecution, which was published by F. V. White (who published all but two of her books). This appears to have been the title she was best known for during her lifetime; advertisements for her later books tended to refer back to it, which suggests no subsequent title was as successful.

Two years later, F. V. White published *Mistress Bridget*. The story is that of nineteen-year-old Bridget Conyngham, daughter of Squire Conyngham, who is left to fend for herself when her parents rush off to look after the squire's dying twin sister. Abandoned in the Manor House at Rithycombe in Somerset, with only her old nurse, her nurse's husband, Joe, and her servant, Timothy, to look after her, Bridget is forced to protect herself against pillaging soldiers, on the hunt for treasure during the aftermath of the English Civil War, and then violent, prejudiced, witch-obsessed villagers, inspired to action by the doings of Matthew Hopkins, Witchfinder General, who is going about the country torturing anyone he doesn't like the look of. The supernatural element comes in the form of the ghosts of 'Madam' and a captain of the Parliamentary Army, who both haunt the manor where most of the action takes place.

Historical accuracy was extremely important to Ehretia, and it is obvious from the level of detail in her work that she carried out a great deal of research before writing her novels and short stories. For example, in *Mistress Bridget* there is a scene in which a ritual for curing the 'evil eye' takes place. The incantation used during the exorcism and the description of the ritual itself are based on details of actual practises carried out in Somerset, as described by John Cuming Walters in *Bygone Somerset*, which had appeared a year prior to the publication of Ehretia's novel of witchcraft and witch-hunts.

The following two years saw the publication, again by F. V. White & Co., of the Gothic novel *Sarolta's Verdict: A Romance* (1899), which seems to have received very little attention in the newspapers, and *Vanity's Price* (1900), which is about a girl who happens to have been born without a heart. Attempts to fix that problem leave her incapable of ageing physically. The critic in the *Graphic* wrote—and if this doesn't make you want to read it, I don't know what will:

'The novel contains many excellent morals, concerning the vanity of Vanity, the expediency of kindness to dumb animals, the inexpediency of joining murder-societies, the imprudence of trusting to quacks, and the folly of being born without brains.'

Two years after *Vanity's Price* was published, Digby, Long, and Co. published *The Monk's Shadow*, 'a romance of a proper old fashioned sort, with horror piled upon horror from beginning to end',[55] involving a lost will, secret treasure, and a monk's ghost that walks the hallways of the Priory where the latter is hidden. Though described as 'an attractive story, well told' by the *Irish Times*, it appears to have received very little attention elsewhere.[56]

At the time *The Monk's Shadow* was published, Ehretia and her children were living at The Cottage, 6 Church Lane, Bitton,[57] about four miles from their old home at Doynton Rectory. Ehretia, by then sixty-three years old, continued to take an active interest in politics and remained part of the community that her husband had served until his death. She was on the committee for the annual flower show in Wick (located about a mile from her old home in Doynton),[58] which she'd been involved with since its foundation in 1889; during its inaugural year, she was the judge for the wild flowers section of the show's competition.[59]

Following the publication of *The Monk's Shadow*, no new novel by Ehretia Yolland appeared for five years. Then, in September 1907, F. V. White published *Under the Stars*, a tale of vengeance that begins at the outbreak of the Morant Bay Rebellion in Jamaica in 1865. Like its predecessor, it received little attention, and that which it did receive was lukewarm. The critic for *The Graphic*, feeling that the book was 'needlessly long', suggested that 'too rapid and fertile an imagination [had] proved the author's bane'.[60]

In 1912, Lynwood and Co. published Ehretia's final novel, *The Struggle for the Crown: A Romance of the Seventeenth Century*. The story is constructed around the various misfortunes of the 'Winter Queen', Elizabeth Stuart of Bohemia, daughter of James I, and her husband, Frederick V, Prince Palatine. However, it is Elizabeth Sarrell, the queen's favourite maid of honour, who is the real heroine of the tale, and it is her stirring adventures that are the main focus of the novel. The book received very positive reviews in the newspapers; one critic wrote that the details of Elizabeth Stuart's life were 'portrayed with vivid accuracy', and the description of London in the Stuart period testified to 'considerable antiquarian research.'[61] Another wrote of Elizabeth Sarrell's adventures:

'Truly the difficulties of her love story were marvellous. There is the plague, and there is a room filled with coffins and skeletons. There is a scoundrel lover who abducts her and makes rendezvous with her in horrid places and by horrid methods. There are cossack raids and highway robberies, and a dramatic incident on nearly every page.'[62]

By the time that *The Struggle for the Crown* was published, Ehretia, who was seventy-three years old, was living alone at 42 Aberdeen Road, Redland, Bristol, with a single domestic servant.[63] Her oldest living daughter, Beatrice, was working as a self-employed 'Lady Gardener' at the time; rather appropriately, her middle name was Flowers.[64] Beatrice never married, but Ehretia's youngest daughter, Mary, had married five years earlier and had a young daughter and baby son of her own; her husband, Francis Gurney, was also a horticulturist; he was a specialist in carnations.[65] Ehretia's youngest son, Henry, was a self-employed insurance broker and had moved in with Mary and her family at their home in Bitton.[66]

I found some of the above information within the census returns for 1911, and I found something else of interest while checking them. While researching Ehretia's life, I had my copy of *Mistress Bridget* beside me, and I often wondered about the author's name on the cover; it had the look of a signature. The census for 1911 was taken on 2 April of that year, and it was the first to be completed by actual householders rather than the census enumerator. The 1911 schedule for 42 Aberdeen Road, Bristol, was filled in and signed by Ehretia herself. And it confirms that the gilt-stamped signature on the front cover of *Mistress Bridget* was indeed that of Ehretia Yolland.

By the spring of 1921, Ehretia, now eighty-two years of age, had returned to the village of Bitton in Gloucestershire and was living with her daughter Mary, who by then had another young son. The following year, on 9 March 1922, just a month before her youngest son was due to get married, Ehretia passed away at the age of eighty-two. She was just shy of her eighty-third birthday.

When I first began trying to uncover the true identity of E. Yolland, I didn't have high expectations. I had so little to go on; it seemed to me that an attempt to put flesh on bones that had themselves long ago disappeared was likely to fall flat before it got going. As it is, we now know that she was a wife and mother, an educated woman with a keen interest in history, horticulture and politics, that she suffered great loss during her lifetime, and that it was in response to one such loss, that of her husband, that she began writing for publication. The writer is reunited with her writing at last. And now, when we read her novels and short stories, we are able to see how much her own personal experiences, of loss and loneliness in particular, informed her writing.

The works of Ehretia Yolland are incredibly hard to come by these days; her short stories, in particular, are almost impossible to get hold of. It is my hope that, with this current publication, Ehretia will find a new modern audience, and an appreciative one at that... that this long *lost* Victorian author will at last be *found*.

Notes

1   *England & Wales, National Probate Calendar (Index of Wills and Administrations), 1858-1995*. Probate: London, 25 April, 1922.

2   *England & Wales, Civil Registration Death Index, 1916-2007*. January to March, 1922. Although the register records her age at death as eighty-three, she was just shy of her eighty-third birthday.

3   General Register Office: 1839, Apr/May/Jun, Volume 12, p. 146.

4   Though the sixth child (of ten), her brother Richard had died in infancy the year before Ehretia was born.

5   J. Bernard Burke (ed.), *The St. James's Magazine: And Heraldic and Historical Register* (London: E. Churton, 1850). Vol. 1, p. 32.

6   Charles Howard Burnett, *The Burnett family: With Collateral Branches; Also Historical and Genealogical Notes on Allied Families and Biographical Sketches of Various Eminent Burnetts*. (Los Angeles: privately published, 1950), p. 265.

7   *1851 England Census* for Chelmsford, Essex.

8   *Chelmsford Chronicle*, 11 May 1849, p. 1.

9   *England, Select Births and Christenings, 1538-1975*.

10 *Exeter and Plymouth Gazette*, 27 December 1845, p. 3.

11 *Exeter and Plymouth Gazette*, 7 July 1827, p.3.

12 *Oxford University Alumni, 1500-1886*, 1715-1886, Volume IV, p. 1627.

13 *Saint James's Chronicle*, 20 March 1860, p. 1.

14 *Colne Engaine Parish Magazine*, July-August 2020, p. 35.

15 Royal College of Surgeons of England, *Plarr's Lives of the Fellows*.

16 *Colne Engaine Parish Magazine*, July-August 2020, p. 35

17 *Essex, England, Church of England Marriages, 1754-1937*.

18 *Lincolnshire Chronicle*, 3 January 1862, p. 5.

19 *Cambridge Chronicle and Journal*, 15 February 1862, p. 6.

20 *England & Wales, Civil Registration Birth Index, 1837-1915*, 1866.

21 *Essex Standard*, 25 January 1867, p. 3.

22 *Essex, England, Church of England Births and Baptisms, 1813-1921*, 1869.

22 *Chelmsford Chronicle*, 4 March 1870, p. 6.

23 *Chelmsford Chronicle*, 17 December 1869, p. 5.

24 *Essex Herald*, 1 March 1870, p. 5.

25 *Essex Standard*, 21 April 1871, p. 2.

26 *Salisbury and Winchester Journal*, 3 June 1871, p. 3.

27 *England & Wales, Civil Registration Birth Index, 1837-1915*, 1871.

28 *Chelmsford Chronicle*, 16 February 1872, p. 8.

29 *England & Wales, Civil Registration Birth Index, 1837-1915*, 1874; 1939 *England and Wales Register*, 1876; *England, Church of England Births and Baptisms, 1813-1921*, 1878.

30 *Essex, England, Church of England Births and Baptisms, 1813-1921*, 1880.

31 *Chelmsford Chronicle*, Friday 22 July 1881, p. 3.

32 *Chelmsford Chronicle*, 17 February 1882, p. 5.

33 *Chelmsford Chronicle*, 29 December 1882, p. 5.

34 *Essex Newsman*, 26 July 1884, p. 3.

35 *Essex Herald*, 11 October 1884, p. 4.

36 *Essex Standard*, 25 July 1885, p. 5.

37 *Essex Herald*, 21 September 1885, p. 7.

38 *Chelmsford Chronicle*, 25 September 1885, p. 7.

39 *Essex Herald*, 28 September 1885, p. 5.

40 *Chelmsford Chronicle*, 2 October 1885, p. 7.

41 *Chelmsford Chronicle*, 3 September 1886, p. 1.

42 *Chelmsford Chronicle*, 1 October 1886, p. 7.

43 *Chelmsford Chronicle*, 29 July 1887, p. 5.

44 *Essex Newsman*, 18 April 1887, p. 4.

45 *Chelmsford Chronicle*, 20 May 1887, p. 7.

46 *Bath Chronicle and Weekly Gazette*, 26 May 1887, p. 5.

47 *Chelmsford Chronicle*, 12 August 1887, p. 1.

48 *Bristol Mercury*, 18 December 1888, p. 7.

49 *UK, Clergy List, 1897*.

50 *Bath Chronicle and Weekly Gazette*, 4 September 1890, p. 5.

51 *England & Wales, National Probate Calendar (Index of Wills and Administrations), 1858-1995*. Probate: 6 November 1891.

52 *Western Daily Press*, 23 November 1891, p. 1.

53 *Frome Times*, 3 August 1881, p. 1.

54 The Cagots were an ethnic minority that inhabited certain areas of the Pyrenees Mountains in France. They were outcasts, shunned and subjected to hateful discrimination.

54 *Graphic*, 29 September 1900, p. 36.

55 *The Scotsman*, 10 April 1902, p. 2.

56 *Pall Mall Gazette*, 29 May 1902, p. 3.

57 *1901 England Census*, Bitton, Gloucestershire.

58 *Bristol Times and Mirror*, 10 August 1892, p. 7.

59 *Bristol Mercury*, 1 August 1889, p. 3.

60 *The Graphic*, 14 September 1907, p. 30.

61 *Bayswater Chronicle*, 25 January 1913, p. 8.

62 *Dublin Daily Express*, 27 February 1913, p. 7.

63 *1911 England Census*, Clifton, Bristol, Gloucestershire.

64 *1911 England Census*, Sussex, Buxted.

65 *1911 England Census*, Somerset, Bitton.

66 *1911 England Census*, Somerset, Bitton.

"Ring out wild bells to the wild sky.

*   *   *   *   *   *

"Ring out a slowly dying cause,
    And ancient forms of party strife;
    Ring in the nobler modes of life,
With sweeter manners, purer laws.

"Ring out the want, the care, the sin,
    The faithless coldness of the times;
    Ring out, ring out my mournful rhymes,
But ring the fuller minstrel in.

"Ring out false pride in place and blood,
    The civic scandal and the spite;
    Ring in the love of truth and right,
Ring in the common love of good."

In Memoriam

Tennyson.

MISTRESS BRIDGET

Anno Domini, 1897

I.

Introduction

HOW THE BELLS BEGAN

"On the floor are mysterious footsteps,
There are whispers along the walls."

—Longfellow.

ONE of the Western Counties of England stands out in bold relief for all time as the home of the earliest Church, and for possessing for centuries the richest Abbey. With the long line of saintly records of religious strife in those far gone ages, we meddle not—all histories teem with them. The rich red soil, the fertile pastures, the sheltering hills, no doubt prompted the Welsh to bestow the name of "Gylâd-yr-Haf"—"The Land of Summer," upon the well-renowned county of Somerset, with its 1,049,815 acres, and ever-varying population. Well renowned truly, but with murky clouds of persecution, death, and disaster forming the solid background; possessing from the Past to the Present age, a rich store of Legends, hardly if ever equalled by any other county belonging to the English realm, over whose dominions the sun never sets.

      *   *   *   *   *   *

Belonging to Somersetshire, yet at no great distance from the Devonshire border, stands a tiny country church, with thick white-washed, unadorned walls, just a few simple benches (pews if you like to call them by so dignified a name), a small recessed chancel with narrow lancet windows, and one or two memorial slabs on the floor and walls. Also what was perhaps the most valuable thing in the building, a beautiful old carved chancel screen, with its rich colouring of red and blue showing little traces of age. Underfoot a rough, uneven pavement, with gaps and holes from missing mortar; and above all, beyond all, a pervading smell of damp and dry rot. So far the inside. Outside, a tower large for the body of the church, possessing a peal of somewhat rusty bells, whose frayed ropes hung limply down in varying lengths from the dark cavity above, crowned in its turn by a rotting platform, from whose once sound summit many a beacon fire had blazed forth in the days that are no more.

A half stumble on the floor, a curious glance for the cause, and a stare of surprise at a queer little oblong, dust-filled space at my feet, caused the natural question to the showman sexton (a cheerful old man of eighty):

"And what is that?"

"Nobbut a bit of tin, that caused folks' feet to trip, so I tuk hur into the vestry, where you can see hur for yourselves if you are curious like."

The vestry was large for the size of the church, and maybe a trifle lighter, without quite so many creeping ivy trails over the thick glass.

The brass was the smallest I have ever seen, and though worn and defaced by age and ill-usage, still outlined a woman's form, with hands piously joined together, and garments hanging in severe folds.

"Ay! 'Tis Madam herself, the Squire put it up to her; he thought a deal on her he did, so I've heard my great, great grandfather said, and he should have known, seeing he lived at the same time; though it's true he was but a young lad when that brass was new. Beg pardon, ladies, did I hear aright? Were you asking who 'Madam' was?"

An uneasy glance around, an instinctive ruffling of the silver locks, a distinct sidling nearer the door, warned us the subject was evidently regarded as one of nervous thrills, believed in, almost worshipped, even after the lapse of centuries up to our own days.

The story of the past follows in due order; the traditions surviving at the present day will more fitly form the Introduction. At any rate so it came to us, and so we hand it on, even at the risk of being accused of putting the cart before the horse.

The bells that still hang in the old church tower are dusty and dull, and quite useless; no mortal hands can wake an echo from their ancient sides, no vigorous pulling of lusty men can make the clappers swing. They rang their last, it is said, all by themselves when Madam died; and sound of awe and fear as those muffled bells had become long before *then*, not a feeble echo had sounded since all down the ages! Pray God *never* again would they be heard, for awful would be the sound, certain the warning.

Whilst the tower itself resisted the passage of Time, by common consent the bells would remain, for no Somersetshire man would dare to brave unknown evil by removing them. The old man pointed to a queer yellow chart hanging on the western wall, which in crabbed fine writing and much-faded ink, described the mottoes on the bells above. Curiosity and interest combined made us peruse the same.

Legend on the Storm Bell

Voce meo viva depello conte nociva
2nd Bell—Ave Maria Gracia Plena. R. S.

3

3rd 𝕭ell— 𝕴 sound to 𝕭eid the sick repent.[1]

In hope of life when breath is spent.

𝕭ig 𝕭ell—𝕴 to the 𝕮hurch the living call,

And to the grave do summon all.

𝕿hese 𝕭ells were consecrated to the 𝕲lory of 𝕲od and for the 𝕳oly 𝕾ervice of 𝕳is 𝕮hurch by 𝕭ishop 𝕲rant   1479.

Then came some unreadable lines, and again clearer—evidently added at a later date—

In conformity with the 𝕾ociety of 𝕭ells lately inaugurated at 𝕭ristol, a fine of sixpence will be enforced on any ringer forgetting to kneel down and pray before entering the belfry, for the first offence, for the second, banishment from office.

Silently the old man waited until I had reached the bottom line, and turned to him with the obvious question *why* the date of the consecration of the bells had never been filled in.

"Well, ladies, it was after this manner. There had been a deal of talk about the new bells, how handsome they were, good tone and shape, far too grand for such as we, some said; but there was a rumour afoot that the Squire who gave the bells, used what now folks call conscience money, else he never would have given so much, as all counted him as rare and close-fisted. Be that as it may, the bells were reckoned a noble gift, and his generosity lauded to the skies. It was to be a grand affair altogether—wrestling and grinning matches,[2] and

---

[1] Beid: bid.

[2] Face-making matches. The most fearful grimace wins.

such like popular diversions, with dancing and feasting thrown in of course, so naturally every soul in the place took a holiday with leave or without.

"Bishop Grant was an old man, though hale and hearty, but the sun had been fierce, and he looked tired and hot as he began the solemn Benediction Service, called the Baptism of the Bells.

"Carefully he washed them all with salt water, dipped his finger into the oil for the anointing, which, ladies, you know preceded the dedication with the sign of the Cross, Latin benediction, and the final censing—all that is put down in order on that old document, only 'tis not easy to make out now.

"Well, he had just dipped his finger into the oil, when he gave a start and a gurgle, and fell down in a fit of apoplexy. The ringers—hemmed in by the crowd, excited by liberal potations, and altogether confused, thought from the movement amongst the bystanders the service was concluded, so gave the guiding ropes the required jerk, and the bells swung up into the belfry.

"That is how we tell the story now, and the bells have therefore never been consecrated, and 'tis not their fault if the Devil uses them now and again. The Bishop died, and if anyone ever thought of another service for the bells, no one stirred in the matter; and were it not for the date in the prepared chart being omitted, few would know there was a reason why our bells are not quite like others."

A modern bell on a sturdy hempen rope (whose tin-kettle, feeble clink could form no faintest comparison with the deep musical chime silent above its head), hung from a pent-house above the clock face, and jingled the villagers to church.

"Strangers often jeered, and said 'twas folly and worse to give in to such notions of superstition," the old man volunteered, but whilst the Manor House stood in the vale, with the weathercock with its golden initials turning in the wind, standing out clear against the sky, and Madam's little brass was visible, he was positive the tale of Madam's wanderings would remain.

Yes, oh! yes, we should have the whole story as perfectly as he knew it, and with all due respect none could tell us more, seeing that his great, great, great, grandmother had been Madam's nurse; but he must ask our patience a little longer, as first he must beg us to look at the time-worn stone in a quiet corner of the small God's Acre, and note the deep-cut inscription to "Reginald Markham, Captain in the Parliamentary Army, who died in the Service of the Cause, 1659, at the Royalist Manor of Rithycombe."

Simple the words, plain the statement, and yet what a world of tragedy lay below!

That was the Rectory yonder, with the tall, thick hedges of yew and box, between which, in the shades of night, a lady's white-robed figure passed, with a silver lamp held high in her hand, intent on a secret search. It was broad daylight *now*, but up to the present day, no one who knew the tale of the past cared to wander alone after nightfall in the Rectory garden.

Neither was it to everyone the story of the place was told; strangers likely to scoff were often put off with careless remarks about "things" being seen, and the such like; few took the trouble to sift and enquire as to the origin of the spirit that walked— walked as truly as you or I, with flowing garments, and dark, steady eyes, looking—for ever looking for what it never found.

The story being really a true one, highly prized by the villagers, any ridicule thrown on the subject was greatly resented, and when did a spirit—call it wraith, ghost, or spook—what you will—appear before a mocker?

Matters had got to a fine pass in the last century, so far as the Manor itself was concerned; not a maid would remain beyond her hiring-time, and a certain dormer window, high up in the steep-pitched roof, could only now be used as an apple loft, because in the northern sense, it was never "alone."

"Had no one ever attempted to lay the uneasy spirit to rest, did you ask, ladies?

"Ay! indeed! more than one such endeavour had been made, only to prove a failure."

The first, the village wise-acres had organized themselves, using an old and infallible charm for laying a ghost to rest. On Hallowe'en the whole place turned out, with seven men and seven maids, and an immense length of silken withes.[3] Placing the cords in a double circle on the ground in the middle of the Rectory walk, full in the light of the silver moon, they waited with peering eyes and silent tongues, for the clock to strike the witching hour of twelve. All were on their oath to shut their eyes on the first stroke, or else the charm would fail. It came at last, with a "boom" on the silent night, and then both ends of the silken circles were drawn sharply together, with the object of enclosing the restless spirit; and the chosen men and maids pulling the ropes along, guided only by the blind fiddler, tramped away to the nearest pond, and flung the silken bonds well into the middle, where the water swirled speedily over them. Some declared they heard groans and sighs, others that the weight was awful; but the pond was in a dark corner, and all fled with their best foot foremost, and never willingly passed the place except in daylight.

After a short interval, the figures became visible again, and then authorities declared someone must have peeped, that such a

---

[3] Ropes of twisted, flexible twigs, especially of willow.

reliable cure should have failed. Finally, they consulted the Parson and implored his aid, and after hunting through various tomes, he promised to do what he could by a solemn Requiem service. Before that, he advised that a thorough search should be made for hidden treasure, for everyone knew that if valuables were secreted anywhere, the house would be haunted until all was found, when the wandering ones would rest in peace.

He made one of the search party himself, and when, after much tapping and banging, they *did* find a few jewels and a spoon hidden in the upright of an old carved bed, and a little secret panel in the dormer-room, empty of all but one thin coin that had crept into a crack, which prevented the spring snapping tight, else very likely no one would ever have found the cupboard out, it was such a splendid hiding place; but the coin bore silent witness to the fact that treasures had evidently been stored there at one time.

There was great exultation that now the trouble would be ended without any further bother. But no! Again in the gloaming the ghosts passed—oftenest, but not always Madam alone, who remained watching from her dormer window until the broad light of day caused her gently to fade away.

Then the Rector tried his solemn service, held on a far distant hill with silken cords drawn duly all the way, to the measured chant of psalm and hymn. The torches flared around on the white-robed clergy and chorister boys, as in earnest, reverent tones the priest banned the wandering spirits by bell, book and candle, not to come nearer the Manor lands than by one cock's stride a year!

A solemn silence, and a great awe fell on the listening crowd, then a huge bonfire blazed redly up, on which with a sign of the Cross the silken ropes were laid, and all waited motionless till nothing but a heap of ashes remained. These the Rector scattered to the four winds, with a parting earnest prayer, that God in His great mercy would now allow these poor troubled spirits to sleep quietly in His Almighty keeping until the Resurrection morn.

Then the procession reformed and returned to their various homes, as the first red streaks glowed in the east.

"Did that answer, ladies, did you say?

"Ay, surely, and as long as the figure keeps her distance no one minds her walking, but 'tis many years agone, and so often has Madam now been seen again in the Rectory garden, 'tis certain in her cock's strides she is so far on her return to the Manor, for 'tis a bee-line from yon hill to the old house in the vale.

"When she reaches that, a new generation will exist, who will deal with the matter according to their lights, and probably pretend to scorn the means our fathers used!

"All right, Martha, woman, I'll be along directly. It is my missus, ladies, come to say our bit of dinner waits; maybe you'll like to give a glance round. Look in at the old Manor, see the screen and the window, and hear what Mrs. Collins has to say on the subject. Then, if I make not too bold, and you still wish to hear the whole story, my missus will be proud to have a dish of tea ready for you, and I'll tell you all I know."

The offer was too tempting to refuse. We took the old man's advice, found all he had told us quite matter of fact, and spent most happily the rest of the afternoon in his sweet brown cottage, with its quaint corner cupboards and octagon-shaped rooms, listening to the ancient story of Madam's life and death.

Anyone who doubts what a vivid personality she possessed, has but to journey to that quiet Somersetshire village, and if they return unconvinced that there are more things in Heaven and Earth than our philosophy understands, then this story is not for them —headstrong, wilful sceptics!

To this day the spirit walks: no one will pass alone between the box-tree paths of the Rectory garden; the weathercock turns in the wind with all the initials in view, and fragrant apples strongly scent the dormer chamber, always called "Madam's Zimmer," wherein no doubt to those whose ears are listening for it, the hum of a wheel can be heard in the stillness of the summer night, and were there eyes to see—a slender form and delicate fingers spinning the web of fate.

None of the old family remain. They are completely died out, only the ghost of a bygone day keeps faithful watch and ward!

*   *   *   *   *   *

So far, only modified in language, and greatly altered in style, was the preface the old sexton gave us, of the story set forth in length in the following pages, interesting to us so deeply as we stood on the actual spot, that it seemed likely others might like to hear the tale of what had given rise to the haunting of the past and present, which it seems probable will still continue into the vast mysterious future.

Will the treasure ever be found? *Where* and by *whom?*—and if so, will the old man's surmise prove correct, and the ghosts visit no more that peaceful little village?—are questions Time and God's Providence will alone make plain.

In the Year of Grace 1659

II

MADAM'S ZIMMER

"Nor think to village swains alone
  Are these unearthly terrors known;
  For not to rank nor sex confined
  Is this vain ague of the mind:
  Hearts firm as steal, as marble hard,
  'Gainst faith, and love, and pity barred."
                                    "Rokeby"—Scott.

"BLESS my soul, what are we to be up to now?"

Squire Conyngham ran his hand through his scanty grey hair in grievous perplexity, the effect of which was, of course, to make it stand up in a kind of halo round his fine old head. The summer sun was shining in all its power through the open window of the Manor dining-room, bringing out a few dabs of colour from the faded rugs strewn over the polished boards. Great jars of oriental pottery held sweet treasures from the walled flower-garden, and a beautiful bowl of roses flanked a corresponding one of cream on the soft damask table-cloth. A rich old carved screen extended the entire width of the room at the bottom end, leaving a passage way behind from door to door.

The outside of the house was gabled and most artistic, with latticed casements and deep-set eaves. The once bright red tiles, toned to a rich brown crimson, that showed picturesquely through the various greens of the trees between the tiny church and the small hamlet over which Squire Conyngham held sway.

High above one pointed end a quaint old weathercock formed of the initial letters "B. C." on two points, and the date "16" and "40," on the two others, turned with the wind.

A few miles off and several market towns were within reach, and from any of the rising hills a good view of the sea itself was to be obtained, with the queer old weather-beaten pier itself, on which on stormy nights the Whistling Witch held wild revel, and with her high-pitched notes distinct and clear above the tempest's din, lured and enticed unwary mariners to their death. Huddled in a heap in her dark mantle, the Siren would laugh in mad glee as she saw the wandering lights, with their baneful gleam shining clearly out from dangerous rocks and cruel reefs, as the wreckers followed her evil example and made ready for their wicked work.

Smugglers, too, had a home of their own amongst the many caves, and lively times were those when the Excise men and the freebooters had a tussle together.[4] The country people were so often mixed up in the contraband trade, it was greatly to their interest to hide and help the reckless desperadoes; and surely few counties could give them better vantage ground than the highly superstitious one of Somerset, with its steep hills, deep vales, and dark, lonely lanes that rivalled Devonshire itself in their narrowness and wild luxuriance. A mere handful of men could guard and keep one of these winding ways against heavy odds, as was often proved when the "boys" were out.

---

[4] Freebooters: pirates.

Just now the whole country-side was in an uproar in the disturbed period that ensued before Charles II gained his father's throne. Everyone was fighting-mad, some even in ignorance of what they were struggling for; and utterly dependent on the news-monger's own views on the subject, they frequently got rather confused as to the rights or wrongs of the subject under discussion.

On those rare occasions when a silk-tied packet arrived post haste for the Squire, there were sure to be a few loiterers hands to the porch door on the chance of picking up a few scraps of news or gossip. The jovial old man was not one to keep information to himself in those stirring times, and few went away on such days without gaining their object. There was always the plea of wanting Mistress Bridget to write a letter for them, should the curious stumble against Madam, who was all for keeping herself to herself, and therefore, by no means a popular person.

So stood the picture on that sunny day of summer, when through the village had galloped, on a smoking horse, the bearer of the letter that plunged in one moment the Squire and his family into a sea of perplexity, and broke up for ever their happy home life.

"What is the matter, John? You keep us quite in the dark—what has chanced to startle you so?"

"And you too, my lady, for hearken! Eliza lies at death's door, and prays without ceasing to see me once again. Thomas says I have not a moment to lose; immediately on receipt of his tidings, sent by his quickest messenger, I must start at once, not alone, he trusts, for Eliza would dearly love to bid you farewell; but that they leave to us, for Bridget has to be considered. He adds a warning that the roads are none too safe. I had best not forget pistols, but beyond and above everything, to remember time is life! There now, wife, do you wonder I called out?"

"Not in the least; I should have, in your shoes, but now we must be off at once. Will you order the horses, and ask Richard to see the pillion saddle is buckled on better than last time we rode, when it was so loose it kept on sliding, and took the skin from poor Jenny's back? Richard will have to get ready also, for he must ride the pack-horse; and Bridget, will you come and help me with the valise?"

"Then I am not to go, mother?"

"To go, child! Who ever thought of such a thing, in these unsettled times? You are far safer at home, where none will harm you. We only take Richard, really for fear of any mischance to Jenny, when we should go forward on Lucifer, and he would bring the mare back. Supposing we thought of your going, you must ride pillion behind him, and then, if Jenny cast a shoe, or went lame, what in the world could we do with you?"

"I understand, mother. Then I remain here?"

"Why, of course, Bridget. I leave you in charge; if Martha had not marred last week, she would have taken care of you: indeed, anyhow, I wish you to send her word she will be conferring a great favour upon me if she and old Joe will come here and stay during our absence. It will be company for you, and the maidens are too flighty for my taste. There is another matter I wish we had seen to, and that is the hiding of your father's prize-money, and the bits of plate he sets such store on. We have been meaning to do it any day for months, and now it will have to be left to chance, unless, Bridget, you can manage it yourself. If you do, tell no one where you put it, and be a steady lass, and not afraid. Now, child, there's your father calling. Give me my hood and mittens, and send Richard up for the valise. If only James was at home!"

Never once did the idea strike Madam of remaining at home with her daughter; in every thought or action her husband came first. So many happy years had sped in the quiet Manor home before the little daughter's arrival some twenty years ago, that for her to step between the devoted couple could never be. They were all in all to each other, and she was a most precious treasure to both. Certainly she favoured her mother mostly, and the villagers spoke in awe of her great learning. Few of them could read a word, and therefore her most ordinary knowledge grew into something peculiar.

The adieux were very brief. A great longing to go with them seized Bridget's heart as her father folded her warmly in his loving arms, and tears were very near when her mother kissed and blessed her. There was nothing for it, however, but to gulp down the choking sob and wipe the tear-dimmed eyes, in time to give them a parting wave before the whispering avenue trees hid the last glimpse of the riders.

Then she donned her hood and kerchief, and started off to Martha's cottage, burdened with her mother's message, which she felt bound to deliver in person. Her nurse Martha had begun her married life in the keeper's cottage across the common northwards; quite a good step away, and a lonely path. *That* was nothing uncommon thereabouts, however, and it was but a pleasant walk in summer-time.

Martha was busy washing, and her hands were covered with soap suds, as, all in a hurry and a flurry, she hastened to throw wide the gate on catching a glimpse of her nursling approaching. Her greeting was very warm, but her face fell when she heard of Madam's wish.

"There now! Did ever anything happen more contrary?" she cried. "'Tis but last night Joe settled with Captain Fosbrook, up at the Grange, for us to take charge of the place during his visit to London, and he starts to-morrow for an indefinite period. Only that Joe was married, he would not have had him at all, but very likely he can get someone else to do for him just as well; and Mistress Bridget, my child, I need not tell you we'll come and take care of you with al the pleasure in life. Ay! and there are troubles ahead, if my old man speaks truth; but don't you be afeard, we'll look after you all right. I'll go at once and find Joe, and we'll be up with you long before dark."

Bridget sauntered slowly homewards, hardly noticing how the bright sun had clouded over, and what heavy clouds were coming up before the wind.

The villagers were principally at their cottage doors, which were frequently decorated with yellow oil-skin coats freshly greased.

She entered the tiny church with its tremendously thick walls, and sunken windows, with just sufficient forms for the village proper, and carved work on the choir stalls. Tired with her hot walk, she sank into her accustomed seat and fell into a doze. Outside the ivy creaked and tapped impatiently against the window, but it was a long, dismal howl that roused her up from an unpleasant dream at last; then a cautious black nose came pushing the old narrow door open, there was a joyous bound on to her lap, and a little hot tongue began licking her hand.

"Why, Rough, how came you here? I would not take you with me, the sun was too fierce, and I thought you sound asleep. Well, now we must be off, or the storm will overtake us."

One long, lingering glance round the familiar building, and the two set off on their return home.

With colour heightened and hair blown wild Bridget looked the picture of health, as she passed up the stately avenue and crossed the velvet lawn. There was a sound of loud talking as she approached the door, and the three maids were standing in a group, but on seeing her, came rushing forward, all speaking at once. When she could make sense of their remarks she made out that, taking advantage of their mistress's absence, they had begun gossiping busily with the villagers, when all of a sudden a band of soldiers had ridden through without drawing bridle, and looking stern and fierce.

Roundheads, of course, but what the errand that took them through the quiet village who could say? Hard upon their heels, only with jaded steeds and dusty garments, passed a company of Royalists, who yet had time for a jest and a word, and seemed reckless and wild in the extreme.

Frightened, in spite of themselves, by the bold glances and random words, the maids had come running home, heedless and careless of the fact that several pairs of keen eyes noticed the direction they took, and promised a speedy return.

Now what did Mistress Bridget wish them to be at? Was it safe for them to remain?

"Safe!" and the young voice had a keen edge of scorn. "What was it they feared?—who would hurt them?"

One maid nudged the other to speak, and then all began at once.

Had she forgotten, maybe, that each time soldiers had been seen about, tales of pillage and robbery had been leaked out, whilst rough words and rougher deeds had abounded? Truly, so far they had escaped wonderfully, but perhaps it was their turn now. Would it not be better to fly whilst there was time?

"The Royalists will not harm us; we shall be pleased to treat them well, and the Roundheads may never come; so why be scared at shadows?"

The maids withdrew muttering audibly, and Bridget watered her flowers, and tidied her mother's room. All in a minute her dream in the old parish church came clearly back into her mind. The dread of it had been on her when Rough's tongue had awoke her.

She had hidden the treasure in secret, and then a great crowd came round the house, shrieking and shouting strange words, whilst they piled up faggots in the courtyard round a stake, to which a figure dressed in her cloak was led out; but the form faded away as she looked, and a dog's eager bark sounded near.

Nothing more could she remember, only such a horror and trouble, it seemed too heavy a burden. If only she had stayed awake, her nerves would not have been all in a quiver, as bad as the foolish maidens.

One thing she could, and would do, before daylight faded, and that was, hide the money where no strange person would think of looking. Quietly she lifted her mother's heavy châtelain,[5] and passed into her father's dressing-closet, where in an iron-clamped box, the family treasures were kept.

He had done good service to his country as a young man, and, in spite of his wife's wishes, had always kept his prize-money by him. Even when parting with most of his handsome plate, to aid the martyred King's cause, he never would touch a sovereign of that bright pile of gold. It was the child's dowry, he said—the best he could do for her, and neither for King nor country would he rob his little maid.

Only a few thick mugs, old-time spoons, and quaint snuff-boxes, with a battered salver, were kept in the house, besides a

---

[5] An ornament, usually worn at the waist, with chains bearing hooks on which to hang keys, seals, purses, scissors, etc.

certain amount in daily use. The best had been melted down for the King, so that Bridget had only one journey to make to carry her treasures away. Up the wide old stairs she went, two flights, and along the narrow passage that led to her gabled room (immediately under the glittering weathercock proudly bearing her initials aloft, put up in honour of her birth), with a view from the casement surpassed by none in the house.

Deciding in her own mind that the recess seen in her dream was as good a secret hiding-place as she could find, she decided to use it for the present. It was in her mantel-piece, simply an old-fashioned oak one, that had never struck her as possessing any individuality.

She felt it carefully all over; it seemed solid and ugly, with no carvings to hide springs, or knobs to press to open cupboards. Once, twice, she failed, and then she sat down in front of the fire-place, and gazed fixedly at the simple shelf, supported by brackets with plain wooden jambs, that baffled her completely. It was the frieze *below* the shelf that ought to move, if there was any truth in that queer dream of hers. Deliberately she rose, and going to the side of the chimney, pushed against the wooden jamb with all her might.

Quite useless! It would not move! Hot and tired from her exertions, Bridget was in two minds as to whether to try again. Hating to be baffled, she went round to the other side, and pushed the frieze from there.

It gave way! Very slightly, most unwillingly it moved a trifle; then after a more vigorous push, slid well aside, leaving visible a carefully-made cupboard behind it, in which lay a queer old book, with brass clasps and mountings, and yellow leaves, covered with faded writing.

True daughter of Eve as she was, Bridget seized the book, opened the time-stiffened fastenings, and gazed eagerly within. Full of cookery recipes at first sight, and then concoctions of herbs and simples for wounds and bruises, love philtres,[6] charms for man and beast, evil spells minutely described, poisons of deadly effect and untraceable origin, with their antidotes marked against each—the pages in that hurried glance seemed strangely to fascinate her, and it was regretfully she closed the book at last, determined to study it at leisure.

Why it should be hidden there she could not guess, and hardly troubled to think just now; the fact that the treasure would be secure was the great thing that mattered. There was plenty of room and to spare, and a safer receptacle could hardly be found, to her thinking. The designer had done his work well, whoever he might have been.

Lost in thought, Bridget stood gazing from her window out over the tall tree-tops swaying in the summer breeze, to the misty, distant hills behind which the silver sea rippled and danced in glee. How she loved her home! she felt as if she *could* not live elsewhere, she would rather die than leave.

A hurried step on the stair, a nervous knock at the door, warned her she had other things to do that brooked no delay. The time for musing was not yet, action must come first. Part of her morning's dream had so far stood her in good stead. What of the other and darker half?—the memory of which alone brought a sound of crackling wood in her ears, and a wild red light before her eyes!

Bridget shivered as she crossed the floor and flung wide the door.

---

[6] Love potions.

"Please, Mistress Bridget, Martha is below, in a terrible taking, wanting to see you at once. Can you come?"

"Surely," and the dainty high-heeled shoes tripped lightly down the shallow stairs.

"Oh! Mistress Bridget, my dear, did you ever hear tell of such bad luck? Captain Fosbrook had started for London when my Joe got to the Grange, and had left a message for us to say he had been called away suddenly, and had every confidence in us. Joe says we must keep our word, sorry though he is at disappointing you, but if you feel nervous and frightened, suppose you come up to the Grange along of us? Not but what I believe you are safe enough anywhere. I should dearly like to have you, child, all the same, and the idea of harm coming to you just makes my flesh creep."

"Oh! No! thank you, Nursie dear. I am really not afraid, only mother said I was to ask you, and I have a bit of spinning in my mind to do as a surprise against her return, so shall have no time to think I am lonely or dull."

"Suppose Joe's brother Timothy sleeps here during the master's absence; he's a good lad and trustworthy, with all his wits about him. Give him my old room, dearie, and then I shall sleep in peace. Now do, honey, just to please me!"

"I don't mind, Martha, one way or the other, but I expect the maids will feel happier for knowing there is a man on the spot. So please ask him to come and take care of us."

"That I will. I'll go at once, and just you make him of use, my dear, now mind."

III

OUT IN THE NIGHT

"Scorn the whispers of fear;
Be righteous, and bravely bide on."

—Waugh.

AFTER that topsy-turvy day things settled down wonderfully for a bit; then ugly rumours reached even Bridget's ears of cruelty and wrong done to innocent people.

Some argued all was fair in love and war, others declared when hot blood caught fire, who stopped to count the cost?

Troops of reckless soldiers seemed everywhere, and bands of private robbers often finished in brutal fashion what the soldiers began. Incendiary fires lit up the darkness of many a night, sending a spasm of fear and dread through timid, anxious hearts, as the fiery sparks and crimson glow warned them *their* turn might come next.

Several times dead bodies were found in unexpected places. One day this happened in the Manor avenue, and the maids, scared and frightened almost out of their wits, declared it was a warning only the foolish would neglect, packed their trunks in haste, and leaving them for the next carrier to call for, departed forthwith to their homes. In such a panic for their own safety, they could not even spare a thought for the young and beautiful girl they left behind.

It was Timothy who told Bridget of their flight as the evening shadows grey long round the old timbered house, and then in silence he stood before her, twisting his soft hat in his hands with a troubled look on his rugged face, waiting for his slow words to come.

"Will you let me see you to the Grange, mistress? There may be rough work here before long, not good for maids to see!"

"And what about you, Tim?"

"I thought maybe you'd trust me to do my best. No harm shall come nigh the place that I can help, and I shall be all the freer, having no petticoats to look after."

"I can't do it, Timothy, really. I should not have a moment's peace, and if harm befell you, I should always fancy at least I might have helped you somehow. Now please let us lock up the house before it gets quite dark, and then we can settle what is best to do. *Is* it my fancy, or is there distant shouting? It sounds like tipsy men!"

"I hoped you would not notice it, mistress; the inns have been crowded all day, and this is the outcome. Also a riotous lot of soldiers rode in a while ago, ripe for any mischief."

The light faded slowly, the stars came glimmering out, and night drew on apace. Bridget sat in the silent hall, listening to the song of the clock and Rough's loud breathing, as he lay asleep in his mistress's lap.

In the kitchen hard by Timothy smoked over the open hearth, with his honest face a mass of puckers, as he thought on his difficult post. Loaded pistols lay at his elbows, and a great knotted club leant against his knees. At last, what he had been waiting for came to pass—the sound of horses trotting and a heavy tramp of feet. Shouts and cries, and bits of songs heralded the approach of a lawless band in the calm silence of the night.

Quietly the man arose, put his pistols into his pockets and grasping his stout stick, walked into the hall.

Bridget had risen to her feet, and was standing listening, still clasping Rough in her protecting arms.

"They are coming, mistress."

A nod was his only answer, as the girl listened intently. Then came a banging on the door, and shouts to open, or an entrance would be forced!

Rough oaths were largely interspersed, and voices broken by hiccoughs grew threatening in their tones as no answer came.

The door was giving on its hinges when Bridget found her voice, and asked Timothy to throw it back and enquire what they wanted. Very unwillingly he complied, blocking the entrance with his body as well as he could.

"Your pleasure, sirs?"

"Riches for the Royalists!" shouted some. "Wages for the Army!" yelled others. "Treasure, treasure!" howled those who cared little for either.

Then a sudden rush was made, and Timothy was ousted from his post. Plunder certainly seemed the chief object of the visit by the way the things were seized on and hurled outside, and many a mocking jeer was pointed at the girl who stood motionless looking on.

Timothy was terribly knocked about, and soon lay a helpless heap on the floor, and Bridget made out the place was to be fired when emptied of all they required; but that would not be to-night, as they had another job on hand that would not keep as well as *this* one, which they had simply taken *en route*. So with oaths and laughs, telling her to expect them to-morrow, the rabble followed the blustering soldiers out of the desolate home, under the lofty avenue, down the narrow lanes.

Bridget waited, listening intently, until silence reigned again, when she stooped over Timothy and tried to discern his injuries.

The moon shining calmly through the open door, with the peaceful stars around her, gave plenty of light to see the confusion and disorder all about and around; and also showed, to her untold relief, that her faithful henchman's eyes were wide open and clear.

"Where are you hurt, Tim, poor fellow? Can you tell me?"

"I think, mistress, 'tis mostly bruises; they pounded me well-nigh to a jelly, and in falling I suppose I hit my head, and it stunned me for a bit. Now, my lady, we've no time to lose. Can you go for help? If Joe would give me his arm, I could crawl to a place of safety; and *you* must not be here when they return. You say they have gone further afield, probably to Marshfields, where the old miser lives. Then *now* is our chance, if your heart is brave enough, and if not, then Gold help us!"

And the honest fellow groaned in anguish at his helplessness.

"What am I to do, Tim?"

"Start at once for the Grange, and send Joe back to me, but for the love of Heaven return not yourself; the moon will have set, and the roads no fit place for you."

Bravely the poor fellow smothered his groans until out into the now silent night his mistress stepped, and with feet that would falter, and heart that would flutter, started away over the lonely common in search of aid for both.

Rough ran close beside her, and his companionship did great things for the trembling girl. Never had the common looked so wild, or the hollows cast such shadows.

Suppose she met the ghostly three that nightly walked and watched on the edge of the disused chalk pit, or what if the Wild Huntsman galloped by, with all his pack behind him? Surely, surely, she should die of fright!

Well she knew no maid of their would willingly pass down their own avenue after dark, though what they expected or feared to see they would not say; and now, here she was, alone on the wild Somersetshire moor, without a creature near, and with countless fancies taking shape and form in the over-excitement of her brain. Again and again she glanced nervously behind her, and watched Rough's ears in an agony of fear; if they pricked up, then something must be near!

Up they went in sudden straightness, and out came a quick, short, warning bark. Over the hill in front came riding a troop of men, and by the moon's silver light on their weapons Bridget made out they were soldiers. Alas! alas! Then she was too late to save poor Tim. Useless to hurry on, or try to hide, where concealment amongst the short heather was impossible. As well meet her fate now, as later.

As they came riding nearer, Bridget saw this was no disorderly band, but men riding steadily with an officer at their head.

That it was the hated Roundheads she also noted at a glance; the next moment a sharp word of command rang forth, and all came to a sudden halt.

"Who goes there?" came the challenge. "Friend or foe?"

Trembling greatly, Bridget stepped forward to centre of the red road, where the moonlight fell full upon her, and lifted her white face to the captain's.

"A woman, and out at this hour! Mistress, you should be at home. *What* is it you say? Help! That you want help? From what, may I ask you? Rest assured I will do what I can to aid you if you will explain the matter."

As briefly and steadily as her faltering tongue would allow, Bridget explained what had occurred, and the soldier's brow grew very dark as he listened to her tale. Half his troop he sent off at once to Marshfields, with strict orders to avoid bloodshed, if possible, but to secure the ringleaders; and with the rest he escorted Bridget home. Placing her on his own horse, he walked beside her at a quick pace, keeping his hand on the bridle all the time, for he saw how shaken she was, and the horse was not used to a lady.

Rough was quite content to run alongside, and if the troopers wondered at their errand, they were too well accustomed to obey orders to trouble their heads at the why and wherefore. Poor Tim's heart sank very low as he heard the soldiers dismounting, and he could hardly believe he saw aright when Bridget and the captain came in together. He was nearly black and blue by then from his bruises, some of which were greatly inflamed.

The captain proposed to leave a few men as guard, whilst he, with the rest, pushed on to Marshfields. He must be prompt, he said, or his regular work would be thrown out, and of course, his time was not his own. He promised faithfully to return, and said he would consider very carefully in the meantime what could best be done. The whole country was so unsettled, it was absurd to look on one place as safer than another. Hordes of wild soldiers on both sides were swarming everywhere. The force of arms was the only power that prevailed.

He spoke very quickly, so as not to frighten the girl, and seemed greatly distressed at her friendless condition. He rode away as speedily as might be, and Bridget, assisted by a compassionate soldier, did her best to make Timothy more comfortable.

The night passed over, and in the clear morning light the Roundhead captain rode again to the door.

Very grave did he look as he told his anxious listeners that horrible deeds had taken place before *his* men reached the lonely miser's house, and the Royalist soldiers had ridden off before their arrival. The old man had been murdered, and terrible pillage done after the red-coats had departed with all the portable valuables they could lade themselves with, but as the darkness passed a sullen shame had fallen on the rabble of peasants, and they had slunk away like beaten curs, cowards in very truth, in the pure light of day!

He had but waited to give what little help he could to the frightened family at Marshfields, and then rode his best to reach the Manor.

"Now, mistress, I have here a signed safety warrant for my own family, given me by the Parliament in recognition of my services. I am on oath only to use it for them, so cannot give it to *you* unless my poor scheme seems at all possible to you."

He spoke very softly as he drew her gently into the quaint bay window, whilst he finished his tale of sorrow and bloodshed.

"I am but a rough soldier; my tongue is not used to fine phrases, fit for a dainty lady's ears. One day, maybe to-day, a pistol shot or a sword slash will finish me. Very likely you many never see me more, but as the only protection I can give you, to shield you in the present and the future, will you consent now—at once—to marry me, a poor but honest man, with a whole heart at your service, and a strong and willing arm to protect and help you as long as life shall last? It is but a rough wooing, well I know, but what else can I do? If you but grant my humble prayer, then the signed warrant will hold you sacred from my side, and I can leave *my wife* a guard to protect her from all else, should need arise. The Grange is burnt to the ground. I rode that way to enquire if your trusted nurse could come to you, but no one knows where she has gone. To leave you here unprotected, without a woman by you, is an awful thought, and yet I am so pressed for time I know not what to do if you say me Nay. Indeed, mistress, I would treat you well, and my mother longs for a daughter."

Bridget looked at the face bending over her, at the smile in the eyes, and the look of self-reliance in the mouth, and made her decision on the moment.

"I will be your true and faithful wife, sir. God bless you for your thought and care for me. Few would have troubled what became of an enemy's daughter. Civil wars make hard hearts."

"When a man has it in his power to help and shield a brave woman, believe me, mistress, he counts it high honour, side with whom she may. It is truly no time for forms and ceremonies, yet even I, Roundhead as I am, do not go the lengths that some do, and though I would not willingly break any law, yet I would fain have the Church's blessing rest on us. I sometimes think the day is not far distant when I would gladly turn my sword into a ploughshare, so sick and tired am I of endless petty quarrels and jealousies even amongst our generals. Had Henry Cromwell been the senior to meek, gentle, easily-frightened Richard, the reins of power and direction would not have slipped like waxed ropes through *his* fingers, judging by the tact he had displayed in Ireland. Is there anyone here, either who has taken the oath of agreement or not, who would run the risk of uniting us, now at once?"

"In this quiet spot, sir, our own old Rector lives unmolested at the Rectory and has held his services much as usual. The people love him, and until lately we have had no agitators to stir up tumults amongst us; but my faithful servant, Timothy, told me yester-morn that Dunstar,[7] our nearest town, is in a state of terrible excitement, and riotous meetings have been held in the market place, the clergy

---

[7] Variant spelling of Dunster, a village in the civil parish of Somerset.

prohibited from entering the church, and virtually imprisoned in their own houses. So that before long we may be in the same case. Will not marrying me bring you into trouble with Parliament?"

"That I will gladly risk if we can manage the business anyhow. My troop have served under me well, and would, I fancy, hardly care to play informers; and by the time the idea had entered into their heads of making any disturbance, the deed would be done. But I must warn you of the heavy penalty strictly enforced for using the so-called Common Prayer Book, which might fall heavily on your old friend at the Rectory."

"No, sir, that cannot touch him; he is very nearly blind from specks in his eyes, and years ago learnt the services he required off by heart, to our great advantage these last few years."

"Well! that is good for us; many of the best of your clergy have done, and are doing the same, so that their people should yet have the comfort of their familiar prayers, even if in a modified form."

"And you a Roundhead, sir, to speak so moderately!—you puzzle me!"

"Ay, mistress, but my mother is a Royalist, and mainly for that reason I procured the safety warrant I shall leave with you; and for her sweet sake, I trust my zeal, in what I believe to be the righteous cause, will never turn me into a fanatic. There are many moderate men like myself, serving in the Parliamentary army, quite as wide awake to our shortcomings as any Royalist can be; but a truce to such outside matters, a soldier's first duty is to obey. Now I must to your village pastor, and see if he will help us. Kindly tell me how best to find him, and will you of your charity make your own way, with two of my fellows for witnesses, to the little parish church hard by, in half an hour? Nay! look not so slightingly at your dress, it is all that I could wish; a fairer maid I ne'er beheld."

"One moment, sir, I pray you! Should my parents object to this sudden action of mine, will it cause you ought of trouble?"

"They will *not* object when I explain my motives fully, and my reasons for what seems, I grant you, like hot haste. Nay, more, they will understand no other course was open to me, on my honour as a gentleman. And now, farewell! time flies!"

With quick strides the soldier disappeared from Bridget's view. No fear but what she watched him out of sight; as godly a man to look on, as would be found in a long day's ride. Ere long he passed up between the high-clipped laurel hedges that bordered the Rectory gravel drive, and knocked on the porch door, half hidden in its bower of roses.

A night-capped head peered forth, with ideas of infant baptism required, put swiftly to flight by the solder's brief words. Then came a hurried tumbling into the best Sunday-suit, a stock very much under one ear, and an old, old man shambled side by side of the young one, down to the tiny church across the road.

A smaller party was not possible for legality's sake, than just those few men and the girl, who looked a winsome bride indeed, in the simple white muslin dress she had found time to put on, to do honour to the brave soldier, whose smile of thanks and whispered words of approval fell softly on her ear as he led her up the church; whilst the Rector shuffled helplessly into his smocked surplice wrong side foremost, with no watchful clerk to put him straight.

Quietly, but very reverently was the service said in the early summer morn. The soldier placed on Bridget's finger his own signet ring, all too large for her small hand, and did not again loose his clasp until they stood in the old vestry to sign the register. Then he wrote a few lines swiftly, which also he called on his men to witness as his will, and filled in the Parliamentary warrant in all due form. Well under half an hour, and all was finished.

At the church door, when the pair came out, all the captain's troop were drawn up in order, and of their own accord, after saluting him, each man respectfully did the same to his bride, who went from red to white, and back again, as she recognised the hour of loneliness had indeed returned. How should she bear it again?

Clearly, coolly, did Captain Markham detail the men for the special duty of guarding his wife—how proudly he said the words!—and then in sight of all, stooped, bareheaded, and kissed her on the lips; sprang briskly into his saddle, gave the quick order to trot, and was out of sight before Bridget quite took in what had happened. The old priest offered her his arm, and respecting her silence, walked quietly homewards, whilst the few specially-selected soldiers walked their horses behind.

Timothy's unfeigned satisfaction at what had taken place did more to rouse Bridget from her musings than aught else; and after she had attended to him, she went up to her own old chamber, and stood for hours gazing out of the latticed window along the winding road over the hills the soldiers had taken that morning.

No hum of her spinning wheel vibrated that day on the clear air, and when she went to her rest, her simple robe was laid with unusual care aside, to wait for another gladsome day that should see a simple, honest man return in peace and love!

Ay! wrap it up with every care, and strew sweet lavender around, to set rust and moth at defiance, but never more will you robe yourself, fair lady, in its soft folds, or look again as you looked erewhile in that tiny village church.

A few peaceful days followed, during which Timothy made good progress, and quiet returned to the village. It was but the lull before another storm!

Disorderly bands of soldiers came frequently sweeping by; some, warned by the sight of the soldier-guard at the Manor House, passed on their way with jeers; others, those of the Roundhead persuasion, respected the safety warrant; but one rampageous lot, fired with the thought of treasure, outnumbered the slender garrison, killed two, wounded more, and ransacked the place from attic to cellar. Even Madam's chamber was not respected, but underwent the most searching scrutiny of any. Flooring was pulled up, walls tapped, backs of cupboards wrenched down, and the chimney fired up all in vain—not a coin could be found. Savage and disappointed, at length the lawless lot rode off.

In those previous quiet days Bridget had studied attentively that quaint old mystic book, and hearing the soldiers had been very brutal in their conduct to the villagers, went down to offer her aid.

Was it shame at their past behaviour that caused such glowering eyes and sullen murmurs to reach her on all sides? Mothers snatched children hastily out of her sight, and once she caught a murmur of "Bewitched—the evil eye!" that only made her smile. She called on the old clergyman, and found him in such a shipwrecked condition after the soldiers' rough visit that she obliged him to return with her, on plea his company would be protection.

And so the hours sped, and the shadows lengthened.

One day a letter came from her absent parents, full of regret and alarm for her, and saying how thankful they were to have come alone, for the country round her uncle's place was like a volcano—no peace nor rest for man or beast. Her aunt still lingered on—every day the end seemed imminent, and then would come a rally, and hopes of recovery quickly revived. With so many counties in open revolt, any prospect of their return seemed far distant, and the Squire himself was so ailing, he was not fit for the journey, had all been plain sailing. It was often the way with twins, she added; if one was ill, the other surely ailed. Bridget might rely on her sending as frequent tidings as could be managed. Their hearts were full of her!

Timothy was out and about again when Martha and her husband walked quietly in, and took possession of the kitchen. After doing their utmost to save the Grange for Captain Fosbrook, they had, under cover of the confusion and darkness, escaped to the shelter of the woods, and remained there until all danger to themselves was past—then came straight to the Manor.

Timothy at once offered to go home, but Madam Bridget had learnt to rely on him so thoroughly that she would not entertain such an idea for a moment, and two trustworthy men were none too much for a household in such troublous days.

One morning Tim came in with a very long face, and said he had heard a rumour in the village that there was expected to take place in a day or so, a great organised Royalist rising, only a few miles off, to meet which, on the other side, General Lambert and a strong force were coming from London.

Bridget's heart beat very fast. Would her soldier husband be in the thick of the fight—should she see him first—and what if he fell?

Day by day, for hours together, she watched that winding road from her dormer window, until her eyes ached with the strain, and her brain wearied with the suspense. Except for her visits to the village on errands of mercy, and the morning tendance of her mother's pensioners, accustomed to come at a certain hour to the servants' hall, every thought was occupied with the coming fight.

Young and enquiring, she tried some of the simples and recipes mentioned in the little old book, and found them more efficacious than her mother's usual remedies. Encouraged by this success, her belief in the book grew, and in one or two cases of fever she ventured to treat the children by its directions, strong though the remedies seemed. Martha was too pleased to see her occupied with anything to mind what it was, and the villagers' opinion of her powers grew apace.

One morning, as she entered the hall, she saw a silk-tied paper lying inside the open door. The direction was firm and distinct, and the first time of seeing her new name in writing sent the blood in a flush to her white face. Only *one* hand could have penned *that*, and every letter was so carefully formed, it was evident that pleasure and pride had both taken part in doing so. With elaborate care she untied the fastening and read the few brief words.

"Keep a brave heart, sweetheart, and farewell!"

How or when it had come none knew, but Bridget guessed it had been sent off on the eve of the fighting, and by now might be the last token from as brave a man as ever held a pen or used a sword.

Every possible minute of that weary day found her watching from her window, whilst memory retraced those few brief hours of her wedding-day that had fenced her round with a strong man's watchful guard; and fancy sped ahead, picturing a manly form laid low, and a loving husband and heart cold with the chill of death.

Timothy had gone off somewhere long before she had awoke that morning; she felt no shadow of doubt to do her service, in some faithful fashion or other.

It was a perfect day, with a heat haze hanging over the blue hills; too hot, almost, for even the buzzing insect life to keep awake, and the flowers in the garden looked quite faint and languid.

35

Was ever day so long!

The shadows lengthened steadily, the birds awoke and sang their evening hymn, and with the prospect of a heavy dew ere long, the roses lifted their heavy, perfumed heads, and reigned supreme once more.

Over the crest of the nearest hill through the mist of warm vapour, surrounded by clouds of dust, rode a few horsemen slowly. Then one detached himself from the others, and urged his jaded steed to a quicker pace down the winding, deep red road, straight for the Manor gates.

Bridget knew then, in one swift moment, that she had need of all her courage to meet the news so near. Timothy was coming to tell her as gently as he could that her soldier was dead. Dead in the path of his duty; dead in the prime of his life!

Calm and white she turned and left the room, whilst another thought sprang into life; if her great fear was true, surely, oh! most surely, there would have been a bier! Her faithful comrade would never dare to face her if *that* had been left behind on a field of sackage. If *he* was not still alive, why came these soldiers here?

Down with speed to the entrance door, a few hurried words to Martha in passing—for a room to be opened, and a bed made—and then another pause of anxious waiting, broken at last by Timothy's voice as he stood close beside her.

"The captain is here, madam. It was his greatest wish, though the doctor said it was an awful risk, with such a wound! He *is* alive, thank God, and that is more than we expected when we started, but once the doctor told him it was only a question of hours, no chance would be thrown away by coming, he would set off at once. Lambert has won; the Royalists' losses are very heavy, and they are utterly routed. Take courage, madam, for *his* sake."

Slowly the horsemen came on, one riding behind his officer, holding him up in his arms. So weak, so white, so helpless, that they had to lift him like a baby, and lay him down full length on the polished floor of the hall. Bridget feared he was dead as he lay with his head upon her lap, but when a strong cordial had been given him, the eyes opened bright and clear, and a smile that was not of earth stole over the quiet face.

Involuntarily and swiftly the troopers bared their heads, whilst Martha and Timothy sank on their knees.

There was a convulsive quiver all over the recumbent figure, one feeble, faltering word—"Sweetheart!" and Reginald Markham, brave man and true, lay numbered with the dead.

When they came to undress him, and robe him for the grave, they found the bandages had slipped on the ride, and his clothes were simply soaked in blood.

Timothy was very clear that the doctor had said *nothing* could save him, when Bridget, with hands clasped and quivering lips, had grieved over that awful ride. How gladly would she have gone to him, had there been time, only just *that* was wanting. Timothy had not arrived until the fight was really over, and the victorious army in pursuit of the flying Royalists. Most fortunately, he had speedily fallen in with some of Captain Markham's troop searching the ground where they had noticed their leader fall in the thickest of the fight! Amongst the many riderless steeds wandering over the field of carnage, one weary beast stood still, with drooping head and relaxed limbs, who whinnied every now and then in a hopeless, melancholy fashion that speedily attracted the solders' ears.

It was Sultan, the captain's charger, cut and bruised not a little, with his coat all clotted with dust and blood—not his own! Captain Markham was clear enough then to pray them to take him at once to the Manor, and it was not until they had seen the hastily-summoned doctor's grave shake of the head, that they had realized the gravity of the case.

Very quietly he was laid to rest in a sunny corner of the old graveyard a day or two after his death, and only her altered name and the signet-ring remained to remind Bridget, if she needed it, of the romance of her life. His will left all he possessed to her, but in such unsettled times no steps could be taken to claim her rights.

IV

CAUTION

"There's a track upon the deep, and a path across the sea;
But the weary ne'er return to their ain countrie."

—Gilfillan.

"HEIGH-HO! It is a weary world, nothing but trouble and sorrow from the cradle to the grave!"
Half under his breath the words came from Squire Conyngham's lips as he stood in the autumn sunshine, with hands folded on his thick stick, and his keen clear eyes fixed wistfully on the far distant hills, beyond which lay the home he loved so well. Beside him stood his wife, trying with all her might *not* to see how sadly the fine old man had wasted away in the last few weeks. His twin sister's illness seemed really some ill-defined and happily rare form of consumption. Some days she was so wonderfully better, all felt hopeful; others so bad the end appeared imminent.

Any hint as to her brother's departure was sure to bring on an exhausting attack, so that it seemed absolute cruelty to the Squire and his wife to insist on returning home, though they were really not required to assist at Ellesmere. There were plenty to do the little possible for the invalid.

Openly to herself Madam Conyngham owned the relief it would be when they could leave, for without their usual occupations both felt lost and dull. Madam perhaps in particular; hers was such an active nature, busy from morning until night indoors and out.

The memory that the brother and sister had been such veritable twins, rare then as now, and the old doctor's warning at the time of their birth that one would hardly outlive the other, repeated solemnly to her by her mother-in-law, often awakened a feeling of dread in her heart that she kept to herself.

Only two brief letters had found their way in safety from Mistress Bridget, and the interval since the last had been of great length, neither had they been fortunate in finding trustworthy messengers to her. Tired of inactivity Richard had enlisted.

Another half-checked sigh, and Madam could bear it no longer; laying her delicate hand with its glittering rings on her husband's arm, she begged him to tell her what the trouble was that lay so heavily on him.

"The truth is I am worrying about Bridget. I fear we acted unwisely, and without due thought in leaving her alone. How shall we forgive ourselves if owing to our carelessness harm befall the child? *We* shall be to blame in the sight of God and man, for neglecting our nearest duty to take up with one further off."

"Surely, you take too strong a view of the matter. What else could we do but come?"

"Ay! Ay! Dear wife, so it seemed best to us at the moment, for you and I have always been so much to each other, having no chick for so long, that when at last the baby came, she seemed a thing right outside our lives; we never realized till now that she was the very kernel of home!"

"Now surely you are talking rubbish, what greater fuss was ever made of any baby than of ours! Did not you feast the whole place for miles around?—were not the bells a nuisance from the way they chimed? *Now* what is the matter?—you have gone so white!"

"You reminded me of what in truth I had no right to forget —the muffled peal that all in a moment tolled through the joyous strains, and then was gone!"

"I told you at the time, and I tell you again, something quite simple would account for that accident; it shows how out of sorts you truly are to hark back to that!"

"Ay, you didn't hear it, wife; it was gruesome, only thank the Lord, the chimes rang true again to the end, and so, if my belief is correct, it is a warning sent that in the midst of life, our winsome maid will suddenly meet Death: and I comfort myself with the notion that, as the joyous strain rang out again, it was but maybe a passing illness, and Life conquered!"

"If it gives you any comfort, pray think so. I don't believe in such old wives' fables myself, as you know!"

"Well, it is hard *not* to believe in them when so often in the family records a muffled peal is mentioned; not always, though generally, happening at some great event in the lives of our ancestors, who died suddenly and unexpectedly, it is true.

"I had a great fancy for old records at one time, if you remember, and in them I found one or two peals mentioned, when trouble worse than death fell on our belongings. Also I found noted amongst the papers another queer thing that I kept to myself until now, and that is really what I am fretting about; so as we are on the subject, I may as well tell you about it. Whether some old curse was the origin of the muffled peal that I have heard now more than once, ringing out in the still night air when no mortal hand could have been on the ropes, or whether it was intended as a kindly warning by the Great Powers above, or simply due to some unexpected cause, I know not; but as surely as the bells ring out, on whatever *day* of the month, the corresponding *year* of the person's life connected with that day will bring, and always has brought, trouble—sorrow—maybe death—to the member of our family concerned.

"Therefore our Bridget's trouble is fast approaching for the muffled peal was last heard on the day of her birth, the twentieth of February. Remember, wife, if I am not at hand, that very great will need to be your faith and patience then, and give good heed to the child!"

"*Why* did you wait till now to tell me all this? It is a more serious matter than I thought for; would it not be well for Bridget herself to know?"

"Most certainly *not!* Keep the child from ever hearing of the old tale if you can. So far as I know, there is nothing uncanny or doubtful in the way of papers at Rithycombe. My father told me he remembered well a huge bonfire on the terrace when he was a lad, into which books and papers were hastily thrown with looks of fright. What these books were I cannot say. I have never come across any suspicious ones. I know there was a long story about one of my aunts, but that I told you years since; no need to go into it now, and see—yonder rides a messenger!"

With more alacrity than his appearance promised, the Squire hurried to meet the armed letter-carrier, bearing papers from one part to another. He had quite a packet for Ellesmere, and amongst them one from Mistress Bridget to her parents. Eagerly they scanned the closely-written pages in which, in simple, quaint language she told them of her recent experiences. How, to save her from harm and trouble, the brave soldier had shielded her with his own name, and left her a military guard. Of how she waited for their home-coming, and how long the days seemed in the present quiet period; would they not soon return to her? She could not speak too highly of Timothy's carefulness, nor of how kindly Martha and her husband looked after her. She said she spent hours at her wheel up in the old dormer room, and anxiously awaited the reply from her parents. Humbly she hoped they would approve of the important step she had taken, and give their loving sanction to what indeed had seemed the best and wisest course to take.

No doubt at so great a distance they would consider such haste unnecessary, and maybe undutiful, but not at all in excuse for herself, simply to clear Captain Markham's name from any idea of self-interested motives, she thought it fair to state that the old clergyman had warmly approved of the step; and Martha had declared none but a good man would have acted in such an unselfish manner, and that some of the soldiers had spoken most heartily to Timothy of their leader's upright, honourable character and stainless name.

With her loving duty, and earnest trust her parents would forgive her for acting so entirely on her own responsibility, she signed herself for the first time, their loving daughter, Bridget Markham.

In silence except for deep breaths both parents read the closely-written sheets, realizing very vividly that, no thanks to them, their child had been protected and cared for, even at the present moment, by the brave heart and generous act of a total stranger.

But themselves could they have blamed if evil dark and dread had fallen on the flower of their house?

"God bless him!" murmured the old man, as he passed his hand over his dim eyes, whilst Madam's lips moved in wordless response. "My little lass, my little lonely lass! Ah! if we were but with her, we would part no more! I have acted on impulse more or less all my life, and now it had led us into this mess."

"But John, my man, your sister's prayer was very urgent for you to come at once. How could we guess or imagine the poor thing would linger so long? She worked herself nearly into a frenzy yesterday because I let fall the merest hint that we were wanted at home; she knows neither peace nor rest if she fancies for one moment you are out of call. Truly it is a difficult position, for granted that it was an error of judgement to start off quite so suddenly—and at the time you acted only on the dictates of your own warm, loving heart—can it be right now that by our own will, we *are* here, to get back home at once, willy-nilly, and accelerate poor Eliza's death by so doing? Two wrongs can never make a right. God in His mercy has guarded Bridget so far, can we not trust Him still? See, there is Thomas beckoning to you; what a sheaf of papers, to be sure."

"I thought it would surely interest you to hear that had you not got here when you did, it would have been folly and worse to attempt doing so later. The accounts in these papers of the terrible state of the country are something awful, and make one shiver for the wickedness that stalks abroad.

"Murder—ruin—cruelty—torture—pillage—and worse, have spread like an evil blight over our peaceful land. Those who are sober are wicked, and those who are drunk are reckless! My tenants are refusing to pay their rents on the ground that their crops have been so ruined by scattered bands of soldiers passing over them, that there will be *no* harvest, and I have no right to expect to fare better than my neighbours.. Then I have a letter from Moberly saying the county bank has been broken into, and besides all available cash being carried off to pay the army, papers and deeds of great value were wantonly burnt. In vain the respectable townspeople made a stand, and tried to save their property and keep order; the riff-raff who had no interest at stake were only too enchanted to have a row on, and joined heartily in the work of destruction, which would possibly have attained even greater dimensions had not a man suddenly ridden in amongst them, shouting that a fine old mansion some five miles off had just been fired, and there was loot enough for all!

"The clearance was something wonderful, but with all their speed they only found an empty shell and no treasures. The place had been raided days before; it was only a ruse on the messenger's part to try to save the bank. So far, so good—the scheme was a daring one, and deserving of success, but unfortunately the man himself, trusting the darkness of the night, and the excitement of the people, to prevent recognition, had not hidden himself, as would have been only common prudence. The mob surrounded him at once on their return, and literally tore him in pieces; so that though the loss, as far as *I* am concerned, is no light one, and puts me in an awkward position, when I think of that poor fellow's terrible end, I feel afraid to grumble. There now, like a true Briton, I am all the better for such an outpouring, tell me your tidings?"

Eagerly they repeated their news.

"Married! That *child!* You don't say so—to a Roundhead soldier, alack-a-day![8] What could have possessed her? His motive is very clear, forsooth—a pretty lass, and a heavy purse, both to be had for the asking! Take my word for it, brother and sister, he's a regular scoundrel working on the maid's fear like that. Just taken advantage of your absence—a made-up plot the whole thing. Be very sure there was some irregularity that when it suits him our fine gentleman will bring forward in triumph, and then how will it fare with Mistress Bridget? But I can find out about him from my friend Colonel Peter Robertson, who made the blunder of following Cromwell, so he's sure to know something of this fellow if he's,

---

[8] An exclamation expressing regret, sorrow or alarm.

as you say, in Lambert's command. When I get an opportunity, I'll make a few enquiries, and you'll see I shall come out right."

"I don't know about that; it is rather hard to condemn a man you've never seen, without hearing his version, and I don't see how he was to know Bridget would have a halfpenny. Did you tell the child where to hide the dowry, wife?"

"No, I had not time; indeed, we had never settled on a place, if you remember. I only told her to tell no one where she put it, and I dare say it is all right."

"John, I think you are an uncommonly lucky fellow to have got off so lightly at Rithycombe; only the furniture banged about and broken, whilst Fosbrook had his place burned, and at Marshfields they suffered so heavily."

"You forget Timothy's injuries."

"No, I don't—not a bit; but they didn't kill him, as they did the miser, poor old man! He never went out anywhere, did he, of late years?"

"No; shut himself up so completely, that for days even his wife never saw him, and the windows of his private room where he spent all his time were never opened; indeed, rumour said that they were screwed down for safety. His sole amusement and occupation, his wife told me once, was fingering and counting his treasures, not only money, but plate and jewels as well; and Bridget says in her letter, when the raiders burst into his room, there he was, with all his secret places open, and his possessions heaped around him in confusion. Of course, they carried off everything, and murdered him cruelly into the bargain."

"Did you know him?"

"Formerly. Before this craze grew to such a disease, he was a pleasant man enough, but so close, his wife had the greatest difficulty to manage on the pittance he doled out. She was his housekeeper, certainly not his lady, but a very nice woman, and it was always supposed he married her for fear she should talk about his wealth."

"Well, I mustn't stay gossiping here any longer. I have a lot of business on hand this morning, and by rights should be off to London, but I can't possibly go with poor Eliza in this state, so it makes things complicated."

Madam thought her husband seemed decidedly more cheerful than before the messenger's arrival; it had given him something fresh to think about, but presently he again reverted to his worry about Bridget's birthday. If his sister went on like this, should they be kept here until then, and not be able to watch over the child; he thought it would drive him mad. With both of them to keep her in sight all day, how *could* harm befall her?—but if absent, it was a very different pair of shoes. Argument and remonstrance alike failing to comfort him, Madam went indoors to her sister-in-law, more disturbed than she cared to own, by this haunting fear of her husband's.

So passed a few more days, and then very quietly Eliza died, bidding *all* farewell except the twin brother seated close beside her, with one of her thin hands held in his.

Madam breathed a sigh of relief as the hours rolled on, and her husband went about much as usual; not looking well by any means, that he had not done for long, but still not feeling ill or complaining in any way, but, poor woman, she rejoiced too soon.

The weather had been very dry, and in consequence of the unusual heat of the summer, many settlements had taken place in doors and walls.

Returning from the funeral, as Squire Conyngham and Thomas Melville passed under the portico, without any previous warning a heavy mass of stucco fell full on the Squire's head, sending him flat to the ground on the instant, and killing him on the spot.

No one had noticed the cracks widening steadily day by day, and it was an accident that might have happened to anyone, and for which no one was to blame.

Not that that idea gave much comfort; it is always a satisfaction to declare it was someone's fault such and such a thing happened.

Poor Madam for long refused to believe her husband was dead, neither would she leave his side night or day for a moment, until, almost by force, they had to carry him away, to bury him beside his sister.

Thomas Melville made all arrangements, but dare not risk taking him home. Indignity to the dead was too awful an idea, and the roads were really unsafe for the living.

Madam collapsed altogether, when her state of terrible excitement had literally exhausted itself. Utter oblivion fell on the tired brain, and she lay like a log, from which state, after long days, she recovered, with memory for the time completely gone, and vitality much impaired. The doctor said they must give her time, and the clouds would lift from her mind, but that the rousing must come naturally, not be forced in any way, or permanent blankness might remain.

Should she ever worry too much over events that seemed dreamlike and vague, it *might*—he did not say it *would*—bring such a strain on her over-taxed brain, terrible consequences might ensue.

V

THE TIDINGS SENT

"On by moor and mountain green,
　Let's buckle a', and on together,
Down the burn, and through the dene,
　And owre the muir among the heather,
Owre the muir among the heather."

—*Jacobite Song.*

ONE fine autumn day, when the country round had subsided into a semblance of quiet that deceived *no* one, Timothy started to carry a letter to Captain Markham's widowed mother.

It had been no easy task for Bridget to write, and the shaky writing bore testimony to the effort made, as kindly and sadly she related the little she really new of Reginald Markham. She told of the lonely common—of the chivalrous soldier who had gone out of his way to help and shield her—and how in the few minutes they had had together he had confidently assured her his mother would give her a warm welcome for his sake. Perhaps in the unknown future, if peace ever came again, Madam Markham would pay her a visit, and see the flower-decked grave that meant so much to them. Dearly would Bridget love to tend and wait upon her.

News of her parents came but seldom, and she was *so* lonely, though she tried her best not to be selfish in her sorrow; her nerves seemed all upset, and the slightest noise made her jump nearly out of her skin. The house was too large and dreary for its few inhabitants, and a blight seemed to have fallen on the place.

That was the substance of the sorrowful silk-tied missive that Timothy secured in his leathern belt, handed up to him as he stooped from beautiful Sultan to receive from Bridget's slender fingers the letter that had cost her much to write, and must and would cause bitter grief and sorrow when read. It always made her wince to see him on the glossy charger, and yet no other horse than her husband's was at her command, and she counted it a sacred duty to speed the sorrowful tidings to the lonely mother waiting, for tidings that never came.

The horse knew her well by now, and stooped his strong neck to her to stroke his soft nose, whilst jealous Rough, unheeded, went barking at his heels.

So through the high wild lanes and over the wind-swept common, Timothy made his way, dreading the end of his journey in no slight degree, and yet knowing well that Bridget had purposely selected him on account of his admiration of her husband. He noted for himself the neglected state of the farms, and the trampled crops in the fields, and there was a sullen look on the faces he passed that struck him as something very unusual. And the smells from neglected drainage and choked-up ditches were something awful. The public inns in Crampton were full to overflowing, and such filthy songs issued forth amidst yells of hideous applause, the simple fellow blushed all over, and thanked his stars his lady was not with him. The same spirit of reckless idleness, ripe for any mischief, was abroad in the old market town of Dunstar, or Dun Tor, the towered hill, to use its quaint old name, from whose ivy-covered castle gateway one fine day in 1413 the fair and gentle wife of the haughty lord of the castle, in her flowing robe of white, barefooted in the dusty road, started to make as long a circuit as she could to win a common for her people. Doubtless she had tried all forms of persuasion first, before half in fun, half in mockery, her husband promised to give her as big a piece as she walked round with her delicate feet bare.

Above the gateway he stood to watch her descending the steep rough pathway to the tiny village green below, the only bit of open ground the poor possessed, and that but a few yards square.

In his rough way he loved his gentle wife, but to a nature like *his*, it was impossible even to fathom the shrinking and the faintness that filled *her* gentle heart when she saw all the place was astir to watch her painful progress. For the flints were sharp and rough, and burnt like hot coals from the power of the sun, and even before she reached the level, there were ugly red marks left behind her. But her courage in its way was equal, if not superior to her husband's. and with head erect and smiling lips she persevered. Women, children, and finally men, rushed to strew sand on her path, and to scrape the stones aside, but when she saw their object she bade them desist; it was not in the bond she was thus to be helped. Respectfully they obeyed her wish, only the pitiful tears streamed down the women's faces as they saw how she winced with agony, and almost crawled back to the ivy gateway. But the piece of ground she had encircled was a goodly size—a right noble gift for all time to the inhabitants of the market town. The brave spirit carried her to within a yard of the ascending path to the castle, but could do no more; and even as her husband sallied forth to meet her, she fell fainting almost at his feet, and the spontaneous cheer that arose fell unheeded on her ears, as she was lifted from the ground. It was weeks before she could stand on her cut and bruised feet, but from that day the townspeople almost worshipped her, and she felt well repaid for the effort she had made, when she found how highly her husband praised her courage, and how proud he was of her.

51

Timothy knew this story well, and looked with special interest at the frowning gateway, sheltering amidst thick trees on the side of the steep hill—that very gateway that in the form of a picturesque photo adorns our railway carriages to-day.

Desolate rides over ruined lands were his portion for many days, with nights spent at village inns, where queer bits of news fell to his share; how the people all over the kingdom had refused to pay taxes—how Monk, at the head of seven thousand veterans, had marched into England from Scotland, holding his own counsel as to his intentions—how that milk-and-water copy of a great original, General Lambert, had hastened northwards to encounter this army —and how a rumour had travelled straight from London town itself that the only choice now left to the nation was the rule of the Stuarts or of the army. Timothy heard this last report in the fair city of the severn hills; his goal was nigh at hand, but a few more hours and his journey would be done. Had he wished to linger then, his steed would have refused, for his strides grew faster as he came on familiar ground, and Timothy rode with slack rein, leaving the way to him to choose.

Through a quiet, picturesque village, up a steep bit of road, and then Sultan stopped at lodge gates that were at least a welcome sight to him, with the surety of a nice warm mash to eat, and a fresh soft bed to roll on. The sound of the prancing hoofs brought a clean-looking woman hurrying eagerly out to the gate, with her face in a glow of pleasure, and a smile of welcome ready on her lips: how quickly the latter faded as she saw a stranger riding Sultan, whose name she called out in greeting, in the shock of a great surprise.

"I have news for Mrs. Markham," said Timothy very quietly. "I suppose I can ride to the house?"

"The news is bad, I take it, for *you* to ride the horse?"

"Yes, bad as it possibly can be. Is your mistress able to hear it?"

"Poor soul, she has lived in terror of this day; *any* news must surely be a relief, for she has been half beside herself, fearing she knew not what. Walk Sultan quietly up, and I'll go on ahead. Ay, that is well done," as Timothy threw himself off. "To see *you* in her son's place would be too sad and sudden. Poor Master Reggie! All loved him here! There, I must not keep you; she has the first right to your sorrowful news. I shall hear all in time."

Wiping her eyes with her apron, she hurried up the drive, and Timothy slowly followed, marvelling at the trouble in the world allowed by a merciful God for reasons only know to Him.

A white-haired, frail old lady stood framed in the doorway by the time he reached it, with the few slow tears of age trickling unheeded down her face. One soft withered hand stroked Sultan's glossy neck, and it was very evident the creature recognised a friend from the way he pushed his velvet nose into the palm of her hand, where in the long ago, sugar or apples had often lain.

Timothy waited respectfully until she turned to him, when, with his best reverence, he took from within his doublet the packet entrusted to him by Bridget.

"You will rest and refresh yourself, my good friend, and then I shall love to hear all you can tell me. My old man-servant will see to your comfort, and Sultan's mash must be ready. Ah me! it was not for nothing—it *never* is—that our best apple-tree showed flower and fruit together this season;[9] I thought it a sign for myself, that I should rest in my grave before next spring, but now it seems it was for my boy, my only child. God help me!"

---

[9] It was widely believed that a fruit tree flowering out of season was a sign that someone would die. *Notes & Queries* 9, vol. 12: 133, 1903.

Alone in her own quiet room, the poor heartbroken mother untied the silken fastenings of Bridget's packet, and gave a little gasping cry as she saw an enclosure addressed to her in her son's well-known hand. The outside was disfigured by an ominous stain, sad for a loving heart to see, and it had needed some effort on Bridget's part to leave unread the open letter, that *she* had sealed with the signet ring. Her own letter was simple and sad, but it touched a chord of sympathy in the old woman's heart, that a more ceremonious narrative would have utterly failed to arouse.

Her son's letter was written on the eve of the fight, when a sure presentiment of disaster was weighing him down. He said most unexpectedly he had had a sudden chance given him of getting a line to the Manor—how, he had pledged himself not to say, for every man's hand was literally against his brother, and the friend of to-day was the foe of to-morrow. If all went well his mother would never read this, for there was, at present, no safe opportunity of getting it to her; but should he fall, it would, he knew, be no small comfort to her to have a parting word from him. Briefly he related what a hold the fair and gentle girl had taken upon him, left as she never ought to have been, well-nigh unprotected; that had he searched the whole world through, no more suitable daughter, or sweeter wife could he have found, than the girl he had encountered on the lonely common in the silence of the summer night. That all he possessed he had willed to her, for the estate itself was entailed, and his mother amply provided for. Perchance, in the providence of God, he should yet lead his bride to his mother's side, but if not, then surely he knew he had but to commend Bridget to her loving care, and, given time and opportunity, she would not fail him.

And so in love and charity with all men, ready for life or death as pleased the Lord above, he signed himself her faithful,

loving son whilst life lasted; and if it might be so—beyond.—
Reginald Markham.

It was hours before Timothy received his summons to the oak
parlour, where whips and weapons hung around told him most
plainly whose private room it had been.

Mrs. Markham looked sunk and aged, but her voice was as
gentle as ever as she asked Timothy to begin at the beginning, and
tell her all he could of her son and his wife.

Be sure that Bridget had full justice at her trusty servitor's
hands, and he told his tale so well that Mrs. Markham could almost
fancy she saw it all—the old timbered house in its lonely vale—
the rough village near—the tiny church—the hurried wedding—
and the last sad scene of all, when, in the quiet early morning,
they had laid her soldier son in his peaceful grave.

Timothy said the soldiers had carried him along, and Bridget
walked behind. The old parson's voice was very shaky, as again
from memory he recited the proper prayers, and his eyes were
dim from more than age as he thought of that other service so
lately held.

The hour had purposely been chosen before the village
should be astir, and no volley was fired, by Bridget's wish. There
was no saying what unseemly conduct would have taken place,
even amongst the peaceful dead, if the rough, ignorant folk had
got wind of the fact that a hated Roundhead had been buried in
the churchyard.

Wreckers, smugglers, robbers, and Royalists, *when* it suited them,
but Roundheads, never!

Mrs. Markham asked him many questions about Bridget, all
of which he answered truly. He told of her tendance of the sick and
suffering; how she spent hours spinning at her wheel in the high-

pitched gable room, which commanded such an extensive view of the country round; how very seldom tidings came of her absent parents, and of what a terribly superstitious part theirs was.

Then he lowered his voice almost to a whisper as he told her what even Bridget had not heard; that when the captain lay on the blood-stained ground, whilst the soldiers who were to form his escort bustled around, and wandering figures that boded no good were dancing here and there amongst the dead and dying, robbing some, killing others, Reginald Markham had solemnly asked *his* promise, poor, ignorant fellow as he was, to watch over and guard his youthful bride whilst danger threatened.

"And God help me, so I will, madam; with you goodwill I will depart in the morrow. I can get a lift from here for part of the way, perhaps as far as Bridgewater, and methinks I shall but fidget till I see the golden letters of our weathercock standing out clear against the sky. Without taking this journey, I never could have imagined the country was in such a state, for we are in a very quiet part, and news reaches us but seldom. Why, madam, as I rode over Bristol Bridge I saw a huge placard, with great printed letters, offering large rewards to any person or persons who should give such certain information as should lead to the discovery of a witch or witches, and such crowds pressed forward to read the same, it struck me it might be something new. The Bible words 'Thou shalt not suffer a witch to live' were quoted."[10]

"I have not heard of it before in Bristol, but for the last fourteen years there has been a great outcry made about witches, and I have heard cruel tales about their sufferings; but if it is true that their power is almost unlimited, I certainly agree with those

---

[10] Exodus 22:18

who endeavour to rid our land of them, though any cruelty in the matter would be very wicked. And now tell me if my new daughter is loved amongst the poor around her."

"Mistress Bridget is more feared than loved, shame on our ungrateful folks that so it should be, always ready as they are to ask her aid, and then abuse her behind her back. If the Squire had but had a son to follow him, things would have been surely different; folks will put up with plain speaking from a *man*, when they call it interference in a maid. If I had any say in the matter, none of the cottages in the village should my lady enter; the people are not worth it."

"Timothy, I think you are wrong; it is but our simple duty to help our neighbours, and if my young daughter has the power and the will to do so, it would be a sin to hinder her."

"Well, madam, you should know best, but maybe I've not made my meaning clear. A few weeks ago, a sudden, sharp storm came on; the sea rose in fury, and the breakers thundered on the reefs. A poor ship was caught in the gale, and *purposely* lured on the rocks. Her cargo was known to be spirits and tobacco, which the people around decided should never pay the customs' dues. They got her smashed on the reefs sure enough, on a rock we call the 'Shark's Tooth'; some of the crew found a precarious footing, others were seen clinging to the rigging. Only one was carried alive next morning into our village, the nearest to those particular rocks. Mistress Bridget, busy tending a sick child, immediately followed him in, to see if her help was needed, and he—poor foolish fellow!—out and told her of the false lights that had lured them on with hopes of harbour, strangers to our coast as they were; and that to the fact of the Excise men suddenly appearing he owed his life, for the wreckers had not time to finish him, and conceal the cargo, neither dared they leave him behind to give evidence against them. With dark looks and threatening words they had handed him along byways and noways until the cottages were reached. Mistress Bridget was terribly upset, and she spoke out her mind to those present, heedless, fearless of possible consequences. Sullen silence answered her, and she left, fancying *her* words, poor maid, were strong enough to impress reckless men, who, when I passed through a while later, were talking in a very ugly fashion of serving out someone or other, for meddling in matters that concerned them not.

"A Somersetshire man can bide his time, but he keeps his word!

"Had they had the faintest notion that directly the whisper reached *me* that the Whistling Maid was abroad, I up and went at my best pace to the Excise officers' quarters, and told them to be spry, for the wreckers were out, a ship in distress, and the crew would be lost—let alone the cargo, it is certain sure *my* treatment would have been rough indeed, but for my lady's sake I had taken uncommon good care that none save the bats and owls should know of my warning visit.

"Young Mistress fretted sorely all that evening to think of the brave lives lost for lack of a little help, and I sat tongue-tied like a fool, for well I knew it was no uncommon accident on those cruel rocks of ours. Early in the morning I met her dressed in hood and cape ready to sally forth, and on my asking what could take her out so early, she lifted her great dark eyes to mine, and said she had stayed awake all night, regretting she had not said the rescued sailor must come to the Manor; so now she was off to beg he might be brought up at once and she would tend him. I prayed her earnestly to go on no such errand; if need be, I could take any message for her; the villagers had spent the night in drinking all too freely of the stolen spirits, and their cottages would be no fit place for her! She drew herself up in a haughty scorn at first, and said she feared no one; but at last, by humble prayers, and by using the captain's name, I got her to say I might go instead.

"Well, madam, I went, but not even to you will I tell all I saw or heard, but *nothing* you could imagine could beat the reality. The sailor was dead—*how* boots not the telling. Was it likely that a crew of desperate men would let such a witness to their last night's lawless, wicked deeds live? And moreover one who had already blabbed? Not they! His doom was sealed from the first word he spoke to Madam Bridget. The Excise men about us are not sharp enough for the work they have to do; and maybe it is excusable when one thinks for a moment that every mother's son of them has most likely brother, cousin or friend, on the other side, to lay hold on whom would bring vengeance on them and theirs in very decided fashion.

"Pardon me, madam, for talking so much, but I wanted to make it clear to you, what only this long ride of mine had brought home very forcibly to me, that of all unsettled parts, ours is probably amongst the worst, ripe for any crime."

"I hope you will urge your lady to be careful; it seems to me she is over brave; and, Timothy, I need not remind you that my dear son looked to you to guard her well, the pretty creature. Give her my dear love, and say if God sees fit, not many months shall pass before we meet in person. I have much to settle and arrange before I can leave this place, but the moment I am free shall see me on my way to her. Now you will like to have a look round the house and grounds; it is a fair and lovely place that after *me*, alas! must pass to a distant cousin."

Timothy wandered all over the house, escorted by the trusty old butler, who eagerly drank in any details of his master that the messenger thought fit to tell. Then he told of the conflicting feelings abroad in the towns and villages he had ridden through in his long ride over one hundred and eighteen miles. How some people were sunk in a sullen stupor that savoured strongly of a violent reaction from lawless words and deeds; villages, desolate beyond description, with silence everywhere, and blackened ruins bearing witness to the vengeance wreaked. Some few folk professing a light-heartedness they did not feel, whilst women wept, children starved, and men drank deep to drown alike the thought of their own ill-deeds, and the misery of their once happy homes.

It was not a bright look-out by any means, but what could you expect in such unsettled times?

Eagerly the servants listened to his tales; he was a great traveller in their eyes, and we all know how pleasant it is to have a good audience. Timothy, in spite of his sad errand, enjoyed himself vastly, and was quite sorry to find the evening gone, and the hour of rest at hand.

But sleep he could not, in spite of his long ride; fears of he knew not what weighed him down, and he was thankful when the light grew strong enough for him to rise and roam abroad.

In the morning light, the traces of shock and sorrow were very visible on Mrs. Markham's face, when she summoned Timothy to say farewell, for trouble like hers is not fully felt in the sorrow of the first hearing; it wears into the mind and body far more heavily when there has been time for full realization that never more will the loved ones pass before our eyes, or hand of theirs grasp ours—gone without even the sorrow of an illness to prepare the mind—gone in the pride of manhood's strength, while ailing, feeble bodies exist on to extreme old age, not even sometimes considered welcome to the smallest share of home by those they have brought into the world, and cared for in their tender youth.

Timothy was soon on his way to the village inn, where the carriers bound for Bristol stopped to water the horses, and he was greatly struck by the general sorrow at the tidings he had brought, expressed by the villagers waiting to see the lumbering waggon well on its way.

"Eh! He was a good sort, Master Reginald; we could have spared many better, and the leddy herself, 'tis a grievous trial for her, poor soul! Most of young Master's troop was made up by men from these parts, and 'tis certain sure any one of them would have died to save the captain's life; but that was not to be, worse luck!"

VI

PERSECUTION

> " 'Twas a rough night
> My young remembrance cannot parallel
> A fellow to it."
>
> —*Macbeth.*

I T was an awful night in late November. For hours church bells had been rung to ward off, if possible, the violence of the coming storm, and to restrain the power of evil spirits wandering wild. The wind howled as if in pain, the rain poured down in floods, the bare trees bent before the cruel blast, snapping and breaking in all directions. Not a night for a dog to be abroad in, much less a human being.

Along a slushy lane, a ponderous, heavy cart jolted and jerked; a miserable scarecrow of a horse was between the shafts, all unequal to the heavy load, and no sawing at his mouth, or lashing his thick, rough coat with a heavy whip, could move him out of his monotonous jog-trot. It would have been far quicker for the solitary passenger to have alighted and walked, had he known his way, but that was just where Timothy was at fault. He had already come miles out of his path, and lost valuable time by taking what he understood would prove a short cut.

His return journey bid fair to be far more difficult than he had expected, or maybe, he had not realized that with Sultan at his command, he was free to travel at what pace he chose, and he had taken little heed as to whether the ordinary carriers' waggons were to be relied on or not. Many times that day had he bitterly regretted his pig-headedness in refusing Mrs. Markham's repeated offers of a mount. Over and over again he had represented how easily he had come, and that the roads were quiet and safe. In such a tiny hamlet as hers, there was no one to say him Nay, and suggest difficulties.

All had gone well at first; believing only that he had missed the regular carrier, he got a seat in a waggon at Bristol, which took him far as Watson, twenty-eight miles, and then his troubles began. He could not hire trap or horse, and found all public conveyances were suspended. The people in that part had struck for no taxes, like the rest of the kingdom, and he was quite jeered at as a fool when he asked about carriers' waggons. None had run for months; mounted messengers—often untrustworthy, carried the news, and if you had no horse of your own, you might go walk, and welcome.

So Timothy did, finding entreaties and bribes alike thrown away, but whether by malice or accident, he was wrongly directed, and tramped all day only to find he had well-nigh made a circle, and was back where he had started from. Never very sweet-tempered, he then promptly lost the small remnant of control that yet remained to him, and from angry words, he and the men who had misdirected him, would soon have come to cruel blows, the end of which might have been disastrous, if an old, shaky carrier's cart had not pounded by. The driver promised to take him on after an hour's rest, if he made it worth his while, and Timothy sullenly withdrew inside the tavern, and flung himself angrily into the settle by the fire.

His late antagonists scowled heavily at him, and slouched into the stable. A low whistle, muttered voices, and Timothy fully awoke to the peril of his position, for which he had mainly himself to thank. In the dusk of a November evening, he had risked more than he had thought of, by his want of self-control.

Darkness outside, gloom within, a stranger to the place, friendless, alone, in a solitary building; what were his chances?

The muttered voices grew louder, hob-nailed boots struck sparks from the rough stones without, a gruff, thick voice said "Good evening," and the old carrier stumped in, and banged down with a clatter the pail with which he had watered his horse. No doubt he was as bad as the others; what good to appeal to him?— how worse than foolish to let those wretches know he had money on him when he tried to bribe them to find him beast or conveyance?

The carrier stepped quietly up to him, and whispered in his ear:

"Take my hat, and muffle this scarf round your chin; put this stone in your mouth, and rub the horse down with yon wisp of hay; then bolt when *they* come in, straight along the road, and lie in the ditch somewhere, until you hear me coming. It will give you half a chance, and is the best I can do for you. Only you mind me of my own poor boy, dead in these wicked fights, I'd stir not hand or foot to help you; why should I? It's none of my business. Haste and be wary."

"And you? They will kill you!"

"Not they. Old Sam has cut his wisdom teeth, and knows every turn and passage in this rabbit warren of a place. Go!"

With temples throbbing, Timothy rubbed and scrubbed at the jaded old beast, with his bent knees and heavy coat, feeling sure all the time he resented a stranger's touch, and finding the minutes hours, as he listened to the plans for his own death and burial, before those three thick-set ruffians went inside the house to finish *him*. Yes! There was no doubt of it; he had heard enough of their mutters to know that, but for Old Sam's assistance, his life would have been taken, and none the wiser! Like a hunted hare, he panted breathlessly along the dark road, not willing to remain in the near vicinity of the "Cat and Fiddle," and while he lay in the deep ditch and listened to the gathering storm, vowed to be more cautious in future, for his dear lady's sake.

When at length Old Sam lumbered up, he asked him eagerly how he had fared, and the carrier quite chuckled as he said:

"It was just child's play, and nothing more." He had lounged in, mopping his face, at the end of the hour, and asked for his passenger, when all three speaking at once, told him he had left some while ago—curse him!

Then the two fell to gossip and Timothy was surprised at the tales the old fellow told him of misery and violence, that in his work he came across. He strongly advised him to be more wary in future, if he cared to keep his head on his shoulders, and if possible, to walk the rest of the way, and only by daylight.

At last the lights of Lyng came in view—Timothy's route, but not old Sam's—so he had to leave his friendly refuge, with many thanks, and plod on on foot. It was a town of some importance, and though now quite late in the evening, the narrow streets were all in a bustle, and full of muffled-up men and women, in twos and threes, hastening along. In answer to his enquiries, he was told that the great Witchfinder, Mathew Hopkins, had arrived there yesterday morning. The inhabitants had eagerly paid his heavy fee of twenty shillings, to free their town from the pest of suspected witches. His first court of enquiry was to be held *now*, in the town hall, when the results of his preliminary investigations would be open to examination before the public, who would thus be able to judge for themselves of the strict justice shown. Curiosity impelled Timothy to join the passing crowds, who all surged one way, evidently bent on the same object.

The town hall was crammed by curious folk, and badly lit by vile-smelling oil lanterns. The magistrates of the district were all present, with the town councillors in state, and the ruffian Witchfinder, and his cruel band, faced them. They were an ugly lot to look at, any time, but now, in the flickering light, they might well have passed for demons, with their great bare arms, and greasy leathern aprons.

Hopkin himself was a short, thick-set, powerful brute, with fierce eyebrows almost meeting, wide mouth, from which a few yellow teeth stuck out, protruding eye-balls, and enormous ears. But more than anything else, the cruel expression of the face made Timothy feel chilly down his spine. It was not likely that the assistants, selected in all cases by Hopkins himself, would be far behind him in cruelty and coarseness.

Beside this repulsive group a few of the "toys" of their trade were piled; chains, irons, vices, weights, thumb-screws, pinchers, and a cat-o'-nine-tails, that evidently had seen service. Tortures of all kinds were Hopkins' speciality.

The oldest magistrate on the bench opened the proceedings. His nose was a dark purple, and one foot, swathed in bandages, was supported by a stool. He told the people that more than three thousand witches in England had been put to death during the Long Parliament, in the earnest hope and endeavour of freeing the land from what *he* considered an awful curse; that in spite of this wise measure the canker was spreading fast, and no one could possibly feel secure from an evil eye blighting them, unless a vigorous and united effort was made in the cause of humanity at large to exterminate the mischief. There had been published and proclaimed in every town of note, the order from the Privy Council for clergy and squires alike to band together, and uphold the law of James I in this matter by burning all witches, *real or suspected*, in their own districts; and he called on his fellow-townsfolk to aid and abet

Mathew Hopkins in his absolutely necessary, and unpleasantly dangerous calling. Few of them would care to brave what *he* did daily—nay, often hourly, for the benefit of others; they owed him their warmest thanks and their deepest gratitude for his self-denying efforts in this painful duty, and must endeavour to let no personal private feelings interfere with the public good.

He ceased, amid loud applause, but Timothy felt there was another view of the subject as he gazed on Hopkins' ugly face, and watched his hideous sneers.

Timothy had by now elbowed and pushed his way into a good place for seeing and hearing, and listened to every word, with mouth wide open and staring eyes.

Now before the expectant gaze of the crowd a heavy curtain was drawn back, revealing the group that awaited judgement. Hisses loud and frequent greeted their appearance. What a crew they were!

Wild, unkempt, unwashed, dirty hags for the most part, some screaming in terror, others swearing hideously. One between two men, was never allowed to stand still one moment, but was dragged and pushed backwards and forwards without intermission. Her eyes were dull and glazed, her swollen tongue hung out of her parched mouth, whilst her long black hair was caught and torn frequently in her keeper's clutches, as they pushed her along. She was out and away the youngest of the miserable group.

Another poor wretch, huddled in a corner, proved to have his great toes and thumbs tightly tied together, and in this cramped position he had now remained for hours, with the cords actually cutting through his swollen flesh to the bone.

The others were as yet unbound, but these "obstinate ones" in Hopkins' sight required extra discipline, and a cruel smile of triumph played round his thin lips as he glanced now and then in their direction. They had refused to confess, and nothing, therefore, was too bad for them.

A man rose suddenly from the body of the hall and asked for the law quoted to be cited.

"In the year of grace 1603—

"Anyone that shall use, practise, or exercise any invocation of any evil or wicked spirit, or consult or covenant with, entertain or employ, feed or reward any evil or wicked spirit to or for *any* purpose, etc., etc. . . . Such offenders duly and lawfully attained shall suffer death."

There was silence for a minute, then another man rose, and said, to be quite in order he must read a statement, most fairly drawn up, that would show to all how serious the evil was.

A learned writer whose book he had lately had the pleasure of reading, said that there were no less than twelve distinct methods adopted in bewitchings, but they were set forth at such length it would be impossible to read them through there, and also quite unnecessary; their evil practices were too well known for a publication of the systems to be desirable. Starting, therefore, from the acknowledged belief that all forces of the earth, water, air, and fire were under the witches' control, and that laying diseases on man and beast, intercourse with the devil, etc., etc., were part and party only of their evil work. To be brief, many there had suffered much from sorcery or witchcraft, taking sometimes the form of ruined crops, robbery, house-breaking; was any punishment, torture, death itself, too bad for such wretches?

Here such a storm of shrieks and yells arose, Timothy felt deafened; hats were waived, hands held up and shouts of "Burn all such hags!" rang round the building.

Then the brutal Mathew Hopkins strode forward, and in his harsh voice said he would read the list of those he had discovered practising magic. With the help of his "toys," and with the bribe of life, several had at once owned to their close dealing with the devil; others, more obdurate, had required sharper handling, but the people could judge for themselves. An old, wrinkled hag was pulled forward, who was accused of being a body-snatcher, on the evidence of some powders made from human bones being found in her hovel, marked "Enchanted Powders for Love and Life."

Whether they were reliable love philtres or not, anyone present was welcome to try, but he had little doubt on the subject himself, and had had her thrown into the river that morning, and she had floated—sure sign of guilt—although she vehemently protested the powders were made from chicken bones, and she had never violated a grave in her life.

A laugh of mockery and derision from the audience showed their view of the case, and brought the poor creature to her knees, praying and begging for mercy.

Not one person called for pity on her, Timothy noticed, though the man standing jammed against him muttered "Shame!" audibly. A heavy flump on the platform made him peer behind Mathew Hopkins, only to see the poor walking witch had, in spite of tugs and rough pulls from her keepers, fallen in a heap on the stage, and lay there moaning miserably.

For fear pity should awaken, the Witchfnder said she had been guilty, some weeks ago, of throwing a dead hand into the peaceful home of one of their best-known residents, and the portended doom had so preyed upon the inmates, several had gone out of their minds in consequence.

A hiss curled round the building; what hope or room for mercy was there?

"Her doom is settled," proceeded the strident voice, "but always and fair, I call on any witness to prove my statement false."

To Timothy's surprise his neighbour pushed by him, throwing back his heavy cloak as he did so, and displaying a well-shaped head with decided, clean-cut features.

That he was well known was evident, for exclamations of "Doctor John" were frequent. He strode upon the platform and faced the room, holding up his hand to enforce silence.

"That poor wench, Margaret Finch, is absolutely ignorant of any crime or witchcraft whatever, as, if you grant me time, I can make clear to you very briefly."

Here Hopkins tried to drown his voice by calling out he was misinformed, and the proceedings must continue; but the doctor was a match for the bully, and, being a favourite, had the people's ear, and calmly made his statement, whilst Mathew swore at his subordinates for having told him the doctor could by no possibility be there, as he had been summoned elsewhere.

Dr. John said the woman was a tried and faithful servant in his house, with a service of many years' standing, devoted alike to him and his. One or two invalids of slightly-affected intellect lived in his house—had done so for long. Coming in one day with his wife and two of the hysterical ladies, Margaret had just opened the door to them when she started back in horror, pointing out to them the bleached skeleton of a hand lying on the doorstep. The invalid ladies promptly had hysterics; one of them had not yet got over the shock to her nerves, he doubted if she ever did so, the other was all right long ago. After some trouble and private search, he found the hand fitted the skeleton of a criminal hanging in chains at the cross-roads outside the town, but the object of the deed he had not discovered, or the doer of it. It might have been mischief or malice. They had tried to keep the matter quiet, and quite hoped, as it was now some weeks ago, that they had succeeded; but to his sorrow, on returning from a long round and an anxious day's work yesterday, he had found his faithful servant had been mysteriously carried off *where*, his wife had failed to find out. Had it not been for a soiled scrap of paper, thrust into his hand that evening by someone unknown, with "Try the Town Hall" on it, he might never have known her fate, poor soul! Private spite, or the hope of the reward, had wrought her this evil, for a more guileless creature never breathed. He requested that she should be released at once, and the people, led by his good influence, shouted "Set her free!" with one accord.

Ay! But she *was* free—free from all care and trouble, free from the life on earth! When Dr. John stooped over her and lifted her listless hand, he laid it gently down again with a sigh, and rose to his feet. Very stern was his voice, as he asked the two men who had been her keepers a few brief questions, and then turned again to the audience.

"For thirty-six hours that poor creature has been kept on the tramp, foodless, waterless; God knows what else she had to bear: with all the anguish and fear of a horrible fate before her, her heart has failed, and she has gone to the Better Land, where God Almighty will surely prove a more merciful judge than her fellow-creatures have been. Take warning that these pitiful trials which long ere this have made *my* heart ache, run not into wanton cruelty."

In vain Hopkins tried to stop him, the doctor *would* finish; then signing to two men he knew to lift the poor woman from the platform and follow him, he left the building by a door at the back.

Timothy had now but one wish, and that was to get out as speedily as might be, but this was very difficult, and he had to listen

71

to many charges and see several so-called tests applied before he really gained the door, and found himself in the pouring rain. A man brushed hastily by him, almost knocking him over; with a hurried apology he strode on, then turned sharply on his heel, and looked up in Timothy's honest, perplexed face.

"Had enough of it, eh?—or are you on the lookout for more poor creatures? Pah! It makes my blood boil. I'd rather ten thousand times be an honest fool than a clever rogue like yonder blackguard Hopkins. Ay, it's true!"

"Sir, I am but a country fellow, and my brain is sick with yonder scene. Could you but tell me some decent inn, it would be a real charity."

"Yes, go down Brick Lane, through Blindman's Court, and—there! You'll never find it such a night; you'd best come with me, and when I've done my night's work, I'll set you on your way. It is a positive disgrace the way these streets are lit, or rather *not* lit. I am all too late as it is, but I was on my way to this case, when the paper I mentioned in court was thrust into my hand, and Margaret was worth saving, poor wench! What thought you of the play?"

"I liked it not, but knew not what to think. Why, sir, they ran huge pins through the poor creatures' eyes, hands and bodies, and they never called out; surely they *are* possessed?"

"Not they, poor souls! The pins went back into the handles, I misdoubt not, but proof I've none; only when a wretch like Hopkins promises life and liberty if free confession be made, often under tortures too horrible to mention, what wonder if the poor frantic creatures own to anything and everything they are accused of, and then awake to the fact the stake still awaits them at the end? I know the game, I've seen it played before, but am powerless to prevent or help. See that cottage; it is for a sick child in it I am

72

sent for, said to have been bewitched, and under the influence of the evil eye pining away. Fancy how late it is, why, there goes twelve."

The cottage seemed brightly illuminated as they approached it, and a curious sing-song sounded from within, and came out through a cracked pane of glass.

With his finger on his lip Dr. John beckoned to Timothy to look in, and a queer scene met his gaze.

A huge fire was burning hollow on the hearth, in front of which, on a spit, a sheep's heart was roasting whole, stuck all over with pins—large, small, straight, crooked, black and white. In front of the almost furnace sat an old couple continually throwing salt on the fire, and chanting monotonously the following incantation:

"It is not this heart I wish to burn,
But the person's heart I wish to turn.
Wishing them neither rest nor peace,
Till they are dead and gone."

A group of friends in the window end of the room watched to see the result.

Only a minute had the doctor and Timothy watched the weird ceremony, with the fitful flames playing over the intent faces, when something black sprang sharply out of the fire which, already quite hollow, fell together with a sudden quenching of the bright light, and caused an immediate rising of thick smoke, which must have been nearly suffocating. The old woman tumbled backwards in her chair with fright, whilst the old man promptly joined the watching group in the window, who loudly applauded his pluck in trying this famous cure for the evil eye, and assured him they could all swear, the black cat, with his eyes flashing and claws distended, had jumped out and vanished in smoke. Now all would be well and the child cured!

"Why, it was only a bit of charred wood fell out, I saw it myself," said Timothy, turning in surprise to find Dr. John had gone indoors, so he waited outside, wondering much how people could really and truly persuade themselves to see what they wished. Often had he heard of this well-known cure, but never before had seen it tried, and naturally he felt a little sceptical of the result in this case.

A nervous dread was taking hold of him, an awful fear clutched at his heart. Suppose that brutal wretch came their way, who was rumoured to possess the evil eye amongst them? Mistress Bridget! Mistress Bridget! Mistress Bridget!"

He started as if shot; who had whispered that name in his ear? What letters of fire were these dancing round him? What business had he loitering here, when trouble might be stalking near her, and not at hand to give what help he might?

"Why, man, I believe you were asleep; you jumped so when I touched you, and called out so scared—'Mistress Bridget!'"

Timothy told in few words how worried he felt at the difficulties he found in getting home, and Dr. John gave him counsel on the same, repeating very strongly the old carrier's warning only to travel by day. He said the last news was that the Parliament and the Army were at loggerheads, and the nation well-nigh distracted, a condition of things that allowed liberty of all sorts to highwaymen and the like, with no one to check them or call them to order. Seeing Timothy's preoccupied air, he kindly asked him what further was troubling him.

"Surely the last scene has no power over a sensible fellow like *you*, my man! Why, only that I was so late, nothing of the kind would have occurred, but getting impatient and excited waiting so long, that old couple were easily prevailed on to try the famous exorcism of the evil eye. The child will soon be better, and their belief in the charm stronger than ever. I come in for queer things in some of my long rounds, and crossed Hopkins' path not a great while ago, and under the influence of fear and torture saw and heard men and women confessing to anything he put in their mouths, riding broomsticks, changing babies, mildewing crops, and the rest of it. Alas! some of his wicked cruelties are too bad for me to relate; would to God I could forget them. It is the same with those folk who have just left; their will power is so small, they have given themselves so entirely up to the idea the child has been bewitched that they now actually believe it. Saucers of water everywhere, quite a row of horseshoes, a large bough of rowan wood, with dolls stuck full of pins, surround that little helpless boy, who only needs care and kindness, and the strong stuff I have given him will work its own cure; but the pin will have the credit, not the medicine. Enough; I'm fagged out."

"Pardon, sir, but could you not have stopped that wretch taking possession of the town?"

Doctor John passed his hand wearily over his worn face, ere he replied.

"I did try my very utmost when the offer was first made. I said, all too hotly, I fear now, that anyone possessing an ounce of common-sense would agree with me to manage our affairs ourselves, without a paid informer, but against superstition who can prevail? No one backed me up; all were in favour of Hopkins. In disgust and anger I left the building, refusing to sit on the committee, or act further in the matter; hence I was *very* doubtful whether I could save my poor servant or not, and dare not move in the business half as speedily as I wished to, for fear of losing all. I was prepared to use bribery, if necessary, as a last resource, but as it happened, my townsmen bore no malice for my hasty words, and would I believed, have backed me up most heartily. Here we are at my house, and it is so late we must find you a shake-down somewhere. Ah, Caroline, is that you? How late for you!"

"And who could be anything but late, such a night as this, John? It was impossible to go to bed sooner, and I knew how bad you must feel about poor Margaret, faithful soul! How we shall miss her. I never dreamt of such an end as this, and wish I knew who had done this mischief. She went out to see her sister yesterday morning, and I felt sure they had made her stay the night, the weather was so rough. Who is that with you?"

"An honest fellow travelling homewards who finds it difficult to make his way in these disturbed times."

A few questions and answers, and Timothy discovered his hostess was a friend of Mrs. Markham's—indeed godmother to the captain, of whose death she heard with sorrow, and about whom he could tell her much of interest. Mrs. John asked if he knew Sir James Fielding, her nephew, who lived about ten miles, she thought, from Dunstar. Timothy answered promptly that he did, and a right pleasant gentleman he was when last he saw him some years back, when he had almost lived at the Manor, being a prime favourite of the Squire's. At present he did not even know his whereabouts. The children had gone to live with an aunt during his absence. If anyone could be said to possess influence over the rough country-folks, it was Sir James; he had a good word for all, and ready help for those in need.

Mrs. John looked very pleased at such hearty praise of her favourite nephew, and in spite of the sad trouble of the day, took a keen interest in Timothy's adventures and his manifest devotion to his young mistress, all of which she beguiled from him as the two men sat at their late supper; and so kind were both the doctor and his wife to Timothy, that when he left the gate early next morning, mounted on the doctor's cob, he felt he was leaving true friends behind, and that his troubles were mostly over for the present.

Riding carelessly along with a slack rein, he never noticed when his horse put his foot into a rabbit-hole on a wild common, and he was shot suddenly over his head violently to the ground, where he lay in a heap, whilst the frightened horse galloped wildly on, leaving Timothy quite unconscious, with a broken leg and fractured ribs, and no letter or name upon him to say who he was or whither bound; for the small valise that generally was slung on his back was to-day fastened to the saddle so firmly it could not fall off, and in it was all his money and also letters of sorrow and pity from both Mrs. Markham and Mrs. John, to young Madam.

VII

SIR JAMES

"But let no footstep beat the floor
　Nor bowl of wassail mantle warm
　For who would keep an ancient form,
Through which the spirit breathes no more?"
　　　　　　　　　　　　　—Tennyson.

"HULLO, Martha, how are you? Blooming as ever I see; are your mistress and the Squire within?"

"Good gracious, Master Jem—Sir James, I beg your pardon, how you made me jump; it is not thinking of you I was, to be sure, and how are you, sir, and the children, bless their little hearts? But come you in out of the bitter cold."

"Little! Well! Some of them are getting big, I would have you know; they lead me a rare dance, I can tell you. I shall have to get Madam here to take them in hand; she was so successful with me!"

The speaker was a fine-looking man, English to the back-bone, tall and well set-up, with an air of command about him that spoke for a position of authority. Yet trouble had ploughed deep lines on the forehead, and the pleasant smile had a sad edge to it, in spite of the cheerful voice. An orphan from his youth, he had always found counsel and help, with love and care, readily given him in the old Manor House of Rithycombe, where before Mistress Bridget's arrival on the scene, he had almost become like an adopted son; and very likely would quite have taken the place of one, if the wee baby had not entirely altered the state of affairs. That in the far future he might really become their son had been the darling wish of both Squire and Madam, though nearly twenty years lay between the two.

It was pretty to see the strong, powerful fellow submitting to the whims of the little maid, who found "big brother" a very willing slave.

Then the house of cards came down with a crash; a brief summer madness, a few weeks of acquaintanceship, and James Fielding bespoke Madam's love and care for his fair young wife, Hester Brooke.

It was a blow, and yet one they ought to have foreseen, against which no word could be said. The "care" he asked for was always given, even if the "love" was slow to come. Perhaps Madam never realised that it had truly come till a few years later she stood in a quiet chamber, listening to the gasping words in which, very slowly and with falling tears, poor Hester Fielding besought her to fill a mother's place to the children she was leaving.

Sir James was nearly heart-broken, though neighbours openly said it was impossible he and his wife *could* have much in common. She was a mere doll, and he a clever fellow. For a few years he stayed on at Fielding's Court; then a great restlessness fell on him, and leaving his children to his sister's care in Rutlandshire, he went abroad, *where* no one knew. The Squire missed his constant visits greatly, and Bridget, child-like, soon forgot him. Rithycombe was such a quiet little place, with no resident gentry, except at the Manor House, that there was no one in the least to take his place.

Now about forty-one, he stood before Martha at the open door, the picture of health and strength.

"Then you have not heard about poor master?" said she, wiping her eyes with the corner of her apron. "Madam is coming home shortly. Mistress Bridget had a letter yesterday, but *he* has gone to his rest!"

"You don't say so! Dear, dear! Now tell me all about it—he was a father to me."

So Martha told the tale of how, late last evening, a messenger had walked into the hall with a silk-tied missive in his hand from Ellesmere. The news of her father's death was a terrible shock to the lonely girl, and it was an added grief to think he could not be laid with his fathers in the peaceful village church-yard. The country was too much upset, the roads too unsafe for that to be possible; but her uncle told her all he could to comfort her, and said he had purposely delayed sending the heavy tidings until Madam was much better; and that now, on the first opportunity; Bridget might expect to see them, for he should take her mother home himself. He said his sister-in-aw was greatly altered, and it was only by degrees that memory had returned, but when it did, she fretted so ceaselessly for Bridget that, though the cold was great, and the roads difficult, it would be cruel to keep her away any longer. He greatly regretted that he should be unable to stay at least a few weeks with them at Rithycombe, but business of great urgency called him in an opposite direction, he grieved to say.

Martha repeated all this carefully to Sir James, as he sat by the hastily-lit fire in the quaint old parlour, which somehow had lost something of the cheerful look he remembered. Also she told him the messenger reported the travelling coach stood ready packed before he started, so that any day, any hour now, might bring the mistress back. All was ready for her. Mistress Bridget had seen to it herself, poor lassie!

"And how is Mistress Bridget, Martha? Grown out of all knowledge, I expect?"

"You may say that, sir, with truth; though I say it as shouldn't, there's not a fairer maid in Somerset, nor a better, but, Master Jem, she pores over old books all too much, and has grown so quiet-like, she might be my grandmother! 'Deed, and it's no laughing matter; the house is so dismal, a mouse makes me jump!"

Sir James rose, and cast a searching look around.

"No, the old place is not as I remember it; this was such a cosy, cheerful room, and now the furniture looks shabby and broken, as if no one cared."

"You are right, sir, 'tis sadly knocked about. What else could you expect when the rioters played ball with it? The screen that master thought so much of, designed by the aunt whose name Mistress Bridget bears, has got rarely broken. It's a mercy them soldiers did no worse harm here, though, than throw the furniture out of doors; but there, sir, I am keeping you from Mistress Bridget. She went down to the church awhile ago, with some leaves and things she'd been picking. See, the snow is beginning again. Do beg her to make haste; she'll catch her death of cold some of these days, like enough.

"There he goes! It does one's eyes good to see his cheery face again; but only think, I never told him about the captain! If only Mistress Bridget would take a fancy to *him*, there would be some sense in it; but things always go contrary, and I'd best hold my peace."

     *   *   *   *   *   *

Down past the straggling cottages, beyond the "Tabard" Inn, and the Rectory itself, Sir James' rapid steps soon reached the church which, to his surprise, was empty, and he was standing in the porch in some perplexity where to seek or find Bridget, when the flutter of a woman's cloak in the far corner of the little God's Acre caught his eye. A few more rapid strides, and the girl's cold fingers were in his, and he looked down into what he owned to himself Martha was right in calling the fairest face in Somerset. Ay! but with all the charm of the dark, soft eyes, and the thick, long curls escaping from her warm hood, the face itself was white and thin, with black shadows under the pathetic eyes, and a wistful droop of the lips.

Speedily Sir James announced himself, and told her he could share her sorrow, for *her* father had been one to him also.

Bridget looked very fragile in his eyes, and he thought how altered she was from the rosy-cheeked, sturdy little lass he remembered, and he wished, with a sudden impulse, he had been home sooner to help her; for that she had gone through a good deal was patent to the most casual observer. He begged her to come home at once, for the snow was now quite thick, and she willingly agreed, for she said to have anyone heed how she fared was something uncommon in those times; not that she meant Martha neglected her, she was goodness itself, but as long as she had her meals regularly and went properly to bed, Martha was quite content, and hardly knew how long the hours seemed between those functions. Then, looking down at the low mound at her feet, now covered with the White Queen's mantle, she told of the soldier's care for her, and his passing away at the Manor. She had not an idea what her parents had thought of the matter; news had so seldom come, her mother of late being unable to write: but Sir James saw at a glance that she was worrying herself greatly as to Madam's displeasure, yet at the same time aware it was the best that could be done.

"Of that, Bridget, I have *no* doubt," said Sir James, "and your mother will feel the same. It was a brave man's good heart that prompted him, and he had his reward in knowing he had saved you from harm. Poor fellow, that it should have ended so! But now, child, you must hurry, or we shall both be frozen. Now that I am home again, I shall take my place as usual here, and what man can do to help you and yours, will be alike a pleasure and a privilege to me. Don't cry any more, you look quite worn out. Uncle John would not know his little lass."

Bridget had not spent such a happy afternoon since her parents' departure; she had so much to tell James Fielding of the years of his absence, and of her late troubles. How greatly she missed the old Rector, who had been summoned suddenly to a distant relative shortly after Timothy's departure; his gentle presence and quiet companionship had been the greatest comfort. How noisy and quarrelsome the village had become; how often in her ministrations she had met with cross words and scowling looks. Of Timothy's strange absence, and the fear she felt he had come to some harm doing her service.

Then James told of his long wanderings abroad, and the strange places and things he had seen, and how now, when he hoped before long quiet and peace would be restored to divided England, he had returned home with his children to Fielding's Court; of his hope that Bridget would soon see them all; they were full of fun, and so on, so on, until the shadows began to fall fast, and he rose to go, promising to return early in the morning, and see if any further tidings of Madam had arrived.

Martha was very loth to see him go, and declared there was no sense in it. Why could he not use his old room as of yore? She had made it all ready, but Sir James was not to be stayed, and went briskly off for his horse.

Perhaps it was in consequence of Bridget's words, perhaps it was all too evident, but the cheery greeting that used to be his from all about was missing, as he passed some idle men, who stared rudely at him; and his pet aversion, old Nan Crane, stood right in his path and uttered some ugly words not fit to hear. But he was no hot-headed boy to take notice, but a man, fully and keenly aware of the terrible state of the country. So he strode on in silence, troubled not a little at the state of affairs in quiet Rithycombe.

The man who brought his horse out from the stables of the "Tabard" Inn, where, in consequence of a loose shoe requiring attention, he had been obliged to leave him, touched his hat respectfully, and said he was glad to see him back again.

"Your face I know," said Sir James, giving him a keen glance, "but your name I forget."

"Hal Scott, your honour, the same as won the grinning match the year you came of age, when we *were* allowed a few games without being whipped at the cart's tail, or fined a week's wage."

"Ah! I remember now, but the Hal Scott I used to know was a good sort of fellow, not a hanger-on at taverns."

The man's face flushed, and he looked downcast.

"What can a poor fellow do, Sir James? There's no work doing anywhere, and the missus is for ever worriting.[11] The fellows here would give me no peace if I kept aloof, for you see, I know too much, and if I turned sober and *told*, they'd murder me."

"I see—a matter of courage—God save England from such cowards!"

Hal Scott was left rubbing his head doubtfully, lost in a feeble wonder what Sir James had meant, with the ugly word *coward* weighing him down with a very unusual feeling of shame.

Chance words at random sent, sometimes hit the mark. A day was yet to come, when with brave head bent low, and heart on

_____

11 Worrying.

fire, a thanksgiving that those words had found some soil to grow in, went up from Sir James' lips to the God above.

Bridget's voice had quite a cheerful ring in it as she asked Martha to help her fold the napery,[12] made from the thread she had spun so busily during her mother's absence; and it was indeed a goodly pile for one pair of hands to have turned out. Now the wheel was stood back in a corner, and the quaint old dormer-room struck very cold. In vain had Martha begged leave to light a fire there; indeed, when first the severe cold began, she had set alight to the dry logs piled ready on the hearth, without waiting for permission, but Bridget had been so disturbed at her doing so, so really vexed, that at last she had promised not to do so again. The girl said, with no maids at hand to help her, she would not have such trouble taken; she would sit in the hall when cold, the parlour she quite shrank from, it was too large and lonely all by herself.

Many hours, when not at work, she spent at the dormer window, watching the winding road, dreaming her own sad thoughts.

Next day was grey and cold, with the roads heavy, and the skies threatening; if Madam was not well on her way, she would surely be storm-stayed. Sir James rode over as he had promised, stabling his horse this time at the Manor, and stayed as long as he could to get back in daylight.

So a few days passed, and still no tidings came either from Madam or Timothy, and Christmas was at hand.

A sad festival for Bridget, but not as lonely as it might have been, for again Sir James braved the cruel weather, to spend a few hours at the desolate Manor. A smile curved Martha's lips as she heard his firm tread crossing the hall, and she hastened to spread

---

[12] Household linen.

a tempting meal—that spoke well for her catering powers—in the warmest corner she could find. Outside, the wind went shrieking by with a terrible biting sting in its touch, warning folks another fall was close on its way; the clouds were one uniform laden hue, snow lay piled in heavy drifts, and icicles hung from the roofs.

With coat collar to his ears, great wadded cloak to his feet, thick veil over his face all sprinkled with powdered snow-flakes, Sir James would have made a splendid Father Christmas, and nothing but his sorrow for Bridget would have made him venture out on such a day; he begged Martha's pardon humbly for coming in in such a mess. Not that she minded, he could not come too often to please her, and she hoped her mistress also.

In the red light thrown by the logs, Sir James, Bridget, Martha and Joe sat talking of olden times and happier Christmases, when the Yule log had burnt for days, and the long tables at the Manor groaned with their heavy burden. When maskers and mummers had held high revel, with the wassail bowl circling freely; and puppet shows, rope dancing, jigs, and country-dances had been the evening amusements, crowning days spent in bear-baiting, horse-racing, bowls, wrestling and grinning matches on the village greens, weather alone permitting.

"Talking of grinning matches, Joe, what a wreck that fellow Hal Scott has become, a regular drunken sot, and yet I remember him as hearty a lad as you would need to see; and what a splendid grinner he was, to be sure; that double grin of his was unique."

"Ay! Master Jem, and a deal of time he spent over that same diversion, practising some new twist of his lips and jaws that should help him win the prize. His backers were awful proud of him, and the betting was rare and heavy when Hal Scott entered the lists; but it unsettled him like, and brought him into doubtful company. And after all such games were put down by Parliament, when Mistress Bridget here was a wee thing, why, his occupation was gone, and he took to loafing, which ruined him. I don't think he's bad at heart, but so easily led; those that are unscrupulous make a tool of him, and by playing on his fears, compel him to take his full share in their wickedness."

Bridget was very much interested in hearing of these old time sports, of course unknown to her, and wondered if the like would ever be allowed again.

Sir James declared they would, at no distant date, and a good thing, too; it kept the idle out of mischief, and prevented the industrious sinking too much into a groove.

He recalled to Joe's mind the Christmas Day of 1644, decreed by the Long Parliament to be kept from that day forward as a solemn fast, under heavy fines, and how the nation had rebelled to such effect, that one short year only, and this senseless law was repealed.

All were sorry when he rose to leave, he made so light of the ride and the cold, none of them quite realized it was by no means a pleasant, easy thing to do in such weather; but knowing every foot of the way, and being very careful, the danger was nothing to what a stranger would have found it. It was indeed necessary to keep to the high road, where the snow stakes were fairly frequent, and leave the bridle tracks alone, and the former winding frequently amongst the hills, would have made the way long and tedious, if the hope of helping Bridget had not greatly shortened it in fancy.

There was a wild track called the Witches' Ladder, leading up from a gloomy gorge in a very lonely part, that went from Rithycombe to Fielding's Court almost in a bee-line, but that required summer light to be safe, and was impossible except on foot.

The little Fieldings, dressed in their best, were waiting eagerly for their father, when at length he threw back the heavy door, and entered his own cheerful home. The youngest girl, Mona, ran eagerly forward with warm slippers, whilst Ralph, the eldest lad, a tall, slight stripling of fourteen, poured carefully out the simmering posset, over which he had been keeping most careful guard.

Round him, about him, on him, the happy children swarmed, whilst aunts and cousins smiled in the background, waiting ready for what they knew would be a right merry evening. And so it was, a happy time for all, full of fun and frolic, with sweet voices and gay laughter keeping a Merrie Christmas amongst the holly wreaths.

If Sir James' thoughts strayed often to a lonely figure seated in a fire-lit hall, in the silence of an almost empty home, he would not let such private feelings cast a shadow on the children's glee at having him again with them at home.

VIII

THE BLACK BOOK

"I hold it cowardice
To rest mistrustful when a noble heart
Hath pawned an open hand in sign of love."
—King Henry VI.

Y ES! That dark speck crawling on the road *was* a coach, making straight for the Manor. Wrapped in a thick shawl, Bridget watched a few minutes more, then ran lightly down to warn Martha, set alight to the fire in her mother's room, and calling her close companion, Rough, hastened out to the garden gate, long before the heavy vehicle had entered the avenue. Madam was looking out as the chariot drew up, and a cold chill ran through Bridget as she saw how changed her face was. Life—hope—seemed to have gone, only a listless quiet, and indifferent air remained. That was what struck the girl on the moment as she threw her arms round her neck, and burst into a passion of tears.

Madam's calm did not alter; though her soft hand stroked Bridget's face gently, the strange apathy was unbroken even for a minute. Quietly she entered the Manor, spoke pleasantly to Martha and Joe who, tongue-tied, had no word in answer, and had passed up the shallow stairs to her room above, long before Bridget's choking sobs had ceased as she watched her father's valise and other possessions carefully carried in.

Her uncle was very good to her, his own heart was so sore he could truly feel for the child, and putting his arms gently round her, bade her cry in peace, it would do her good.

Then Martha found her tongue, and asked what ailed her mistress, was she ever thus?

"Most ways as quiet; now and again some chance thing rouses her, and she seems quite herself, then that passes and she cares naught. But it is only a matter of time, our doctor says, after the illness she has had, we must have patience. She has talked so ceaselessly of you, Bridget, I marvel much she did not rouse up more. We have been storm-stayed for days, and she has fidgetted much; indeed only this morning with all her old peremptoriness insisted on our moving on, and a weary time we've had; most expensive, too, constant relays of horses, not always easy to get, and in spite of hot bottles, so cold for ourselves, I feel half frozen. Last night we should have been here, only our pole snapped and that hindered us, so now I must move on to-morrow, or lose my appointment. There, child, now you feel better, don't you? Suppose you run up and help your mother as usual, and remember for your comfort she's much better than she was, poor soul."

An hour later Bridget descended to the hall from which the sound of voices reached her ears. Her mother was in bed, inclined to sleep; she said Bridget might go down and get something to do, it was not good for maids to be idle.

Her uncle smiled kindly at her, as she came forward and drew a low stool to his side, where after her greeting to Sir James, she sat and listened to their talk. Thomas Melville had scraps of later news than had reached them; he took a keen interest in things in general, and had many friends on both sides. It was a real pleasure to find such a good listener as Sir James who, seated in the shadow of the settle, could watch Bridget's rapt face as much as he chose, which meant a good deal. He asked her uncle what he thought of the Committee of Safety, formed of twenty-three persons elected by Lambert and the other officers on the 26th of October.

Thomas Melville shrugged his shoulders, and fumbling about in one of his many pockets, produced a crumpled paper from which he presently read aloud the following:—

"I do hereby swear, that I renounce the pretended title of Charles Stuart, and the whole line of the late King James, and of every other person pretending, or which shall pretend to the Crown or Government of these nations of England, Scotland and Ireland, or any of them, and that I will, by the grace and assistance of Almighty God, be true, faithful and constant to the Parliament and Commonwealth, and will oppose the bringing in, and setting up any single Person, or House of Lords, and every of them in this Commonwealth."

"That's the oath all the members of the Committee—some say twenty-three of them, others twenty-eight persons—were sworn in. Fine-sounding words doubtless, but who has the slightest confidence in the Committee thus formed? Monk reinstated the Rump Parliament for his own ends, and they are equally divided as to opinion whether he covets Cromwell's post, or aims at a Stuart King. Inscrutable man, with his silent tongue and secret schemes, he is really at present the pivot upon which the Nation's welfare turns. Lambert has gone northwards to meet Monk's army from Scotland, and it is said he will be fairly mad when he hears the Rump is restored again. I had the good fortune to have a paper given to me to-day where we baited the horses, but I never looked at it; very likely there is nothing fresh in it. Perhaps, Sir James, you would like to see it; the light is none too good for my old eyes. Eh! what have you found, man, you look delighted?"

"Why, just think, here's one notice saying Lambert was abandoned by his troops and taken prisoner. Then further down comes another, saying that on hearing the Rump Parliament was restored, Lambert's *own* troops put him under arrest, and have sent him, with a strong escort, prisoner to the Tower! There! Is not that grand news?"

"Capital. If that milksop, with his selfish aims, is out of the way for a bit, and Monk shows a little activity, there is a chance for peace at last, and the kingdom is in such a hopeless state they will clutch at anything. I would I were at Monk's elbow to hive him a jog. What, are you off? Won't you stay and sup?"

"I must away, but I am most thankful Madam has returned in safety. Mistress Bridget, you will see me shortly, fare you well! And you, sir, a prosperous journey to you!"

"Thanks; and any news I hear I will tell the child to pass on to you, though it will be very stale before it reaches you."

*   *   *   *   *   *

After Thomas Melville's departure from the Manor, and the brief whirlpool of excitement consequent on Madam's return had subsided, the days passed very quickly; except for Sir James's frequent visits, and scraps of news, there was little doing.

The weather was so severe Bridget could rarely get down to the village, and when she did so, Nan Crane was sure to waylay her with such curious menaces and hidden threats, the girl began to dread the sight of the bent figure and shrivelled face, and made up her mind the old woman was going crazy.

Her mother rarely noticed her absences, or, indeed, showed any interest in things about the house, so that one day when Bridget sat in the old settle, in front of a glorious fire, reading from her treasured ancient book, she started violently when Madam touched her on the arm, and asked her what she read so intently.

Bridget held it up in silence, quite unprepared for the sudden start her mother gave.

"Your great-aunt's book; however came you by it, Bridget? I did not know it was in the house, see," and she turned back to the fly-leaf, "Bridget Conyngham. Her Boke."

With manifest curiosity Madam examined the clasps, and turned one or two of the yellow leaves.

"An Undiscovered Deadly Poison, and its Antidote." "Melancholy and Its Cure." "A Lover's Receipt for Securing his Lady's Love." "The Art and Alphabet of Magic." "Witchcraft in Various Forms."

These were a few only of the many headings. Madam read one or two of the recipes, then the flicker of interest and memory died out, and with a tired sigh she sank into her high-backed chair, and gazed at the burning logs.

The book was in Bridget's hands that afternoon as she walked briskly down the avenue to the village; sickness of various sorts was very prevalent, and her time was occupied in trying to help and cheer the sufferers.

The smugglers had been making daring and successful raids. The Whistling Witch had been heard on wild nights, and reckless spirits were abroad in all parts. The illness increased, deaths were frequent, and Bridget's fame faded. The villagers began to look on her with suspicion, and openly spoke of her as a witch.

Black looks, rude words—nay, more threatening ones were used to her, when one gloomy day little Fred Smith died all in a minute under her evil eye!

No good to protect and say it was convulsions. They knew better, and should put a stop to it somehow before all their children were killed to suit *her* pleasure.

Bridget left the village, sad at heart, by no means understanding the mutters she heard, for up to now no whispers even of the great witch persecutions going on all over the land had reached her. If only she had mentioned the matter to Sir James or Martha, they would have taken alarm at once, and implored her to keep at home. Her mother she did tell, but she seemed to think nothing of it, until late that evening, when she roused up suddenly, and asked Bridget to bring her the old black book she was always perusing.

"Be quick, child, bring it at once; let me see it burn *now*. I never saw it until you showed it to me the other day, and with my poor head I quite forgot it was no fit reading for you. I only just remembered it again this minute; for days I have tried to puzzle out what it was I had to say, and couldn't remember. Now hasten, child, before I forget."

"One minute, mother; what do you know of the book? It is surely valuable."

"Your father told me the old tale, and said it always worked ill to those who used it, and it has more lives than a cat. It belonged to your father's aunt, a regular wise woman, and very beautiful. She suffered much from heart disease, and all the family were devoted to her, looking on her as almost a saint. She declared she had found the black book in an old chest, and had taken possession of it, adding recipes of all kinds that she had come across. Some horrid report got about that she was a witch, and she only escaped being burnt as such by being found dead in her bed. It was the sudden shock of the noisy crowd who came thus to repay her countless deeds of kindness that killed her. There has been a Bridget Conyngham for so many generations that your father would have you so called, though I did not like it at all. For God's sake, child, hurry, and let me burn it now at once. I trust your having read it may be unknown, for I tremble to think what may happen if the villagers see it in your hands. Superstitious-mad they all are, and always have been, and we are two helpless women. Oh! dear, dear! I don't know *what* to do, and James won't be here to-morrow."

Bridget was silent; the book had gone often to the village, and only that day Nan Crane had glared fiercely at it in her hand. Neither did she want it burnt, that could always be done.

Could it?

The habit of obedience prevailed, however, and with reluctant feet Bridget mounted to her dormer chamber, and opened the press she kept the book in.

Gone!

What had she done with it? Surely she had not dropped it? Like a flash of lightning it came over her, she could remember nothing more of the queer old volume after that vindictive glance from Nan Crane! Alas! Alas! In vain she searched every available or likely place. Hunt all she might, it could not be found, not even in the mantel cupboard, though, as a last resource, she opened that. She was pulling it to again when the idea occurred to her that often she had heard raiders were more savage if they found nothing than even if their gains were small, so she took a few of the loose coins, and a thin spoon, and, going to her mother's bedroom, concealed them in one of the hollow uprights of her four-post bed. Then it suddenly struck her that the mantel-cupboard opened too easily; either the wood had shrunk, or else the spring was a little slack; whilst she was about it, she might as well find another place of safety for the treasures, so on the impulse of the moment she removed it elsewhere, and closed the secret panel.

Rapid in her movements, she was speedily down in the hall again, and, to her great relief, found her mother had sunk into a doze, and even when she awoke, the book episode had vanished from her mind entirely. Not so from Bridget's. A queer feeling of dread kept knocking at her heart. She thought of little else that evening as she listened to the wind's wailing in the dark night outside.

Rough was very fidgetty; do what she might she could not keep him quiet; he trotted from door to door, whining and growling in a most unusual fashion.

Rendered uneasy at last by his restlessness, Bridget went to speak to Martha in the adjacent kitchen, and as she stood talking to her in the firelight, first one masked figure, then another, came swiftly in through the scullery, until five big men filled up all the vacant space.

Bridget went white as a ghost; her feet seemed suddenly to have grown to the floor, and not for the life of her could she force her tongue to ask their business there. Martha screamed and shrank into a corner, and another shriek came from the hall as the intruders pushed Bridget roughly aside, swung through the door, and tramped noisily and heavily up the stairs, declaring loudly treasure they had come to find, and treasure they would have; they knew well there was plenty hidden, and it would be the worse for all if they did not find it.

Rough flew bravely forward, and fastened so fiercely on the leg of one man, he yelled with pain, and a comrade, raising his heavy bludgeon, brought it down with such cruel force on the faithful little head, that a helpless, lifeless bundle of fur dropped prone at Bridget's feet, as she ran to her mother's side, and she had lost one more trustworthy friend.

Madam was gazing in affright at the crape-covered faces of the robbers, who simply ransacked the place from garret to cellar. Bridget's heart nearly stopped beating when a voice suddenly whispered in her ear:

"I'm here to do what I can for you, Mistress Bridget, though it's as much as my life is worth; tell me how I can reach the big bell in the turret, and for God's sake be quick."

The girl told him in such hoarse, trembling tones none would have recognised them, and added "Oh, Hal Scott, I did not think you would rob us."

"Not I, my lady, though *he* called me 'coward.' You saved my boy for me, and I'd die for you, but betray me not, I pray!"

Then the fierce robbers came shouting down the stairs, vowing life or money they would have!

Madam clung to Bridget's arm and implored her to say where she had hidden their treasure; she did not know or else she'd give it up!

Bridget held her tongue, and watched the men come tumbling down, when loudly, clearly the great Manor bell rang briskly backwards, the signal of a fire. The men started and stared, but still the iron tongue pealed forth with its well-known alarm, and a great thundering fell on the heavy entrance door.

Disappointed, baffled, and muttering evil threats of returning another night, the intruders departed, one shaking at Bridget's head, to her horror, that quaint black book of recipes she had lost, and calling her savagely "Witch!"

When all was quiet and silent save for the swinging bell, Bridget learnt that old Joe, with a club in each hand, was responsible for the thundering on the door, that with the bell had proved so efficacious, and she praised him much; but he said the idea was not his, he should never have thought of it; someone in the dark outside, as he was coming home, had thrust the clubs into his hands, and bidden him bang for his life.

They barricaded every door they possessed, pulling heavy furniture against several, and Joe promised solemnly not to close an eyelid all night.

Madam cried helplessly like a child, but at last consented to go to bed if Bridget stayed with her, and though the girl longed to be downstairs, keeping Joe up to the mark, she lay down beside her mother and kept quiet.

Very gently had she lifted little Rough's body and laid it on a chest; how she should miss him no one knew, and to lose him in such a way?

The fire-bell ceased at last, and Bridget wondered dully no one had come to their aid, but there! in such unsettled times perhaps it was not odd.

Morning came at last, and found them all tired and weary, yet the business of the day had to be attended to.

James Fielding did come over, and was in a terrible way when first told by Joe, then by Martha, and finally by Madam, who seemed quite energetic, of the fright they had had.

In vain he implored them to come over to Fielding's Court at once, and let him take care of them. Madam refused obstinately to leave the Manor, declaring the robbers must have fully satisfied themselves there was nothing to be gained by coming again. After a long conversation on this and other matters, Sir James sought Bridget in the now little-used parlour, and begged and prayed of her to say she would marry him, and let him have the joy of caring for her welfare.

The girl's look of surprise was very genuine, as she stood twisting the signet ring. She said she had never thought of such a thing.

"Oh, Bridget, *do;* it maddens me to think of you here all alone, when I want you so badly, and love you, dear, so much. Indeed, indeed, I would make you happy, and surely I am not so hateful but that you could like me just a little? Your mother wishes it, and she says it was the dream of your father's heart, so pray listen to me, child, and forgive the blundering words that come from an honest heart. Yonder brave fellow saved you once, and *I* have known you all your life, and for all my hopes of happiness and home, do not, do not, say me Nay!"

In vain he pleaded well and truly, again and yet again. Bridget would not say "Yes," and at last, when the short winter's day was closing in, after he had himself seen to every possible precaution, and left his own beautiful collie as guard, Sir James had to ride sadly away, with his bright plans all upset, and a weary ache at his heart, as he looked forward to long, lonely years before him.

His children? Yes, of course he had them, but just now he wanted something more, and though he had plenty of county work to attend to, as a favourite magistrate, he had built up such a home castle of happiness, the downfall was very great. Neither did he think he could reopen the subject to Bridget; her manner had been so decided it was vain to think she would change.

IX

FORGOTTEN

"Whispering tongues can poison truth;
And constancy lives in realms above;
And life is thorny; and youth is vain;
And to be wroth with one we love,
Doth work like madness in the brain."

—S. T. Coleridge.

"TO-MORROW is my birthday, mother; am I not getting old? Martha wants to make me a cake, but I tell her No. I'd rather not."

"Your birthday, child, are you sure?"

"Why, mother, yes, it is the 20th of February. Was it as cold a day as this when I was born, do you remember?"

"*Remember!* Is it likely I should forget such a day as that? What nonsense you talk, Bridget; let me see, that would be how long ago now?"

"Twenty years to-morrow, mother."

"Twenty—and the twentieth day of the month. Dear, dear! I was to remember something *very* carefully when those two dates came together; but *what?*"

And Madam sat bolt upright and looked round the hall for inspiration. "Something so particular it was, too. I wished your father had told me of it before. I can't imagine what it was. Call Martha, Bridget; perhaps she can help me, my poor head is all in a fog. Oh! Martha, what happened on the day Mistress Bridget was born?"

"*Happened*, Madam? Why, that was what happened, and enough too, to be sure! Dear! What a flurry we were all in, and poor Master like one demented, wandering up and down all over the place. I mind well when I carried the baby to him, just for him to have a peep at her, how, all of a sudden he began to shake as if he had the palsy, and I daren't let him take the child for fear he'd drop her, though I had real to shout at him, for the church bells were making such a row, I could not hear myself speak, and he was even then a little hard of hearing."

"Dear, dear, you don't help me at all. I was to be sure to take great care, *great* care, he said, and I don't know of what, but it was something to do with Bridget's birthday; it is *most* annoying you can't help me at all."

Madam's tone was decidedly querulous, and both women tried to soothe and pacify her, not having the faintest clue to what she wanted. After a little doze she woke up suddenly and said she had been dreaming of the black book—a horrid dream; she was thankful to awake and remember the book had been burnt some while ago. "Your father said it carried a curse with it, and he was not the only one of the family who wished it had never existed. After your aunt's sudden death, a great search was made for it, and as it could not be found, it was supposed to have been burnt with a lot of papers your grandfather destroyed when your father was a lad. Tell me, child, how you, her namesake, came by it; only I *know* it is burnt I should not have a minute's peace, and I think it must have been something about that, that your father warned me against. Now where did you find it?"

"In the dormer-room, mother, the day you went to Ellesmere."

"And that was Aunt Bridget's own room; it does seem queer. However, no matter, the thing is gone."

Bridget felt quite a hypocrite as she listened in silence, but as she could not say where the book was, she thought it best to hold her tongue, though to-day her mother seemed more like herself than she had done since her return home.

Only Martha and she herself knew how difficult she had been, and what patience she required. Never once had she alluded to Bridget's hasty marriage, and the lonely time she had had. Not quite realizing her condition, Sir James had asked her consent before speaking to Bridget, and not once, but many times had the girl wished from the bottom of her heart that he had done no such thing, for Madam having agreed, she could not, or would not understand that Bridget had said him Nay; and she harped on at the subject in season, out of season, until it was worn nearly threadbare.

Her confidence that Bridget would shortly come round, so inspired Sir James with hope that again he put his fate to the touch, only to have a gentle but decided refusal. Sore at heart, and very sad, for love for Bridget had taken a firm hold of the honest man, he ceased coming so frequently to the Manor, only insisting that two trusty men of his own selection should always sleep there; and that their doing so should be as little possible burden or extra trouble to the household, they left always at seven a.m. for their day's work, returning again at sundown.

At Fielding's Court the inmates noticed a little sharpness crept into the master's voice, and some said he was not easy to please in those days, others that he was cross and irritable. No one was more aware of the quickness of his temper just then that Sir James himself; little things worried him as big ones never had, and often it was all he could do not to flare out before the children in a way that would have surprised them. They grumbled greatly at seeing so little of him, for to sit still and drink, with the sting of his great disappointment rankling ever in his mind, was more than he could stand; he must out and away, be the weather what it might, and tramp till he was tired out.

Why could not Bridget like him? That was the question faced him morn and night, when with his sore heart he scoffed at himself for caring so much, like any love-sick lad, and bitter thoughts of Reginald Markham tried hard to gain a hold. But against that poor, degrading idea, the better nature of the man fought and prevailed. Where might Bridget have been but for his timely aid? With no thought of himself, he had done the best he could for the girl; need James grudge him her grateful remembrance? *Love* surely it could not be—pity and gratitude together had erected a shrine around his memory; doubtless that as yet had not begun to fade, but that every pulse in her young heart had still to be aroused, as surely as Sir James tossed to and fro, in uneasy slumber, or tramped the lonely lanes, he knew and felt for certain.

But was *he* the man to quicken those heart beats?—there lay his doubt. Slowly, surely, the conviction grew and strengthened that friendship such as theirs rarely changed to warmer sentiment, and that for his own self-respect he must try and be content never to be anything more than the old tried friend, ready and willing to give what help and support he could. And *that* he was indeed, but very likely no need for it would now arise; peaceful times were surely coming on the troubled land.

Bridget missed James Fielding's visits not a little, and she looked so tired and worn Martha felt quite worried about her. A long letter from her uncle had arrived on the 15th, written from London, and contained stirring news.

He said under the pretext of honouring Monk (now rapidly nearing London), but in reality to spy upon him, the Parliament had set two of their number to watch and report his every word and movement. One of them was a personal friend of his own, from whom he had had much information. These men found the great general at Leicester on the 22nd of January, and from that hour, night and day watched him as a cat does a mouse, even to the length of always making, if not finding some hole through door or wall to look and listen. Not very high-class work, according to *his* lights, but still their orders.

The inscrutable man went his own way and kept his own counsel as usual.

It spoke for the state of affairs, Thomas said, that the very day before monk reached London, there was a fight in the Strand between the cavalry and the infantry. An united army had long kept down a divided nation, but the nation was now united and the army divided.

Lambert had broken prison, and called his comrades to rally round him, but was captured and reimprisoned speedily. Great excitement prevailed as to Monk's policy.

Thomas Melville asked Bridget to tell Sir James these important news; he hoped by now they had heard something of Timothy, else he feared they never would. His own plans were too uncertain to mention; he might remain in London, or go home, but the latter would be lonely work, and he had many friends in town. The man who brought the letter was bound next for Bristol, and Bridget spared one of her gold pieces to get him to carry a letter to Mrs. Markham from her, asking what she knew of Timothy, and *when* she had seen him. The man promised faithfully to do her bidding, and Bridget felt relieved. Up to now she had had no one she could send on such an errand. Joe could not be spared, and besides he was too old.

Madam kept very alert all that 19th day of February, asked questions and volunteered remarks as she had not done for long. She expressed herself as greatly pleased with Bridget's spinning, felt the texture of the linen with a critical finger, and said she had greatly improved both in evenness and quality. Nay more, when evening came, and the two sat close to the dancing flames, she told Bridget more of those sad weeks before her father's death at Ellesmere than the girl had yet heard. Once begun, it seemed a relief to her to go on talking, though every now and then a queer gap came of something she had forgotten.

It was very comforting to the daughter's heart to hear how her father had longer for her, and how constantly she had been in his mind.

Bridget began once to say what an anxious time she had had, and how grateful she was to Timothy for his constant carefulness, but Madam looked *distraite*, as if her mind refused to attend to anything she had not herself taken part in. Still she *was* better, and with care might soon be well again, Martha insisted, as later on, when Madam had gone to bed, she came in, and found Bridget alone, seated in her father's great old chair, crying as if her heart would break. She could not help it, she said, as her former nurse, with many endearing words, tried to get at the bottom of the trouble. She was so lonely!

Martha assured her she had only to say one word, and that could all be put right, and a happy home be hers for the rest of her life, but Bridget only shook her head.

Then the faithful maid suddenly resolved on a bit of plain-speaking, and kneeling down beside her, she spoke softly to her as her mother might have done, and asked her if she was right in refusing Sir James for the sake of a memory only.

"Not for one moment, child, would I ask you to forget that brave, honest soldier; treasure up in your heart his care for you to your life's end. But you only saw him twice, and you are young and strong, with maybe a long life before you; surely, surely, the two claims need not clash, your dead lover can have his own place, and your living husband his. Write and ask Mrs. Markham for her opinion, if you doubt the soundness of my advice, but for God's sake don't, *don't*, throw away all your life's happiness for the memory of a dream. Sir James is too proud to keep on asking, but remember he was your father's choice in the long ago. Now, dearie, go to bed and sleep in peace, only think once and again of your old nurse's words, for they are true.

*   *   *   *   *   *

"Dear Nephew,—

"It is only a few hours ago that I heard to my great relief you had come to the end of your wanderings, and had settled down again at Fielding's Court.

"A man brought your uncle a newsletter this forenoon, and said he had lately been at Rithycombe with a London letter for young Madam Markham, who got him to go out of his way with a letter to her mother-in-law near Bristol. Now I can give a shrewd guess as to part of that letter, for I make no manner of doubt at all, it is chiefly to ask her after Timothy.

"Well, I was cudgelling my brains on the subject, when John came in in a fuss, and said a man he knew was going your way, and would carry a letter for me. For weeks and months I have waited and wanted this chance to send word to Rithycombe, and now to have it on the very day I hear you have returned is most opportune, only it minds me to write in such haste, I fear the sense will be none too clear.

106

"Timothy started from here on the Doctor's cob, the very day the first poor witches were burnt and drowned, as you will have seen in the paper, and the whole town was in an uproar. I had been so upset by losing my faithful Margaret through that wicked Mathew Hopkins, that I could not have sent you a letter by him, even had you been at home. Well, hours afterwards, the cob came trotting back, with her knees cut, and her shoulder bruised. I was alone with the maids, with every door bolted and chained. The Doctor was out on his rounds, and the streets so disorderly from wretches shouting and yelling 'Down with all witches!' that I dared not leave the place to find someone to help us, or let the maids go either, for very likely they also would have been kidnapped as poor Margaret's accomplices. I give you my word, when I heard that horse come rapidly up to the door, my knees just knocked together, and my teeth chattered, so frightened was I that it meant harm to your uncle.

"It was very late when the Doctor, tired and weary, came home, and he had come in for some sights that made him shudder. Of he went, however, at once, with the coachman and lanterns, and at length, on the common, a few miles off, they found poor Timothy. One leg was broken in two places, as well as several ribs, and he had severe concussion of the brain. They brought him home here, of course, by as quiet ways as they could manage, and he has been with us ever since. Timothy's leg had been unset for so many hours the inflammation was very great, and at first, your uncle feared it must come off. The poor fellow was, however, such a good subject from having been steady all his life, that by long and slow degrees the swelling went down, and the bones united. But it has been a serious, tedious business, and the ceaseless fret Timothy has been in, ever since he was quite clear, has thrown him back tremendously. He can now limp with a stick, and will start for home the minute the Doctor allows him. Owing to the severe weather and the distracted state of the country, a trustworthy messenger could not be found, though indeed we tried, knowing how fearfully anxious Mistress Bridget must be. Now, will you give her Timothy's respectful duty, and explain how it comes about that he has been detained here. The messenger told me that Madam Conyngham was home again, but that the villagers were a rough set, and had such an evil look about them, he was glad to get quit of the place.

"God keep you from Mathew Hopkins and his crew; he turned this quiet place into a perfect hell, and from the day I heard your uncle had up and said he held not with such cruel and wicked work, he has been a marked man, and I have never had a minute's peace when he was out of my sight, whilst that ruffian stayed here, neither did I venture beyond the garden gate: but that is long past now, he has been touring in other places, and alas! this morning I heard he was making straight for Somerset. Timothy is nearly mad with fear that Mistress Bridget will come to some harm, and on hearing you were home, he begged me to ask you to give an eye to her, and if possible, keep her from the village. He is so excited, I can't make out *what* he fears, and the messenger has just sent in word he can wait no longer; if my letter is not ready, he must go without it, so in haste, dear nephew, fare thee well.

"Your loving aunt,

"Emily John."

*   *   *   *   *   *

In due course, and as it happened, this letter reached Sir James on the 19th of February, after the darkness had fallen, and for hours he paced up and down his dining-room, lost in thought.

One thing was quite clear, and that was, to-morrow, Bridget's birthday, he would ride over to Rithycombe—he had not been there for quite a week. He would take the road through the village instead of keeping to the upper one as usual, and then, if there seemed anything brewing or disturbed, he would *insist*—and the word grew tall as he said it—on Madam and her daughter returning to the Court with him. *Here*, he could keep them safe, *there*, he could not.

The villagers were not likely to be any more evil-disposed to-morrow than they had been to-day, and after then, he would indeed be on his guard and take every precaution, though what particular fear there was for Bridget, he could not imagine. Ah! What about shutting the stable door after the steed is stolen!

In all his many plans and thoughts, he had forgotten the love of talk, and of being, even for a few brief minutes, of importance. As he paced his comfortable room, happy and secure in the belief all was well, the man who had brought his letter was holding forth at the "Blue Anchor" Inn, but a few miles from Rithycombe, to a rough group of men, telling them all the latest news, of course, with the great item of Hopkins' arrival in the county, and the fine times they might look forward to in consequence.

One of the listening men was Nan Crane's idle good-for-nothing husband, Tom, who very speedily bid his boon companions a surly good-night, and tramped, for him, briskly homewards, with evil thoughts and wicked ideas in full possession of him.

X

THE SPEED OF DESPAIR

" 'Once more, art thou determined?'
'I am. Nor is there aught which shall impede me!'
'Then Heaven have mercy!' "

—Byron.

T HE long smouldering ill-feeling against Bridget might have died down completely in time if the rumour that Mathew Hopkins had crossed the Somersetshire border had not suddenly aroused a sort of frenzy against all witches, and their own so-called one in particular; and an eager desire to show themselves clever enough to do without him and his heavy fee, stirred all the worst passions and cruel vices into activity. Starvation from failure of crops, long-continued drought, idleness and laziness on the part of the farmers themselves, had culminated in a terrible state of affairs. Only the taverns flourished, flourished on the ruins of men's souls and bodies.

The night the news reached them, through Tom Crane, that the Witch-finders were drawing near, a group of vile spirits gathered in a small private room of the "Tabard" Inn, and worked up into a perfect frenzy by Crane's wicked suggestions (for which he was principally his wife's mouthpiece), that Mistress Bridget, with her Evil Eye, was at the bottom of all the trouble and misery that had now been their unhappy lot for long, swore in their drunken fury that, the slightest loop-hole given them (and Nan Crane could *make* more than one if she chose), the morrow's sun should not set before *their* witch's spells should be broken for ever, and a handful of ashes, grey and white, be the only remains of the young, fair girl they had known all her life.

Hal Scott, less hardened than the others, vainly tried to stem the tide, and muttered Little Madam had been very good to him and his. They called him coward and poltroon,[13] and swore they'd keep an eye on him that he did not turn king's evidence. The villains were just in that inflammable state, they would side either way, following the strongest leader for right or wrong.

The hours wore on, the darkness deepened, and when the worthless crew reeled home, making night hideous with their shouts and songs, only *one* man lay prone on the dirty floor, sunk in a drunken slumber, and that man was Hal Scott, Bridget's advocate.

$*$ $*$ $*$ $*$ $*$ $*$

It was early morning, and the hush of God's rest lay deep on the land; the mysterious forces of the night had not awoke, the charm of the pure day still held them in thrall, that would last until the silver moon's sceptre was lowered, and her glittering train had all paid their court, and were left with myriad eyes to wonder again and again how man, in his brief day, could spend his life on trifles, and cast not even a heedless thought on the Eternity above.

So still, not a twig quivered, not a dreaming bird twittered; nothing stood in the way on earth or the air above, to check or alter a sound.

Whatever broke the silence would carry far, and must be heard with wonderful clearness, take what shape it might.

$*$ $*$ $*$ $*$ $*$ $*$

---

[13] An utter coward; a worthless wretch.

Out in the darkness of night, clear in the still silent atmosphere, from the old church tower in the vale rang out a muffled peal. No human hands were nigh; the doors were locked and barred whilst the cords swayed and strained, and the plaintive dirge went on—sinking, rising, falling—in solemn cadence, slow and steady, with the strange muffled effect of cotton-wool, making them sound miles and miles away.

The villagers turned on their pillows, starting awake in surprise, the old folks pretending not to be astonished; *they had heard that music before*—when little Mistress Bridget was born. Ay, and before that truly! But there! It was a thing uncanny, best not spoken of aloud; there were sure to be those about whose ears were all too sharp, and luck was bad enough, without tempting worse.

There were others who muttered darkly that it was a sign from Heaven; the time and the day had come.

Only fools would let such a chance slip, another they might not get.

Up at the Manor mother and daughter slept in peace, and heard not the weird music that would perhaps, in the heart of one, have aroused a warning echo, and stirred a dormant fear into activity that might have proved a safeguard.

Madam slumbered soundly, and Mistress Bridget in her dormer room dreamt of her loving father, as in fancy she wandered in bygone years, without a thought of the storm-cloud hovering close above her innocent head.

Was it Kismet or by God's good providence that the warning passed them by?

Would it have altered aught, or only taken their courage away, had they guessed at the trouble close, which yet *must* be faced and met, woven as it was into their life's pattern, to be worked out to the end, even at the cost of their hearts' blood?

*   *   *   *   *   *

The "Tabard" inn was close to the quaint old church, and the solemn peal roused Hal Scott from his slumber on the floor. Roused him sufficiently to sit up and gaze around at the overturned chairs, the empty bottles and battered tin mugs all any-how, no-how, in the confusion of the dirty room, with its heavy atmosphere of smoke and drink.

Sit up. Ay! but with senses dull, and memory blank, listening quite calmly to the deep cadence of the bells, then a wide yawn, a great stretch, an unsteady stagger to leaden feet, and a pause— whilst through his clouded brain the muffled boom forced its way, bringing a dull sense of wonder whose knelling was taking place.

Little Madam's, of course; had he not heard it all planned— *When? Where? By whom?* Ah! friendly deeds are never lost; how quickly he remembered now the frequent kindness shown him by Mistress Bridget and her family. For he was too late; no doubt by now the thick smoke from the dry wood those wicked men had by them, would burn with fierce rapidity.

Too late! Too late! The bells were stopping now; all was over!

Ay! But if so, why this stillness? Surely there would be a great trampling, and shouts and yells of satisfied fury.

There was another boom now; how it started him, though it was but the striking of the church clock close by. One—two— three—*four!*

God save us all! Had he heard aright? Like an animal at bay he glared around, with bloodshot, distended eyes, then tottered from the room, and stumbled along the low passage to the paved court-

113

yard hard by, almost forgetting, poor fool, what he meant to do. One minute more, and drunken slumber would again have chained him body and mind, but the sight of great faggots of timber put all ready to hand, revived in a flicker his wandering senses. Another stumble, and he was on his knees by the pump, with his head well under the spout, sousing himself with all his strength.

Again and again the *douche* was repeated, the cold water worked its cure, and a sober, shivering man stood up in the gloom of the early morn, with one strong purpose well alight—to do his utmost to foil the wicked plot that would soon be put in practice.

Where could he go for help?

Why, there was but one man who *could* do aught—the man who had called him "Coward." It was his only chance, but had he time? Twelve long miles away, over a rough road that wound and wound in useless curves between the sheltering hills.

Hopeless, was it not, almost to try?—for on foot he would have to fare.

Had the Manor stables been full, he would have helped himself without a second thought, but only one horse occupied the stalls now, and *he* was dead lame. Yokels are not good pedestrians as a rule, they slouch along just as it pleases them; continuous steady walking, with even time and pace, is a thing almost unknown to them. Supposing he did the distance in three and a half hours, that would bring it to half-past seven, and then the return on such a rough track, mounted, would mean one and a half, if not two hours more.

They were early folky at Rithycombe, and in this case, if the men should cool off in the light of day, Nan Crane would keep them up to the mark.

Burnt as a witch, that fair young girl; it would be a thing horrible, unknown, unparalleled. In all the witch-burnings and murderings of late, the victims had been old and wrinkled, with most of life behind them and with many sins upon their heads.

The Witches' Ladder! *There* was his chance. Dare he face it with its evil repute, and many tales of woe?—and yet it would cut off miles of his tedious way, and save a lot of time. He knew the spot well, most did, though few had ever set foot upon the rugged boulders that, piled in fantastic heaps, gave just a foothold up the sides of a certain precipice on Hollow Common, above the dark pool of the same name. The stones had slight depressions in them, and bore a strange resemblance to a narrow perpendicular ladder. A cold shiver ran through his frame as he thought what *might* happen if he turned dizzy half way up, but try he must; he could not keep the road and be in time to get help at all. If he fell, well, the water would be his grave, for no one knew its depth.

There was the clock again, and he had lost a quarter of an hour of his precious time. He could but do his best, and no doubt fail at that; and so he started, as quietly as he could, for the village would awake all too soon without extra aid from him. On past the silent cottages, by the old grey church out into the whispering lanes, over the dreary fields.

Down in the vale, deep in shadow, stood the Manor House, its inmates all unconscious of harm or spite, with the ancient trees standing like sentinels, as in the days of old.

He got along well as far as he knew his path in the dim, uncertain light, and felt quite courageous when he deliberately left the winding road, to follow the slender track that pointed straight as an arrow to that narrow dip in the hills, where the cliffs and the ladder stood. Gradually the incline increased, and it was with labouring breath and several pauses, that he at last stood in the cleft in the hills, very dark at that early hour in the morning from the narrowness of the fissure and the overhanging rocks in this particular spot. The cleft widened a little further in, to leave room for the dark, still pool, and there before him stood the famous witch ladder!

With beating heart and shaking limbs he began the toilsome way, that looked so simple till you came to climb it, but really was steep and awkward enough to try a novice sadly.

His hands were cut and bruised from clutching the sharp edges, and his feet were already so sore and blistered, every step was pain and grief. An awful temptation assailed him to give over, and let matters take their course; then realizing rather suddenly that to *return*, to *descend*, was out of his power, he shut his eyes to steady his nerves, and again toiled upwards, but it grew worse, for the top steps distinctly overhung.

Let his body swing into space whilst he tried to drag himself over yon knife-like edge? Impossible!

The faint light was reaching him now from the other side, and just as he felt utterly hopeless, he saw a foothold at the *side* of the beetling rock, and dangling by it a bit of rope. Dare he trust to it?—would it hold?—was it rotten?—would it prove only another form of destruction? Deep breathings, bright eyes, seemed around him; and what were those dark forms suddenly arsing from the ground above, and coming close to the edge to push him over!

No, no! Life was sweet, the rope *might* hold, and in the strength of despair, he seized the frayed cord tight with one hand, steadied himself by the other, made a wild leap upwards by that sideway footstep, and stood safe at the top, in a rough bit of common, with a few poor startled sheep staring in mild surprise at his sudden intrusion.

Great drops of sweat were rolling down his face as the poor fellow paused a moment, to recover his breath. All around him the green hills, below him, well in the distance, stood out the old church of Rithycombe, and yonder to the west Fielding's Court. He must go on—for time was precious, but all was plain sailing now!

A few yards more, a rolling stone, a hasty slip, a sharp stinging pain through his ankle that caused him to fall prone on the ground, without a soul in sight.

*   *   *   *   *   *

"Someone asking for me at this early hour. What sort of fellow, Susan, should you say? The country is very disturbed."

"A decent sort of body, Sir James, but ragged and dusty, with boots cut all in pieces, and clothes sadly stained. He came riding on a poor jaded beast that he said he found straying on Hollow Common, for he had hurt his ankle, and could walk no more. He said it was a matter of life or death, else I would not have troubled you, sir. There! He wouldn't wait, you see, for me to ask your leave, ill-mannered loon; belike 'tis all a parcel of lies!"

"*No*, your worship, it's true, on my soul; but first would you tell me the hour?"

"A quarter past seven of the clock."

"Marry! to think of the time I've been, and I started just after four. Please, sir, order your horse whilst I tell you the tale, and the best you've got in your stables. Don't you know me, sir?"

"Why, as I live it is Hal Scott! Be not so peremptory, my good fellow; tell me your errand first."

"They are going to burn Mistress Bridget, of Rithycombe, as a witch, your honour, early this morning, to save Mathew Hopkins the trouble; but if I wait to tell you all it will cause a long delay. See here, my lord, you shall hang me up by the heels if you find I've told you wrong, only for the good God's sake ride away at once! I've been drinking, did you say? Yes, but not for hours. I'm

117

worn out," and a hoarse sob shook the rough voice, "and not fit for the likes of you; but *murder* will be done if you don't hurry, murder that, 'coward' though you called me, I've done my best to hinder."

Impressed in spite of himself by the man's manner, and alarmed beyond measure, Sir James lost no time in giving his short, decided orders for two serving men to follow him at their best speed; and but a few minutes later saw him booted, spurred, and fully armed, riding at a brisk canter towards Rithycombe.

Better, perhaps, than poor, ignorant Hal Scott, could he realize the awful peril Bridget stood in, if once the notion she was a witch had gained credence, and for his love to be in such terrible danger set his heart on fire.

XI

BURNT AS A WITCH

" Who by aspersions throw a stone
At the head of others, hit their own."

—Quotation.

T HE morning of Bridget's birthday rose bright and clear, with quite a touch of coming spring about it, a refreshing change after the dreary winter.

The clocks were nearing eight o'clock when Martha most reluctantly awakened Bridget, sleeping unusually late after her previous evening's agitation. The girl's long hair fell over the snowy pillows, and she looked so young and fair, a tear dimmed her nurse's eyes as she gently touched her.

"Mistress Bridget, my dear, a happy day to you, child, and many of them. You are wanted in the village at once; there's a poor fellow cut himself so badly they think he'll bleed to death, and have come tearing up for you. Like their impudence, I say, when they have been so glum to you this long while past, and I had a good mind not to tell you, only the woman made such a fuss."

"Quite right, Martha. I'll be very quick; unhang my cloak, yes, and give me that white serge I had on last night; there now, no one will ever see my hair is down with my hood on, and I'll run all the way. A cottage on the green, you said. All right."

It was indeed a horrid cut, from a blunt chopper hacking a bit of firewood. Bridget did her best, and having bound it up very tightly, prepared to start home.

But the smart of the wound was hard to bear, and the discontent of the past few months had gone too deep amongst the ignorant people for matters to end thus.

Excited by fear, no sooner had the girl left the sufferer's bedside than the poor fellow sprang up, tore off his bandages and declared she was burning him with her accursed hell fire; he was *glad* to think his last chopped bit of wood would help to roast *her!*

Out sprang the blood in jets and streams; fright did the rest, and as rough hands were laid on Bridget, the labourer fell back dead.

Oh! the uproar that ensued, the angry clamour, the savage gestures, and brutal threats.

"It ran in the blood to deal with devils," shouted they; "they'd have no more of her black magic, no more murders should be done with *their* consent."

Almost before young Madam knew what was happening, they had dragged her forcibly to the tiny village green, where white-plumaged geese fled in haste. A horde of yelling fiends trooped alongside, fastened her with stout cords and rough words to a handy cattle-post, and piled dry brushwood round her in a close mass higher than her knees, all with incredible speed.

So this was the end; the wood was so dry it would burn fiercely, quickly, and the suffering would soon be lost in suffocation!

So thought Bridget as she stood waiting for her fate, with that strange loss of power in voice and limb she had felt in their night alarm. Only then did she remember how true in every particular had come the vivid dream that had possessed her on that hot summer's day, a few months back.

Perhaps even then there might have been a little delay, and the tide have turned in favour of Bridget, if Nan Crane had not come running along bearing a flaming brand. Then came another mad rush, cruel evil fingers thrusting branches into the torch to assist in firing the faggots. One wretch poured oil recklessly over the wood; and cheered and danced in glee as the blue flames rushed heavenwards, and the yellow and red came curling behind. Smoke in a dense column for a moment obscured the slender figure in the middle, and the air being still and clear, rose up straight to a good height, catching the eye of a galloping horseman, whose steed was flecked with foam, and sides pricked by frequent spurrings.

"Good God! Am I not in time? Ten thousand curses on the brutes!"

In went the sharp rowels again,[14] crash came the heavy whip, and maddened almost into frenzy, the beautiful creature flew over the ground in breakneck style. Up the village street, past the "Tabard" Inn and the quaint old church, to the dark crowd gathered on the village green, whose every thought and eye were centred on the stake.

Sir James Fielding rose high in his stirrups, and shouted with all the force of his powerful lungs, but so great was the noise made by the rabble, and so absorbed were all their faculties, not a head turned in his direction.

Laying his crop about him with a will, the rider tried to force his way through the pack of people, for the girl's eyes were closed, and the smell of burning was suffocating. The horse refused to face the flames, and plunged and reared wildly; but by backing him hard, a passage was partly cleared to the burning pile, though the crowd tried to block it, and he trampled some of the smouldering wood underfoot.

Sir James set his teeth hard—now or never! *Nothing* would bring the horse into such a good position again, and on foot he would

---

[14] Rowel: the spiked revolving disc at the end of a spur.

be powerless. With an awful pull on the curb, he forced the frightened creature to back a foot or so more, closer to the faggots, leant clear over them, and with all the might of a true heart and a strong arm, grasped firmly the stake and swung the girl across his saddle. The chance he had reckoned on, that the fire would have burnt nearly through the base of the post, probably rotten to begin with, was correct, and it snapped off short with the strain upon it, else this would have been impossible, though it might have come wholesale from the ground.

Shouts, yells, curses, blows, even kicks were liberally bestowed by the surrounders on the rescuer and his steed, whose neck they tried to hang on; but the creature kicked out with such a will he left several motionless on the ground, and sprang wildly away with his double burden, in spite of clutching hands, and threatening forms, and went like mad along the Manor road.

Two men servants came galloping up, shouting "Fielding! Fielding!" but their aid was useless, unneeded. Sir James had Bridget safe, though, as he cantered to the Manor House with his unconscious burden, he did not know if it was a living or a dead woman he was supporting. He smelt charred all over, and from the way his hands smarted, ached, and throbbed, soon became aware he was considerably burnt. Bridget's serge dress was discoloured, but there were no visible scars on the face, which looked white enough to have been carved in marble.

His horse was done; trembling violently in every limb, with great beads of moisture dropping from him, with head held low and snorting breath, he still galloped along; but the strides were getting slow, and would soon fall into a weary trot.

Sir James' hands were terrible; exposed to the air as they were, it was just pure force of will that kept them round Bridget, but the sharp pain made him feel faint and dizzy. Would he—could he—hold out to the Manor?

Ay! If he died in doing it!

In at the old iron gates the poor over-ridden beast turned of his own accord, and up the leafless avenue he knew so well. Here Martha was waiting with a look of frenzy on her face, and her hair all flying in the wind. Long before they met, she called out shrilly had he seen her lady?—for such a noise had come up from the village, she knew not what was afoot. Joe was not at hand to ask, and Madam was no use.

Then she caught sight of the helpless burden, and the strained look on his face, as he nodded to her Bridget was there. He reeled in his saddle as he did so, and fear and dread unspeakable filled Martha's heart, as he hoarsely asked her to lock and bolt the entrance gates, and then follow him to the Manor. Just as she clanged them to, the Fielding servants rode up, and told her what had happened, and that it was just a miracle their master had been able to lift such a dead weight from the ground; that they would see to the gates, and be at the house as soon as she.

So they were, and a good job, too, for though the horse stood still enough, Sir James dare not loose his hold from Bridget for fear, helpless as he was, he should let her fall. Neither could he dismount. Carefully, quietly the servants took the poor girl from his arms, and carried her into the old hall, returning to give their master almost as much help, for by now, his hands were simple agony.

Bridget still lay motionless on the settle, and Martha would not have her carried upstairs, for Sir James could not be there and she guessed it would be needless torture to him not to see if Bridget was alive or suffocated.

Most sensible women knew how to treat burns and scalds in those lonely times, when it was a question of hours before outside aid could be procured; and Martha's simple remedies gave untold relief to Sir James, whose coat sleeves had to be cut open to bind his damaged hands. The burns were terrible to look at, though not deep; all the skin was gone some way up the arms, where the flames had crept in between the cloth and flesh. Revived by a strong stimulant that Martha insisted on his taking, Sir James was soon able to direct what was best to be done. He made one of his servants write out arrests for the principal ringleaders, whose names Hal Scott had given him. He had another request to the Excise officers written to ask them to see these arrests carried out immediately, and report the same to him. One man was sent riding away with these, and the other to the nearest doctor, with instructions not to return without one.

Martha trembled, frightened to death, and at last ventured to say was it was wise to take such strong measures in such fearful times? Sir James looked very stern as he said it was his only course; if he let those brutes alone and they went with their lies to Mathew Hopkins, or acted again for themselves, no power of man might save Mistress Bridget.

Crush them now utterly, completely, whilst that wretch was still at a distance, and all might be well.

The excisemen were the only regular disciplined force available, and he believed they would willingly give their assistance, though the work would be quite out of their regular routine.

Without even the farce of a trial the wretches had attempted unlawfully to murder Mistress Bridget; if she died they should swing for it, so help him Heaven!

Martha touched him gently on the sleeve—Bridget's eye-lids

were quivering, and opened wide in a few minutes; down on their knees in thankfulness both sank, for they had feared the worst.

"Yes, Martha, take her upstairs now, if you can. Would that I could carry you, my love; bed is the safest place, please God she is not burnt much! There, Joe, you have come in just in the nick of time to help Martha carry young Madam to bed. Tell me how she seems, my good soul, when you have undressed her, won't you?"

"Ay, surely you may count on me. Now, dearie, I am ready."

*   *   *   *   *   *

Two hours had barely passed, all too long for Sir James' feelings, when the clatter of horses outside, and the jingle of a sword on the stones announced the arrival of the Excisemen, the leader of whom, a fair-haired young fellow, did not look very happy over his job. He came in for Sir James' instructions, and said they were very sorry to be able to spare so few men, but it was useless sending any but reliable ones on such an errand. He quite agreed with Sir James it was the only course for the safety of Mistress Bridget, but he said if the plan failed what then could they do?

"We will leave that to consider until we needs must," said the baronet, deciding rapidly in his own mind there was nothing for it but that he must go himself with the men, and back up this nervous young man.

"You will understand, men, that we need to be quick and firm. With my cloak round me none will guess how helpless I am. The minute I give the order each two of you seize your man, the two oldest taking the first person, and so on in the order that this old fellow," turning to Joe, "points out. Secure their hands, swing them out and away; if you can't mount them behind you, make them run alongside; it will do them no harm, and I warrant you once the people of the village see we are in grim earnest, they will turn round and help us. There must be no time for rebellion, or worse harm may come; we are but a handful. That real old witch, Nan Crane, is the first I mean to secure under their own pretext of saving Hopkins trouble. Besides the attempt at wilful murder, I shall mention the men as her accomplices in unlawful deeds, and if that does not strike terror to the whole place, I'm not a Somersetshire man, but a changeling. We take the party to Dunstar, remember, and lodge them in the county gaol. Now forward!"

"You are not fit to go, sir, and that you know right well, yet it is a serious matter to manage without you."

"All right, Joe, give me a hand with my cloak, and then I'm ready, though I fear I needs must have my beast led. Two of you men must go pillion, for my own horse is too unnerved to mount. Martha, please bar the door."

Away they spun in good style, close together, with pistols ready, and eyes on the alert. The village was still in a bustle, women tearing about, and men in knots of twos and threes. The faggots lay smouldering on the bit of green; no doubt the bonfire had been fine, but the sight alone of the sticks made Sir James feel queer.

He made straight for the "Tabard" Inn, guessing rightly that whether as consolation for the failure of the morning, or encouragement for darker deeds yet to be carried out, most of the evil spirits, men and women, would be congregated there. He was right, and such a buzz of talking filled the stuffy room, no one noticed the horses pulling up, or the jingle of spurs, as they dismounted, so that all the Fielding party were well in the room, with the outer door guarded, before a single man noticed the intruders.

The legal preface to the warrants was lost in noise, then fell such a dead, sudden silence, Sir James' voice rang out clearly and distinctly, saying that by order of the Privy Council and with the authority of the Parliament of England he arrested as suspicious and dangerous characters, Nan Crane, the witch—Tom Crane, John Bowles, George Watkins, and William Smith—accomplices of the same, who had that day added one more crime to their long list, by burning Mistress Bridget Markham, of Rithycombe, whose only fault, as known well to all, had been kindness to them and theirs. For the last crime in particular they were arrested and would be judged in due course.

"Do your duty, men!"

Like flint striking steel, the words rapped out; the women and men were seized, bound and swung by their collars out of the room in less time than it takes to write, Nan Crane making a hideous noise; and though there was a pell-mell rush from the room, in which many knocks and bruises were quickly gained, so sharp had the capture been that they had actually begun to ride away before the foremost bundled out. Again Sir James proved himself right; robbed of the ringleaders, who had dominated the others, the men looked sheepishly after them, muttering it was none of *their* doing, and the women began to whimper, and say it was awful to think they had killed that sweet young Madam!

Such was the state of affairs when a high gig came in sight from another road to that taken by Sir James' party, and the old grey mare in the shafts pulled up gladly at the inn door.

"Why, what's all this to-do?" said the driver sharply; "what are you all loafing about here for? You've had a burning, did you say, and the Excisemen have taken the leaders to prison! And a good thing too. What did you burn, a haystack or a house?"

Silence—no one spoke.

Timothy went very white, and Mistress Markham laid a restraining hand on his arm.

"It was a person then. *Who*, I say, can't one of you speak?"

"*Mistress Bridget.*"

"And you live to say it, *cowards*, not men that you are? Oh! my lady! had I but been here!"

The veins stood out on the man's face, and his clenched hands were white at the knuckles, whilst a terrible look of hopeless despair settled on his features.

The sobs of the women were now supported by the groans of the men, who said it was all the Cranes' doing; they hated young Madam like poison, and had worked on them so, they thought they were really doing the place a benefit by burning *the* one that was said beyond a doubt to possess the Evil Eye. *Now* they knew better, and would gladly walk miles to see Nan Crane suffer the same punishment.

"Ay! but she'd make a noise worth hearing, not take it so quiet-like and silent as little Madam, who had not even said she was afraid."

That was enough. Timothy could stand no more; with curses on them all, low and deep, that in her heart, the gentle lady beside him considered quite excusable, he gave old Nell a cut, the like of which she did not often get, and they pounded away to the Manor in silence; it was no time for words.

Martha very cautiously opened the door, and started back in surprise when she saw Timothy.

"Why, man! I'm glad, real glad to see you, though it's but a sorrowful day you've come on. I thought it was the doctor, and I only waited to throw another cover over Mistress Bridget and run down."

"Yes, it's me, sure enough, and I wish I was dead to have come too late. Was there *no* one to try and save her?"

"Timothy, my man, you could not have done more than Sir James has done, and is doing. God bless him for it! His head is worth any two of ours, and his authority will back him up. Now, come you in and rest, and please tell me who *you* are, madam, that have come on this day of trial. Markham, did you say? What! our captain's mother! How pleased Mistress Bridget would be if she knew! Timothy, what are you groaning about? Have you hurt yourself?—how lame you are, to be sure."

"Always shall be, that matters nothing. Mrs. Markham came to stay with Mrs. John, and as soon as they would let me come, she said she should accompany me, and pay her promise visit to the Manor, and here she is. Take her to a room, Martha; she must be tired out, but can't I just look at Mistress Bridget first?"

"Yes, if you choose, for one minute. Now, madam, please. Why! whatever *are* you doing?" as Timothy, after one glance at Bridget, as she lay in the spare room, covered his face with his hands and sobbed deeply.

"Poor fellow!" said Mrs. Markham. "Don't you see we were told she was burnt, and to find her breathing was too sudden a relief for him. Take courage, friend, whilst there's life, there's hope. Your mistress, how is she?"

"Deed, madam, I hardly know, she is still asleep. I have been in several times, but she does not rouse, she was quite herself all yesterday, and took an interest in everything, stopping up later than usual, and I suppose she's tired out."

"I think we ought to awaken her, Martha; she must need some nourishment, but she has been spared some terrible hours."

"There, madam, there's the doctor's trap. I see it coming up the avenue; he will tell us if she should have her sleep out. Timothy will let him in, and you should rest."

129

"No, not whilst I can help you; take me to Mistress Bridget, and fetch him up."

The doctor examined the girl very carefully; she had some nasty burns on her feet and back, and her hair was like tinder, but they were mostly separate injuries, and not over a wide surface. The shock was as serious as the burns, and she had severe congestion of the brain, and would need the greatest care if she was to live. She would not be out of danger for many days to come, he feared, but youth was on her side, and she would have first-rate nursing, of that he had no doubt! He was so busy he could not come again for a few days, they would have to manage without him. He was turning to descend the stairs, when Martha asked him to glance at Madam, for she slept so late.

The doctor started when he saw her face, lifted her eyelids, felt her pulse, and shook his head.

"This is not sleep, my good woman, but coma; if we cannot rouse her, she will die. There is not a minute to lose. I am afraid I am too late now. This lady, will she help?"

"Of course, and I am well accustomed to illness in most forms, only tell me what to do."

"You have come off a long drive, I understand. Then I must beg you to take some strong cordial at once, and lie down on a bed for an hour, for you will have a heavy night of it before you, and will require all your strength. If you reject my advice, I shall probably have another patient on my hands, but I think you are too sensible a woman not to do as I ask. In the meantime, Martha and I will do our utmost for this poor lady. Did she seem in any way different yesterday?"

"Yes, sire, quite like herself; it was a pleasure to see her."

"Ah! Quite so! A sudden flicker up, too great a strain on

weakened powers, and here we are! Now, madam, please go and rest. I will not leave without seeing you again."

"There is poor Sir James for your other patient, Doctor," volunteered Martha. "I expect he'll return in a fine state."

"No doubt. That man of his was telling me as we drove here what a terrible to-do there had been—disgraceful! It is a mercy Sir James was in time; the man said, when he and his fellow came in view of the green, Sir James was hanging right over the burning faggots. He looked as if he must overbalance, and the horse nearly mad, just backed for those few seconds that saved a life, and then was off like the wind with his extra load. Now, please, to work."

And it *was* work too, hard work, the vain attempts by every means in their power to arouse the poor lady from her heavy stupor. Again and again they gave over, only to try afresh, but it was all of no use, and after a long hour the doctor went to tell Mrs. Markham so.

"She will live just as long as her strength holds out, and then die, most probably very quietly. You are not aware, Martha, of anything shocking or frightening her after she went to bed?"

"No, sir, nothing."

"You will need help. How can I best assist you?"

"Sir James' housekeeper would, I'm sure, spare us one of her maids if I could get a message there, but I've no one to send."

"I will manage it for you somehow, and now I must away. Send for me if you really need me, and if it is in my power, I will come. I have not been in my bed for three nights as it is. Ah! I hear horses; if it is Sir James, I'll give a squint at his hands. I hear him saying good-bye to the Excisemen. I hope he'll hurry."

Sir James looked utterly done as he stumbled into the hall, and sank on a chair, Joe and his own servant following behind.

"Well, doctor, here's a kettle of fish, but I hope we have trodden out the mischief. The village was absolutely quiet as we came through, and those wretched faggots had been carried off. How is your patient?"

"Mistress Bridget is as comfortable as her severe burns will permit; if fever does not set in, I hope and trust we shall do well *there*, but Madam is very ill, as Martha will tell you when I have gone; if you will let me see to you at once and go, it will be a real act of charity! Don't think me fussy or fidgetty, but I have some life or death cases waiting for me, miles away, and I'm nearly dead beat."

"My dear fellow, don't bother over me. Martha can manage."

"Of that I'll be the judge. Wheugh! Well, my man, you must be of Spartan birth; why, you are suffering torture."

"Well I know that; the dressings slipped."

"Slipped—I should think they *had*. Now I shall have to hurt you horribly to get those rags off. I will be as gentle as I can, but I warn you it must be agony for a few moments. Ready?"

"As soon as you please, it will be the quicker over."

"Bravo! That's done, now I shall tie you up properly, and I positively forbid your stirring outside the door till I see you again. You have run an awful risk as it is; it will be wilfully throwing yourself away if you tamper with such injuries. You are sure you have none anywhere else?"

"Certain sure; my clothes were thick, and I was barely a minute. Thanks, doctor, that is ever so much more comfortable. Must you go? All right, I won't keep you."

"Now, Martha, you've something to tell me; out with it—is Madam dying?"

What a relief it was to the faithful soul to pour it all forth, her sorrow for the old mistress and her fear for the young. Timothy's

132

return also took up time, but she had a good listener. Between pain and exhaustion Sir James was very quiet, and Martha chattered on, over and over again repeating herself in her agitation until summoned above to Bridget's room.

XII

HAUNTED

"When troubles come of God,
And men are frozen out of work, when wives
Are sick, and working fathers fail and die,
When boats go down at sea—then naught behoves
Like patience; but for troubles wrought of men,
Patience is hard. I tell you it is hard!"

—Jean Ingelow.

T HE sun sank slowly in a crimson glory to bed and the
moon came up in shining whiteness which, with all the
deep shadows about, made such a beautiful picture, that busy and
tired though she was, Martha paused at Bridget's dormer window
to admire the scene without. She had come up for some fresh
linen she needed, leaving Mrs. Markham by Bridget's side.

Sir James was installed in an easy chair in Madam's room,
for to bed he would not go. Yes! It was very beautiful, but what
messenger was *this*, wearing the uniform of the Roundheads, with
nothing on his head?

Was fresh trouble at hand?

The moon rays glinted on the naked sword gliding noiselessly
over the ground, shone full on the fair erect head, and lit up with
an unearthly radiance, a face with clear-cut features that Martha
recognised on the moment, as with steady unfaltering pace that
soldier figure came swiftly up the avenue.

"Now God in Heaven save us all," cried the faithful woman;

"he has come for Mistress Bridget; it is a sure and certain sign."

Fascinated, powerless to stir, she watched the spirit figure drawing nearer, nearer, then just as he reached the velvet lawn in front of the dormer window, he seemed to fade and fade until there was nothing left.

Even then Martha waited to make sure there would be no re-appearance; satisfied on that point she hurried down, and in a whisper told her tale to Sir James, who nodded his head softly and said, "Faithful as ever."

He was beyond wonder, and could not well feel more hopeless of Bridget's recover than he had done all day.

Still Madam slept her unchanging sleep, only the breathings were heavy and deep.

Timothy crept bare-footed up the quiet stairs, and touched the baronet on the shoulder. "A knot of men at the door, sir, asking for you. I don't know if they are up to mischief or not, but Hal Scott is with them, and they pray for speech of you."

"If Scott is there, I'll stake my life it's all right, and they are very quiet. Open the door, my man, I must see them in the hall."

It was quite a deputation that, with shuffling feet filed in, with such a hang-dog look of shame and despair, it was enough to make anyone sorry for them.

"Look here, your honour," said Hal Scott, limping heavily forward. "The matter is like this. My mates here are real sorry that they went so mad this morning, and knowing as I tried my poor best and failed, to save Mistress Bridget's life, they asked me when I crawled home this afternoon to act as spokesman for them, and to say there is not one of them but is truly ashamed and grieved for that black deed of this morning. They feel as if the memory of it will haunt and curse them all their lives, and rightly too. So now, your lordship understands they would give their right hands gladly to call back this day."

"You all clearly understood that Mistress Bridget was dead, killed by your own acts and deeds?"

"Certain sure, your worship; it was your own words that told us at the 'Tabard' Inn," muttered one of the deputation huskily.

"I said Mistress Bridget had been *burnt*. I never said she was *dead*. Thank God she is alive though in great danger, and the burns are most severe. I am truly glad in these evil times that there are a few Somersetshire men left who are brave enough to be sorry for having played the coward as you all did to-day. You don't need me to say that the only brave soul in that wicked crowd this morning was the girl you have known all her life. If God in His mercy spares her to us, we shall need to be very careful of her in the future, and guard her well. Now shake hands on it, comrades—Bah! what an ass I am! I have no hands to shake with—and swear from henceforth you will be her true men, come good or evil."

A deep murmur that came from hearts, as well as lips, responded promptly to Sir James' request.

"Never will *I* forget how I respect you all for coming here this night to speak to me! Now good-night and farewell."

"God bless your honour! You've taken a load off us, and we've had a lesson to last our lives! See here, sir, when we took them cursed sticks down we came on this, and one of us says as how Nan Crane threw young Madam's book into the flames, and that this is part of it."

So it was—dinted—blackened—bent—half a clasp of the old book of recipes.

Sir James had heard about that book once and again, and had hated to see Bridget reading it.

"Put it on that fire, my good fellow, that is the best thing to do with it. Good-night."

*   *   *   *   *   *

The hours of darkness wore away. Joe slept in his arm chair by the kitchen fire. The Fielding men-servants had been sent to the inn. Timothy went up and down stairs doing anything in his power, with a heart as heavy as lead; and the two regular watchmen snored in concert in the hall. Mrs. Markham had unwillingly consented to go properly to bed; Martha dozed by Bridget's side, and Sir James, in too much pain for sleep, had charge of Madam.

It was very quiet, so still that two villagers knocked repeatedly at the kitchen door before their summons was answered by sleepy Joe. Hal Scott's wife said they had come to see if there was nothing they could do to help at such a terrible time, and the old man assured them there was plenty for all to do. The fires below were out, and he was so stiff from the rheumatics he could hardly move.

What power a cheerful fire has!

The hall looked a different place half an hour later, with the table cleared from yesterday's irregular, snatchy repasts, the tiles washed over, the logs blazing cheerily, and a meal carefully arranged. Places could only be put for two, alas!

Timothy had done his best in the kitchen, so that there was no difficulty about hot water, greatly to Martha's relief, when, hearing the sound of sweeping and scrubbing, she came down to find out who was so busy. Mrs. Markham was quite fresh, she reported, and would soon be down. Bridget had had a bad night, as was to be expected, but was quiet then. Madam looked a shade whiter, and Sir James was sound asleep in the chair beside her.

Probably her entrance disturbed him, for soon they heard him moving about in Squire Conyngham's dressing closet. He spoke cheerfully, when shortly he appeared, thanked the women for coming, and said how nice they had made the place look, after all the dirty boots of yesterday. He and Mrs. Markham made real friends that anxious day; trouble draws people close together.

Greatly to their surprise, the doctor paid them a visit; he said he could not rest for thinking of them, and though there was nothing fresh to try or do, it was a great comfort to them to see him. Again he examined Sir James' hands, and gave a snort of satisfaction as he did so.

"That's going on all right, at all events; now I'll tell you you were within an ace of lock-jaw yesterday, and then there would have been a pretty to-do. You keep indoors now mind, sir, and if it is possible I'll be round to-morrow. There must be a change in Madam before then; if she lives through the day, she will probably pass away before midnight. Mistress Bridget is no worse, though I cannot truthfully say she is any better; still, in her case, to be no worse *is* hopeful."

Late in the afternoon two maids from Fielding's Court arrived, nice, steady women, ready to do their best.

All day long groups of villagers paced up and down the avenue, watching the windows anxiously, on the look-out for any tidings. The sun was sinking fast when Sir James and Martha took up their posts at the dormer window, which commanded the best view of the avenue, and silently waited. The red light had faded, the silver beams were touching the edges of some storm cloud when the soldier's figure came in view. Again the same calm air of conscious power, the dauntless bearing, the unhurried pace, a pause at the edge of the velvet lawn, as if waiting for someone or some signal, and then the slow fading away like last night. Both watchers drew a deep breath, and Martha muttered she did not like it—it was too uncanny.

"Strange, passing strange," was Sir James' comment. "I never held with ghosts before, and should not now, only for seeing him. It would be cruelty to tell Mrs. Markham; we will just watch and see how often he comes."

Madam died about eight that evening. Only the loud breaths coming slower warned her nurses the end was near, and as the doctor had prophesied, it was very peaceful when it came. Two or three days passed quietly away, and then came one so critical for Bridget, a few hours would decide. All those hours the doctor sat beside her, his finger on her pulse, his watch in hand. If collapse came on, all would be over.

Not for one moment of that day did Martha leave her. Sir James sat outside her door, and Mrs. Markham went in and out.

Little groups of waiting men and women stood about all day, though rain fell heavily, and they must have been soaked.

Every evening at sunset the guardian figure had appeared, and now, as the light faded, Sir James signed to Timothy to follow him, and together they mounted to the dormer chamber, the only window from whence they had discovered the apparition was visible.

There now before dusk the figure stood waiting, this time with folded arms and bend head, and he did not fade as usual.

In a whisper Timothy said all the village was talking of the soldier who walked in the avenue.

For quite a quarter of an hour they watched him; then the folded arms fell, the bent head was raised, and the fading began. The last faint outline had just gone, when Martha came hurriedly up, gasped out breathlessly, "It is all right," flung her apron over her head, and began to sob piteously.

Yes, it *was* all right. From the very brink of the grave Bridget Markham recovered. Her mother had been laid in her quiet grave, with a great following of the scattered gentry for miles and miles around. It showed the esteem and respect, also pity and sorrow, felt for the old family of Conyngham.

One of the covenanted clergy read some prayers, cut and clipped from our beautiful Liturgy, it is true, but better than none, beside the open vault; then the concourse dispersed, and only the immediate house-party returned to the Manor. All this had taken place some days before signs of consciousness returned to Bridget, and the frequent mutters of "blood-stained hands" ceased.

Her nurses had no clue to what she alluded, but it seemed to press heavily on her. To their untold relief, when clearness returned she asked no awkward questions, only smiled and thanked them, and took everything else for granted. Very quietly she accepted Mrs. Markham's presence, and it was from her lips she heard of her mother's death. The soldier figure came not again to the edge of the lawn for years, but so many had watched him passing, it was no matter of hearsay amongst the villagers.

Sir James made a good recovery, and his popularity was so well established that when he pleaded at the County assizes that Hopkins should be forbidden all the neighbouring towns, his suggestion was carried with no difficulty, and the wretch had to take himself and his brutal gang much further away than he desired.

As for Nan Crane and her following, had they been set at liberty Lynch law would probably have prevailed, and they would have been torn limb from limb.

But Sir James never intended they should be free, and though, as an act of clemency in such reckless times, their lives were spared, they had a term of imprisonment before them that would see out some of their lives.

*   *   *   *   *   *

The April sun was playing hide and seek amongst the hills, laughing at the swelling buds, tickling the young sap in the trees. Never had the Manor House in the vale looked better, Sir James thought, as he rode up the whispering avenue. It was a week since his last visit, for he had grown weary and sad, this long time past, by never being allowed to see Bridget. It was her whim, and nothing they could say or do, would make her say she would see Sir James. He felt it keenly as she grew stronger, and he heard of other people being admitted to the sick room, and the same answer always met his eager request—"Not to-day."

He knew from the doctor what a strange gap in her memory there had been at first, and while she kept weak, all were most careful not to excite her in any way, but when strength and health came back, and, except for her short, curly hair, she looked like the girl of a year ago, then her persistent refusal to see Sir James did seem odd.

Mrs. Markham assured him it was some strange freak that would surely pass in time, but even she lost hope as March faded into April, and April drew to a close, and still that prohibition remained. By some means Bridget always managed to be aware of his approach, and she was gone from the hall or room long before he entered it.

The old lady hated to see the hurt look on his face of late, as after one swift glance round, he would again miss the one he wanted to find; and she thought so deeply over the matter that one day, after his last visit, she took the law into her own hands, and told Bridget in simple words the whole history, as far as she knew it, of that terrible day to them all—the twentieth of February.

She saw the girl turn very white, and visibly tremble, as she spoke of her rescue from the stake, but she took no notice, and went on quietly with the tragic tale to the end. Then silence fell, broken at last by Bridget crossing the room to kiss her before she vanished upstairs to the dormer-room, where again she had taken up her abode.

"Martha, I can do no more for good, or ill. I have told her *all*. Though the doctor said it would be a mercy if she never knew or remembered the burning; if harm comes of it, blame me not."

"Blame you, Madam? Likely *that*, when you've just been a mother to her, poor child! I think myself it will be a relief to her to know all, and that it was just because there was that queer blank in her recollections, she got puzzled, and made a mess of things so far as Sir James was concerned. It will come all right now, dear lady, I feel sure; only wait and see.

*   *   *   *   *   *

Sir James swung himself clear of his horse, utterly unaware that bright young eyes were watching him, noting with surprise the hoar frost colour of the hair she remembered black, and the lack of spirit in his greeting to Timothy, waiting outside.

Up the few low steps, through the thick oak door into the lofty hall we all have so often entered. Then a sudden flush of red, as a slender figure was noticed in the window, an eager word—"*Bridget!*" two quick strides with ringing spurs, and the girl's small hands were in a grasp so firm and true, the like not often felt.

Bridget looked up in the strangely-moved face stooped over her, and then her eyelids drooped until the log lashes rested on the thin cheeks.

"Forgive me; until a day or so ago, I never knew or dreamt what you had done for me. I thought the fire was all a fever-dream, and that in reality, I had truly seen you kill a man, for what, I did

142

not know. You were riding, and he fell under a blow from you, but that no one else heeded this—to me—wicked act of yours, only made me feel sure you had done that sort of thing before, and even after, when I heard your name mentioned, I saw the mark of Cain upon your hands. Once, long ago, I watched you from the staircase talking to Mrs. Markham, and your hands—to me—looked red with blood, so I felt no doubt at all that what I remembered so clearly had occurred, and that to see you, or to touch you, would drive me nearly mad. Mrs. Markham tells me that if indeed in my unconscious state I *did* distort facts—and somehow I want to think she is right—the reality was an act of bravery I indeed can never be sufficiently grateful for to my life's end. Only to you could I tell this, and the terrible horror it gave me of you. Now I know the truth, from my heart I humbly ask you to forgive me."

"*Forgive you*, child, you tempt me far. What if I say between you and me such a word must never be named? The little that I did was done for love of you—for naught else care I; would that I might have you for my loved and honoured wife. Pause well before you answer, for if again you say me Nay, be it so. I will never ask you more to cast in your lot with mine. Should you in your mercy and—see how I stoop my pride—maybe only in *pity* on your part, give me Yea, then as God is my witness, never, never to your dying day shall you have cause to regret it. One word about my hands, and I have done. You are right, they are often an awful colour; the slightest thing that disturbs or excites me, and they flush scarlet, and burn like furnaces. It may or may not pass in time, the doctor thinks, and is, of course, the effect of the burns."

He loosed her hands as he finished speaking and stood back.

Outside, the birds twittered, the sun danced. Inside, a slender girl put out two trembling hands, with a half-sob, and a whispered "*Not* in pity, James," and Love was Lord of all!

*   *   *   *   *   *

"I was reading a letter from Uncle Thomas when you rode up; he asks me to let you hear the news, so you had better read it, it has been slow to coming."

Thomas Melville wrote to say he had only just heard of her mother's death, and the terrible trouble his niece had been in. He could not bear to write about the latter; it made him shiver even to think of it. But for Hal Scott's gratitude, and Sir James Fielding's courage, he would by now have been a desolate man indeed. Mrs. Markham had written him a full and graphic account, for which he thanked her much, but that under the circumstances the rescue had been effected in time, was little short of miraculous. He hoped soon to take the road, when he should make straight for them, but just then, events seemed marching so fast, he felt he must remain in London for the present, and see what came of it. That he was getting old, and in comfortable quarters, had some thing, doubtless, to do with his laziness, for which he trusted, as she was in such good keeping, Bridget would forgive him. He said:

"When at last Monk broke silence as to his lans, and declared for a free Parliament, the whole nation seemed wild with delight. He was thronged by thousands out of doors, shouting and blessing him. The bells of all England rang joyously, the gutters ran with ale, and the sky for five miles round London was reddened by countless bonfires. The soldiers alone were in a gloomy, savage mood, hating both the title of King, and the name of Stuart. The fury and despair of fifty thousand fighting men was no light thing to manage, but General Monk could do it. Now what would be his next move?"

144

He hoped soon to see Bridget, and find her well and strong, and with his greetings to Mrs. Markham, Sir James, and the servants, ended his newsy letter.

How pleased was Mrs. Markham to find her venture so successful, when later on in suspense and doubt she ventured into the hall, from whence the sound of voices had kept both Martha and herself on tenterhooks for long. What a happy time followed, and how many arrangements were made that sunny day before Sir James rode homewards.

One thing Bridget stipulated for most earnestly, that she should not be asked to leave her dear old home; she said to do so would, she thought, break her heart, and she did not feel as if she *could* live anywhere else. They might call her foolish and absurd, and no doubt she was both, but she felt the power of the old place so strong upon her, that she often fancied even when she was dead, and in God's mercy, safe in his Paradise above, she would often be drawn to earth again, at least in spirit, to visit her much-loved home.

Sir James made no comment or objection to this great wish of the girl's, and so they settled that for the present at all events, Mrs. Markham should reside at Fielding's Court, where the charge of the children would be a real pleasure to her, and Sir James at Rithycombe, with frequent visits between. Martha and Joe would return to their own cosy home, and Timothy permanently remain at the Manor.

Neither was Hal Scott forgotten. Sir James had a good post in his mind, that would give him plenty to do, without coming in frequent contact with the powerful temptations of the "Tabard" Inn. How simple it seemed after all, and what a lovely light shone round the timbered house as Sir James, with glad heart and smiling lips, rode from it that April evening, younger by many years than when he drew rein there that morning.

XIII

THE BELLS FINISH AND THE
GHOSTS CONTINUE

"Bell! thou soundest merrily,
When the bridal party
To the church doth hie,
Bell! thou soundest mournfully;
Tellest thou the bitter,
Parting hath gone by!"

—Longfellow (*From the German*).

L ATE on the evening of the 30th of May, 1660, a man hurrying along the Strand, nearly knocked over another, coming in the opposite direction.

"What *you*, Peter, ten thousand pardons, what a pace you go at. More detective work on hand, eh?"

"Name it not, I beg, the loathsome task to watch and spy from morn till eve. Well, what think you of the world to-day, now *you* are upper-most? Will it last?"

"Last, man, yes, our time and a bit beyond, but such doings just bewilder me. I never saw the like before. The city has gone mad wholesale. I rode along part of the route with the townsmen yesterday to meet the King, and they told me the whole road from Rochester to London was just the same as the bit I was on, one continuous line of booths and tents that looked like an interminable fair. Flags everywhere, bells pealing, bands playing, wine and ale literally flowing, with troops of grinners, performing dogs, dancing bears, puppet shows and the like at every turn; until one's eyes ached with looking, and one wondered whence in such a short space of time all these performers could have been unearthed from."

"How far did you go?"

"Only to the village of Blackheath, where the army was drawn up to receive the King."

"Ah! I heard of that *contretemps*; as things are, it was not politic."

"Not politic call you it? I could use a stronger word, it took me right aback. There was Charles with all the charm of the Stuart manner, looking his very best, every inch a King, on that day of public rejoicing; and though he must have been tired to death with his rough crossing and long ride, bowing all the way incessantly. Then when he halted with his staff, facing that vast body of trained soldiers standing at attention, with their arms grounded and every hand saluting, I thought I had never seen a brighter, prouder smile than what he flashed on them; and they met that pleasant greeting with black, sullen gloom! There! There! It is none of my concern, but I must say I felt for the King, and did not wonder his lips set close, and he turned sharply away to resume his triumphant ride."

"I think myself it was an error, but the army has got a bit out of hand of late to my thinking, and will require a little taking down, though whether Charles Stuart is the man to do it, *I* doubt. I'm off to visit Lambert, poor beggar, and cheer him up if I can, though I have heard on good authority that the King has declared already that two he cannot include in the general pardon are Lambert and Vane."

"Is Lambert still in the Tower?"

"Ay! Only very closely guarded and allowed few visitors. Are you staying on?"

"No. I leave to-morrow to be present at my niece's marriage to Sir James Fielding."

"What, that pretty child I saw once, Bridget—Something? She stayed with you the summer your wife nursed me."

"Conyngham, yes—no—Markham now, I mean. She married one of *you* during the troubles, and he was killed in battle."

"Markham, that good fellow, he *was* a loss; temperate, moderate, clear-headed, and as cool as you like under fire, it is a pity there are not more like him. I remember well going into his tent on the eve of the battle he fell in, to bid him farewell, as greatly to my regret I was ordered off with despatches. Markham was sitting writing, and I laughed at him about it not a little; we were good friends always, though he was of course greatly my junior."

"He said that his mother must hear only from himself, if he died, by letter—if he lived, by word of mouth—that he had married a girl left almost alone in a desolate house, as the only means of ensuring her safety with a protection warrant he had with some difficult secured for his mother; that gangs of disorderly soldiers were raiding the neighbourhood, and it was the best he could do for her at the time. He had done it with all his heart, for never had he seen a better or a fairer maid, and he had come across a good many. Those were his very words, I remember, and he added perhaps for a man over thirty it was ridiculous to say it, but he had really and truly fallen in love at first sight; and if he was spared he had no fear for the happiness of the future."

"I remember laughing at him for taking such a gloomy view of what, after all, was only expected to be a small affair on the morrow, but I could not get him to smile at his fears, poor fellow! In his case they proved to have been well founded.

"He said his puzzle was how to find a reliable messenger, and as, on going into the matter carefully, I found I actually passed through Rithycombe in the dead of night, I said if he would keep his own counsel and not get me into trouble, I would myself leave the letter at the Manor. Poor fellow! How relieved he seemed. I am glad now I did it, though, of course, I had no business to have done it. So I left him to his writing, and only saw him again in the dusk, as I was mounting my charger. He gave the letter into my hand. I could not see the address, so never knew till now that his wife was your niece. I heard, of course, he had been killed, but no particulars. I suppose Madam Bridget is a rich heiress?"

"No, indeed, for the funny part of it is, her dowry cannot be found. It was hidden by her for safety, by the advice of her mother, and then, poor child, she had a time of terrible trouble, and an awful illness, and all that part of her life is an absolute blank. Of late, they tell me, she has tried so hard to remember her hiding-place, she nearly made herself ill again, and Sir James has had to forbid the subject being mentioned; and declares if the money *is* found it shall all be given away, for not a halfpenny will he touch. It was the only way to manage her. An old friend—well, you'll be interested to hear—Markham's mother has seen to her wedding gear, and I am taking down a few oddments, for though the Manor lands are good, it will take years for the farmers to recover, and Mistress Bridget will have nothing of her own till they do."

"Did not Markham leave her anything?"

"All he could, but the property is strictly entailed, and goes to a distant cousin, and the money matters are so mixed up, it will take ages to sort out what really belonged to him."

"And at such an exiting time as this in our Kingdom's history, you can coolly turn your back on it all, and go bury yourself afresh in the heart of the country. Far better remain here and keep in touch with the march of events."

"Thank you, no! I am too old to care for fresh schemes, and am no courtier; maybe, if I stayed in London much longer, the sham and the hollowness of its fashionable life would lay hold on me. Each one for himself first, is the rule here, and those who climb swiftly to the top of the ladder of fame, give not even a glance at those they tread under in so doing. No doubt, in its way, the country is hardly better morally, but there can't, in consequence of the relative numbers, be quite such a mass of iniquity around one."

"These domestic wars, to use a word of my own, have brought the scum to the top in right good earnest, but if *that* is allowed to settle again, how will any lasting good be gained? There, don't let me keep you any longer; remember when down my way, to come and post the country cousin up in the latest town news."

*   *   *   *   *   *

Bridget had indeed almost made herself ill trying to force her mind back, to recall for herself the events tat happened to her during those summer months of the preceding year. The last thing she was clear about was the letter from her Uncle Thomas with its hasty summons to her parents, read as they sat at breakfast in the parlour, and her mother's subsequent charge to her to hide the treasure. In vain she thought and thought, and hunted high and low, wandering about by day, and often at night when all was still, with a tiny silver lamp in her hand, searching—peering—feeling— in any possible or impossible place that suddenly occurred to her.

Martha was quite frightened one night, when hearing someone going down the stairs very quietly, she cautiously opened her bedroom door and saw a tall, slender figure in her white night-dress, with silver lamp held high in her hand, going slowly down the stairs to the hall below.

At first she thought Mistress Bridget was sleep-walking, and held her breath in fear, but no! When she, in her turn, crept after her, she found the girl was wide awake, with a tired exhausted look on her face. She said she had been in bed a long while, and then thought of one place she had not looked in before—in vain, of course—that often and often she had come down like that without disturbing anyone; she was very sorry to have awakened Martha now. If only she could think or dream where she had hidden her father's prize-money, it would be such a relief; it quite haunted her that she could not.

Then it was Martha spoke to Sir James, and he at last prevailed upon Bridget to promise she would give over looking and searching for the treasure, and try and forget, for love of him, that there was any money hidden at all. One day, shortly before that fixed for the wedding, Bridget was talking away to Sir James, Mrs. Markham and Martha being busily occupied in various important and necessary arrangements, when a listening look passed over the girl's face; she stopped speaking, and turned her head towards the door, as if expecting someone to enter; then, to the baronet's no little surprise, sprang up and clapped her hands gleefully.

"James, I remember!"

"Remember *what*, Bridget?"

"Where I hid father's treasure; just suddenly, as if someone whispered it in my ear, it has come back to me. I must go quickly and get it, for fear I should forget again."

"It is all to be given away, Bridget!"

"Yes, I know; but oh, the relief to think it has come back to me. How could I ever forget such an uncommon place? Martha, Martha, come at once!"

"Mistress, dear, I am so busy; should you mind waiting a little while?"

"I can't, Martha; indeed, it is such a very important thing I want you for; to help me carry down the hidden treasure."

"Good gracious, Mistress Bridget, what ails you, honey?"

"Nothing, dear, only I remember now where I put it, and I might forget again. Please be quick."

"Shall I come, too, Bridget?"

"Oh, no! We'll bring it down to you."

Quickly both mounted the stairs, and Martha called out in surprise, when, after a moment's doubt and perplexity, and a little fruitless fumbling and feeling over the wooden mantelshelf in the dormer room, the sliding panel gave way, and the secret cavity stood open, but empty of all save a crumpled piece of paper, on which, when smoothed carefully out, was found written a rough estimate of the coins, jewels, and few bits of plate, not handed over to the martyred King's cause, because Squire Conyngham considered them his daughter's dowry.

Poor Bridget! Her cry of astonishment brought Sir James running up; there was such a baffled, disappointed sound in it, and a very distressed look on the young face.

"Oh, James, it was such a beautiful place! Did you ever see a better? Now I also remember I thought it would be too quickly found, and moved the things elsewhere, but *where* I have not an idea!"

"Then we are just where we were before, and have no wonderful fortune to dispose of to deserving objects."

"It is no joke to me, but a great worry."

"Yes, I know; but that I shall not allow, child, for a moment; so now, if you don't wish to make us both most unhappy, you will think no more of the dowry. After the real troubles God had given us to bear, and helped us through, the loss of a handful or so of coins we shall, I hope, never miss or require, can only be a trifling matter, by no means worth fretting over."

After that the girl grew quite light-hearted, and her happy laugh echoed through the rooms as of old, and so, surrounded by love and care, her second marriage day drew night.

Sir James made all his arrangements for the wedding, as unlike as possible to the quiet ceremony which Timothy, though not an eye-witness, on account of his wounds, described to him as having taken place almost a year ago, and Mrs. Markham helped him greatly.

Very fond had she become of her young daughter-in-law, and, wise and unselfish as ever, carefully refrained, on every occasion, from recalling Reginald Markham to her mind.

The doctor reassured them about the lapse of memory over those few months that had worried the girl so, considering the strain she had lived at, and the awful shock of the burning, without the terrible illness, were quite enough to have really turned her brain: the fact that Mistress Bridget had got through with only forgetfulness and nothing more to dread was matter for great thankfulness, and though, as all were aware, she had been told about those forgotten events, not to remember them for herself was, in his opinion, a great mercy.

*   *   *   *   *   *

So in the quaint old church—whose joyous bells had been ringing since daybreak, rung by many willing hands—before the carved screen, with its rich colouring, Bridget again changed her

153

name. Her soft grey dress, of rich brocade, swept the uneven flooring, hidden as that really was by scattered flowers.

All the village was there, dressed in their very best, so that the building, and out to the road beyond, was just a pack of people, young and old.

Mrs. Markham's hands had trembled slightly as she secured the tiny velvet coif on the girl's short curls with a flashing diamond pin, one of her own treasures; and her thoughts would wander, even during the service, to the new-placed stone in the churchyard corner, where her only son lay buried. The proper registers signed, Sir James led his bride down the old building, out through the crowd of waiting, smiling people to the coach beyond, already packed for a short absence.

In his care for her, Sir James had insisted there should be no shouts or cheers, and that they should go straight away from Rithycombe at once. There was no restriction as to hats and handkerchiefs, and everyone flicked or waved one or the other as, to the music of the bells, the coachman whipped up his excited horses, and Sir James and Lady Fielding turned over a new page in their life's history. On the Manor lawns the tables groaned with the good cheer loaded on them; the Fielding children, big and little, were here, there, everywhere, helping, hindering, in the wildest delight and pleasure possible: and when the evening shadows fell the hall was cleared of furniture, the fiddlers scraped their best, the flutes squeaked, the horns brayed, and the big drum, under Hal Scott's energetic fingers, more than took its own part.

Up and down the middle, in and out the centre, bobbed and bowed and jumped, young and old alike, making up in action what they lacked in grace.

No bonfires blazed as of yore on the purple hills about. No, no! That would not do; *one* too many had been lit in Rithycombe, but the bells rang out their chimes from morn till eve, and when the villagers and tenants of both parties trooped homewards down the avenue, all agreed that never had they had such a happy day in their lives, and all through little Madam! To think that the only wedding present she would allow Sir James to give her, was the pardon of the very wretches who had sought her life. God bless her!

Gossip said Sir James had been slow to agree to this request, and declared it was an unwise step, but had at last given in, only stipulating none of the ringleaders should settle again at Rithycombe.

*   *   *   *   *   *

So in the whirligig of life, the kaleidoscope patterns change from light to dark, from bright to dim, using the self-same shapes and colours arranged only in a different order.

*   *   *   *   *   *

Many happy years went by in the old Manor House in the vale, though in the world beyond trouble and strife, battle and murder, plague and pestilence, took see-saw turns with peace and prosperity, just as they do to-day.

If in 1662 all Englishwomen took a keen interest in Catherine of Braganza, flavoured with a strong touch of pity, all men's minds at the same time were fully occupied with the trial of Vane and Lambert, which concluded, as all know, by the former dying as a brave man, whilst drums beat their loudest round him to drown his voice, lest pity should be aroused in the thronging crowds, and rescue be attempted. The other, Lambert, trimmed his sails so well to the rulers of his destiny that his sentence was reprieved, and, banished to Guernsey, he lived there nearly thirty years, and, changing his Puritan belief, died a Roman Catholic.

For twenty years the happy life went on at Rithycombe, and then Madam fell ill so suddenly it came with a shock on all!

One morning early out rang a muffled peal from the church tower, solemn and slow, with every stroke vibrating to a great distance. Groups of startled villagers listened to the warning note, as in dread and sorrow they waited for tiding in the avenue.

The soldier figure paced slowly up the drive; some said they *heard* his steps, others that he had actually brushed them by; only once he came in vain, the second time before he faded he turned to retrace his steps, and those who keenly watched said a white-robed figure walked beside him.

Certain it was that this time "Madam" was gone! Sir James could hardly believe it, it was an awful shock to him, though he took it very quietly. Lamentations, loud and many, were heard on all sides, the step-children and grandchildren mourned sadly over their great loss, for they had loved her truly. Very simply, in accordance with Bridget's strong wish, were the funeral arrangements made, but nothing could prevent its being a burying the like of which had not been seen before.

So many prayed for the honour of carrying her to the grave that the matter would have been a difficulty had not the step-sons and son-in-law claimed this duty as their right, and so settled it.

From far and near the people flocked, villagers, townsfolk, tenants, tramping for miles and miles to pay the last tribute of respect to "Madam." The bells tolled very slowly; the ringers said afterwards it needed all their strength to get a sound out, but what a volume it was when it came—slower, deeper every time, and then as the long procession waited at the church door, silence—

and silence unbroken on their part up to now. Sir James had chosen the spot for Lady Fielding's last resting-place next to the soldier's grave, with space alongside for himself, in preference to either of the old family vaults; and here in love and reverence beside Reginald Markham's flower-grown grave they laid their lady to rest, loved—regretted—honoured—as falls to the lot of few, the last of her race and name that the old Manorlands of Rithycombe would ever know.

Many a sympathizing hand touched Sir James' as he waited long beside the open grave, waited till all was as seemly as possible, and then turned slowly homewards in the summer sunshine. His kindly face looked worn and sad, and some said he would not be here long; he was just wrapped up in Madam.

His children and grandchildren, with a goodly company of friends, were all beside him when he re-entered the Manor, left for once to take care of itself whilst the servants, young and old, followed in the sorrowful procession to the church.

Had it been left?

That question must remain for ever unanswered.

The hall had a solemn air about it, for there Madam's simple lying in state had taken place, when all who asked to do so, were allowed to look their last at the peaceful face, freed for ever from the lines of Earth, and in consequence looking years younger than her age.

The furniture was all pushed back against the walls, and white flowers were strewn around just as they had been left that morning. Over all, above all, was a strange penetrating chill, that made the strongest feel as if they had entered an ice grotto.

And so still!!

Not one of the footsteps caused a sound, though the floor was bare and the guests numerous. On the spectators fell a strange awe, and all alike felt powerless to move or speak. There were many witnesses to see and vouch for the fact that when standing motionless, in the hall, in the great silence that prevailed, a bright white light streamed forth through the large open doorway leading directly into the kitchen; and it was not the light of the sun, for the room faced the wrong way for that, neither came it from the warm banked-up fire, for *that* could not send out such dazzling streams of light, reaching right into the hall itself, and growing brighter as they looked at it.

Full in this magic light, clearly and distinctly visible, standing close to the hearth itself—nay, apparently bending over a saucepan, stood Madam herself!

And she was quite transparent, they could see right through her, as if she had been a piece of painted glass; and though encircled by such a wonderful radiance, not even the faintest shadow was thrown by her figure. Just as many had so often seen her barely a fortnight ago, in her simple morning dress, with kerchief folded neatly over her kindly heart, and matron's coif resting on the still dark hair. Busy stirring something with a spoon held in her mittened hands, so intent on her familiar task, she had no glance for them.

For a rare housewife had Madam become, taking the greatest pride in her still-room and dairy, and renowned not a little for her simples and cordials.

How long all watched her breathlessly, none could afterwards agree, probably only for a few seconds, that seemed far longer in such a state of tension.

At last Sir James found his voice, and called out clearly "Bridget," when instantly, as if shaken, the bright light wavered and paled; the figure lost its clearness of outline, became dim and misty, and had faded quite away before the last gleam went suddenly out, leaving a crowd of astonished people in what seemed to them for a minute, quite twilight, divided somewhat in opinion as to the details of what they had seen, but certain then and for evermore that, ghost or reality, it was Madam herself they had watched!

The cold feeling was also gone, and the hall struck close and oppressive with so many perfumed flowers all about.

With a heavy sigh, at last Sir James moved and led the way into the parlour where refreshments stood ready.

He went up to an old woman crying quietly in a far corner, and asked her softly if she had seen Madam, and what she thought of the Spirit's visit.

"My child, my child," sobbed the old body; "to see her with the kerchief on that I was ironing that sad morning when she called me and said how bad she felt. And her best silk mittens too, with the vine-leaf pattern. I feel as if my heart must break for grief, and yet how selfish of me to say so, Master dear, when you are so good about it too. It must be with some hope of comforting us that the mistress came back again; surely *we*, knowing what we do about the soldier always watching over her, can believe her object is to show how near the unseen country is where our loved ones pass. No doubt we shall see her often; such a good creature could never return to do harm."

This reasoning comforted Sir James not a little, and helped him through that sad day as maybe nothing else could have done.

Often after that, the maids declared in summer nights a white-robed figure flitted up and down the stairs, or watched from the dormer-window; but Sir James and Martha never saw her again, and inclined therefore to the belief that this was only fancy: but when long years had rolled away, with their constant change, and still the phantom figures came and went, there could be no "fancy" in the matter, and as "fact" it still holds force and power in that little Somersetshire village, where the golden letters on the Manor weathercock turn in the wind, and catch the light of the sun, just as in the days of old, before the haunting began which is said to go on at the present day.

The Short Stories

THE MISER'S SECRET

Belgravia, Volume 79, December 1892.

A WILD and dreary day was closing in with a terrible storm. The rain in sheets was driven along by the howling wind at a furious rate, whilst the waves in maddened fury, dashed higher and higher over the sharp rocks and steep cliffs at Penrhynddu.

The whole force of the gale was felt by the old, half-ruined castle, standing out boldly on the top of the cliffs.

Long bunches of ivy had been torn from the walls they had clung to so long; and from the more ruinous parts harsh shrieks and cries, from disturbed bats and owls, added to the dismal effect.

The old Welsh castle, now falling rapidly into decay, was built on the foundation of its namesake, destroyed by order of the king in 1100, and rebuilt in 1300.

For the next few centuries it frequently changed owners; then came a long, unbroken calm, and, except that no grandson ever inherited in his father's shoes, it had now been in the possession of the Mervin family for over 300 years.

The great-uncle of the present master was a recluse, and somehow the idea got about that he was also a miser; at his death, this notion had to be given up, for, though long and anxious search was made, with the assistance of some aged plans, shewing all kinds of hidden nooks and crannies, old dungeons, and narrow passages, not a single coin or article of value could be fund anywhere.

The need of the family for money being very great, the search was most thorough.

Alone the old man lived, and alone he died, save for one old servant, who on the very day of his master's funeral, having closed and barred the great hall door after the last departing guest, slipped on the old stone pavement, and fell with great force to the ground, hitting his head so badly that he became unconscious.

In this state, apparently, the new owner found him on the next night, when, puzzled at no one answering his repeated rings and blows, he hailed a village lad below, who, squeezing himself in by a tiny, unbarred window, unfastened with many fumblings the heavy door.

The old man never spoke again, but his eyes to the last seemed to the lookers-on to turn in a most wistful way to the pictured face of his master, hanging just over the staircase.

An hour before he died, raising himself with great difficulty, he pointed with his shaking hand in the same direction, then sank back unconscious, and so passed away.

This story of course was often repeated, and gained in the telling many alterations.

The villagers grew to have such a horror of the haunted castle, as they called it, that even at the present time they would go miles out of their way on dark nights for fear they should see any of the wandering lights their fathers had so often described to them; or hear the cries and moans that poor old Michael's ghost was supposed to utter on stormy nights.

To explain to them that bats and owls caused these latter, or that the moon plays strange pranks with light and shade, was labour lost.

The present owner, who succeeded the Mervin that found the poor old dying man, was much loved and respected by the poor folk all about, except on one point only; he had married a Roman Catholic, a widow with one young son, and against this lady and her child, bitter and wicked prejudices strengthened every day. Possessed of considerable means, her money was generously spent amongst them, but nothing altered their cruel hate and determined spite.

Three children were born in the castle, a boy, and two girls; healthy, happy little souls, with merry voices and rosy cheeks, devoted to the elder brother, whose watchful care and pride in them was a picture to see.

Then an act of pure malice on the villagers' part, placed the elder lad's life in danger; and for fear of further evil, the gentle mother sent her boy away, first on a long visit to his father's people, and then to train for the sailor's life he had set his heart on. From that time she pined and drooped, and after a lingering illness passed away, whilst her three babes were all under seven. Her last prayer to her husband was, that he would protect her son if ever he came into wild Wales again.

"My own boy is not more dear to me," he answered. "Madeleine, my wife, trust me, we will guard him well, so help us God!"

     *   *   *   *   *   *

Up in my turret room I heard and felt the full force of the storm, and fancied that the solid walls shook and shivered in the wind's embrace.

A cheerful fire lit up the cosy corners, and I thought as I lay on my comfortable couch, that I was well out of the wind and rain.

The rooms, that I had taken possession of years ago, were those that had been occupied by my old ancestor the miser, and whom in face I was said to take after.

This old man had certainly left his mark behind him, and his chief hobby seemed to have been carving.

Everything was carved that could be, and very proud were all of us, his descendants, of his labours.

165

On entering the hall by the old iron-clamped door, no one could fail to be struck by the beauty of the low, richly-carved staircase, that curved upwards on the left, and, though surrounded by beautiful panelling that reached to the high pointed roof, this staircase had always been my favourite.

Supported by slender twisted columns, a broad rail with wreaths of foliage twined round in cunning art, guarded the low, easy steps, whilst various creatures, perched here and there, kept ceaseless watch and ward.

A hooded falcon, the crest of our family, stood on the rail at the foot of the stairs; the bird's life-like claws, and ruffled feathers giving evidence of the miser's talent.

Next to him my great-great-uncle's favourite hound, "Gelert," reclined; the same faithful creature on whose shaggy head my ancestor's hand rested in the portrait hanging almost above.

In the dog's eyes in the picture there was a steadfast faithfulness portrayed, that had been well caught in the deep-set carven eyes on the stairs.

Above the dog, a grinning monkey held a nut aloft; and mice and a large serpent completed the train. I had been told that on this staircase the old man spent years of labour.

Most of the other carving he had bought, and dove-tailed together, but no hand but his had the credit of the staircase.

That the dog had gained a firm hold on his master's heart was evident; another likeness of him hung over my fireplace, again with the deep-set, sunken eyes, and wistful look. Across one corner of this painting a small plan of the castle cellars and dungeons was carefully drawn.

My bother left his home suddenly, the reason not being mentioned to us children; but some years ago my father told me what had decided my mother and himself to send the lad away.

The people all about were a rough lot, working, many of them, in the slate quarries owned by my father, and others picking up a precarious living as fishermen.

In hard times, want and hunger were frequent guests.

Against my mother and brother, "The Papists," at such seasons, the feeling was very bitter; and at last the worst spirits in the place made a kind of league that, by fair means or foul, the place should be rid of these heretics.

My mother never could master the Welsh language, though she tried hard, and as the poor folk could not understand a word of English, their intercourse was very restricted, and I shall always believe this want of mutual knowledge lay at the root of the mischief.

At last one Winter's day brought a crisis.

My brother spent hours on his pony, riding alone wherever he liked, and one day, returning from a long round, he was crossing a narrow wooden bridge, leading his tired pony, when, with a sudden crack, the centre gave way, and, in a minute, he found himself clinging hard to the slender hand-rail, with his pony struggling on the rocks in the water just below.

Tired and spent, the poor creature was quickly drawn into a foaming rapid, and swept, bruised and bleeding, far down the river.

Harold sickened at the sight, but still clutched hard his rail, and managed so to swing himself along, that at last he had cleared the broken space, and stood, white and shaken, on the bank in safety.

My father went next day at daybreak to examine the bridge, and found, what he had feared he should, that the supports and beams had been so carefully sawn and loosened, that the slightest weight must bring it down.

It was easy to suspect many, but to bring the deed home was simply impossible.

The pony was found next day, mangled and dead, and my mother's face grew ashen white, as she thought that this was meant to be her boy's fate.

My father issued a very stern command that, riding or driving, we were never to cross these little bridges again, but always to go round by the road.

Considering what wild little mites we were, perhaps he was right.

He also gave orders that the broken bridge should be repaired.

My brother left us, and though we missed him dreadfully at first, we soon got used to his absence.

Not so my mother; she faded slowly but steadily away, and at last there came a day when my father led us gently into her darkened room, and bade us kiss her peaceful face, and remember her dying charge to meet her one day in the rest above.

My father was a most reserved man, and it was a rare occasion, indeed, that bought his religious opinions to light; but though of a different faith to his wife, their mutual belief in a Heavenly Father never faltered.

The years rolled on, and, except for our rapid growth, there was little to mark time's progress.

My father spent weeks of anxious thought after my brother's hurried departure, as to whether or no he should permit me to mingle with the villagers, or send me right away to school. At last he decided on having a tutor for me and the sisters, and left me free after lesson-hours to go where I would.

Oddly enough, though my brother had been hardly tolerated in the place, I could do any mortal thing I pleased with the poor, rough folk, and spoke and read Welsh as easily as English.

They took me out fishing, taught me how to manage a boat, to swim, and scale the cliffs like a goat, and watched over me with the greatest care.

Also I knew all the workings of the slate quarries.

One evening, late, I was riding fast home, a storm having rapidly come up, when I found I had taken a wrong turn, and was almost on the fragile bridge that had given way beneath my brother long ago.

Once over that, a few minutes would take me home, only that old promise to my father stood in my way. A promise enforced afresh by him on giving me my first shaggy pony.

I knew I must turn round and make for the long, dull road passing near the cliffs, and yet I waited whilst the wind sent dismal warnings down the valley, and the leaves in the trees sighed and groaned as they muttered to each other there would be no rest for them that night.

At last I turned my horse round, and, through the gathering gloom rode on.

I remember passing Tom, a village lad, a great crony of mine, just my own age, and then, either startled by a bat flying under his nose or the increasing storm, off went my young horse in a mad gallop, with ears laid back and snorting breath.

Soon we reached the track passing over the cliffs, and rushed straight for the edge.

In fancy still, I can feel the sting of the air on my face, as we raced along; then we were at the edge, and an awful temptation seized me to throw myself off!

Jack made a frantic effort to swerve round, and I tried to aid him with all my might. The edge was crumbly and soft, no foothold for the frightened, quivering creature, and in a second over we went to the beach below. A loud shot rang in my ears as we slipped over the edge, and then I remembered no more for many days.

My friend Tom came tumbling down the cliff, which just there was only twenty feet high, and, finding me unconscious and the horse with a broken leg, did the best he could for me.

I had fallen from the saddle in our wild leap, quite clear of the horse, so Tom covered me carefully with his coat, and ran off for help to the fishers in the cove.

All this I learnt long afterwards.

Six words were enough, and all the place was astir.

Lights soon flashed around me, I was laid on a mattress, covered with blankets; vain attempts were made to get a little whisky down my throat, and then with even, slow steps, they carried me home.

The bearers changed repeatedly; men with lanterns walked on either side, and called out warnings of stones and rocks.

Tom started for the castle, after leaving me in the fishers' care, and my father came down the dark road to meet us.

He told me afterwards that the tears were wet on many a rough face, and horny hands shook his as he bent over my poor, drawn face.

What touched him most was to hear men who had never given him anything but a surly word, call him "Master," and bid him not to lose heart.

Then would come a cough, and a choke, and the back a rough hand would be dashed over the eyes.

On entering the Castle, my father desired my careful bearers to carry me up to his own large, comfortable room; then, seeing they could give no further aid, with a muttered "God bless him," the men went quietly down and away; two of their number remaining outside all night, in case they might be of any assistance.

Tom had gone off at once, on our fastest horse, for the nearest doctor, but, in such an out-of-the-way place, all knew it must be hours before he could return.

My father and our old nurse undressed and felt me all over, and could find no broken bones anywhere.

They did not like the absolute motionless of my lower limbs, as I lay stiff and rigid on the bed, moaning pitifully.

If only I had moved, even uneasily, they would have felt cheered.

Getting alarmed at the increasing coldness of my legs, they spent the rest of the night rubbing me with hot flannels, and so in the early dawn the doctor found them.

After one quick glance all over me, he breathed softly, "Paralysed, poor fellow." I was then sixteen, now I am eight-and-twenty.

When I slowly came back to my senses, and my father gently, and very sadly, explained to me that in falling I had come with great force on my back, injuring the spinal cord so greatly that paralysis had immediately set in, and never again should I stand or walk, I buried my face in the pillow, and prayed that I might not live.

I could not bear my life, I muttered, week after week; God was very cruel to have treated me so.

All my dreams of noble deeds and acts of bravery lay buried in the sandy shore below the cliffs.

I made my father's and my sisters' lives a burden to them; and as for old nurse, and the lad, Tom, who had begged to be allowed to wait on me, I treated them worse than slaves. With such bitter repinings and incessant irritability I made but little progress towards partial recovery; and how long matters would have gone on so I do not know, if, six months after my accident, my father had not sat down by me, and talked as I never knew he could.

He put before me the harm I was doing to myself and others, by such rebellion against God's will; shewed me that I was making our once happy home miserable, and cheered me with his strong conviction that there was yet good work for me to do in the world, or my life would not have been spared.

Then putting into my hand a very worn copy of the "Changed Cross,"[15] he left the room, praying me to shew that my bravery was not only skin-deep.

It was a hard and bitter battle, but, at last, thank God, there came a day when I could truly say "God knows best."

For some few years I got on wonderfully; was carried downstairs regularly, and often wheeled out of doors.

Two years ago I had rheumatic fever so badly that it was a wonder I recovered; the doctor warned me never to over-tire, or over-exert myself in any way, as there was mischief at my heart.

The turret rooms were given over to me, and, with my father and sisters always ready to wait on me, hand and foot, life no longer seemed the dreary burden I had dreaded so.

Finding my daily moves shook me a good deal, I remained, by advice, in my own three rooms, where, however, I had no time to be dull. My father was good enough to call me his right hand. All the accounts and business of the estate passed through my hands, thus enabling him to dispense with a bailiff. Writing became my chief amusement.

Times did not improve; strikes became the order of the day; bad seasons ruined the harvests; a spirit of discontent seemed everywhere, and on this stormy night in question, I knew my father was more bothered and worried about money than he cared to own.

---

15 A poem by Hon Mrs Charles Hobart.

The old savage spirit was awake again amongst the village folk, and rumours daily gained ground that the storm would soon burst, but what form it would take no one knew......Elsie, my sister, wants me to leave off writing now, as she says I look so tired, but I shall not rest long, for there is something I want to get written clearly down in case of need...... I am weary of courting sleep in vain, and all my nerves seem on edge, so I must try and quiet them by my old panacea, writing. Half-an-hour after I had laid down my pen to please Elsie, in the midst of the uproar of the storm the boom of a signal-gun startled us all, assembled as we usually were in the evenings in my snug room.

My father went off at once with Tom, lanterns, brandy, a long coil of rope, and a blanket; and my sisters took up their position at the turret windows, and strained their eyes into the gloom without.

At such times as these, it was very bitter to me to feel powerless to aid in active ways, but this night I felt so worn and weary, that the longing to be up and doing seemed dead.

Our coast was a cruel one from rocks that ran far out to sea, and when any vessel by stress of weather was driven on to them, her doom was sealed.

Two hours passed slowly away, and the second had just ended when, dripping from head to foot, with a white, set face, my father entered; and we checked the eager questions on our lips, as we saw how white and weary he looked.

After drinking a little of the cordial my sisters had ready, he told us briefly what had chanced.

A vessel, apparently, a foreigner, was on the rocks when he went down, and the crew could be made out clinging to the rigging.

The force of the waves was awful, and he soon saw she was breaking up fast. It was madness to try to reach her, but for all that he did his best to get a crew together, bribing the fisher-folk, at last, with more money than he could afford. Not a man responded, and my father did not blame them for this, he said, for the attempt, humanly speaking, must have failed.

It grieved him greatly to see the lowering faces, and hear the harsh tones that met him on every side.

The vessel broke up in a minute, so to say, and the next crested wave rose high over the rocks around. There seemed to be faint cries in the air, but this might have been fancy. Soon pieces of wreckage came drifting in, and then some bodies, bruised and bleeding from the blows given them by the cruel rocks as they drifted shorewards.

Only one young man had life in him, and after a little brandy had been forced down his throat, he began to revive, and father and Tom carried him as speedily as might be to the castle.

The men still held aloof, and my father did not like the looks they cast at the poor stranger, so decided to lose no time in returning home.

The stranger was now under old Nurse's care, and with Tom's assistance he would want for nothing.

Father then rose, and asked us all to go to bed, but when the girls left the room, he came back a minute, and touched my hair softly.

"My lad, I have a strange dread on me to-night, and wish I had not to leave you at day-break for that Manchester trial."

"Father, of course you must go," I answered, "why, you are subpoenaed. Trust me to do my best."

"Trust *you*, my boy! Ay, better than myself, and if need arise, remember your dog's secret!"

"I sometimes think, father, we have not got to the bottom of *that* yet."

"Do you think so? Well, we'll see when I return; and now, my brave lad, take care of yourself, and God bless you!"

Long after he had left me, I lay and fought with the feeling of depression that had been on me all day; then Tom came in to help me undress, and told me our strange guest was sound asleep.

He had been so exhausted, and faint, that they thought they should never get him round, but at last, when nice and warm, he fell into the sound slumber he was now in.

Tom also said he did not like the quarrymen's looks at all, he knew they were on short commons,[16] and he heard there was a lot of sickness amongst them.

He left me, and I lay and counted the strokes of the clock, hearing the hoofs of my father's horse as he crossed the courtyard soon after four, and knowing he had gone on his journey with an anxious heart.

Old Nurse brought me my early tea, and I soon saw she had something special to say. She looked at me keenly, and then said very quietly:

"Master Frank, the stranger guest is your brother Harold!"

I exclaimed in surprise, and she proceeded to say that she had had no idea of this at first, though puzzled at his resemblance to someone. Considering the years that had elapsed since we saw him, and that he had grown a beard and moustache, I think she may be forgiven.

Stealing in to look at him during the night, she saw on his arm thrown back above his head, a tattooed cross, and immediately identified him as her first nursling. She said my mother had been

---

16 On an insufficient allowance of food.

very vexed with her for getting a sailor to tattoo the baby arm, but she had had it done to keep evil from the lad.

Just before the bottom end was finished, the baby burst into such a passionate fit of tears, it had to be left undone, thus leaving a jagged end to the cross.

The old woman said she could not imagine why she had not seen the mark whilst undressing him the night before, but being in a great hurry to get warm things on him, the cross never caught her eye.

My next visitor was my long absent brother; ill indeed he looked.

He was coming home on sick-leave, when the vessel ran on the rocks, and, feeble and weary as he felt, it seemed hopeless to think of reaching the shore alive.

A sailor he had been kind to flung a life-belt round him a minute before the vessel sank, and he remembered nothing more until he found himself in bed.

Seeing old Nurse did not recognise him, he felt too drowsy and stupid to announce himself, and drifted off again into sound slumber.

I asked him why he had not written to say he was coming home; but he said it was such a sudden thing he had no time to do so.

He knew how nervous my father would get at his coming to the castle at all, and yet he had such a great longing to see us all again, he felt he would willingly run some risk; besides, surely that old prejudice must have died out years ago? How I wished I could honestly say it had! Tom now came in, and it was easy to see he also had tidings to tell.

He said he had word by a sure hand, that, stirred up by mischief-making agitators, who had now been busy amongst them for some time, all the quarry-men and fishers had arranged a plan to seize the foreigner, marked with a cross! What sharp eyes!

They meant to take us by surprise, and intended no harm to us *if* we let him go quietly.

Tom said the men were half mad, he thought, and quite beyond control. Their object in this proceeding did not seem clear to any of us; those who had urged them on may have had some fixed motive in their minds, or else some personal spite against us; and so, under plausible arguments, and false smooth words, persuaded the poor ignorant people they were doing a righteous act to take the law into their own hands in this riotous manner.

"I will go at once," said Harold, rising feebly from his chair. "Frank, my boy, I am glad to have seen you again. Give the sisters my love; I had better not wait to see them. God forbid I should bring any bother or trouble upon you, for you don't look fit to stand worry."

I thought a minute earnestly. My father had taken his own horse, and the only other one we possessed had gone lame a week ago. How could we send that weak, worn-out man out into the chill, bleak, December day, out of their way?

Then I said quietly, "it is all right, Harold, we can hide you safely; let me just dress, and I'll show you how."

Soon I was ready, and asked Nurse and Tom to carry me in my long chair down to the old hall, and Elsie hurried off to see there was a good fire, and plenty of wraps on my long-unused oak settle.

All tried to persuade me not to descend, but just to tell them what to do, but I felt it was clearly right for me, in my father's absence, to do my best for Harold; and I could hardly have brooked staying up in my turret rooms whilst he was in danger. So, carefully and slowly they carried me down. Stopping them when we reached the carved dog on the staircase rail, I raised myself with difficulty, and pressed my little finger hard into Gelert's right eye.

Then I grew cold and shivered, for suppose my plan was a failure after all!

What more likely than that dust, and rust combined, had done their noiseless work!

Again I pressed, leaning harder, and a click rewarded me.

A carved panel forming a piece of the side of the staircase opened slowly inwards, and disclosed a tiny flight of steps.

Thankful that the spring was still all right, I leant back in my chair, and asked to be carried down to the settle, and that food, blankets, and a small lamp should be collected.

I told them the steps led into a narrow passage running *between* the dungeons shewn on the plans, and ended as far as I knew in a small, well-ventilated room, hollowed out, I believed, in one of the buttresses.

The ivy was so thick that the loop-holes in the wall were quite invisible from the outside. I had tried in vain to find one, and could not.

Madeline and Elsie got quite excited about our wonderful chamber, and I felt glad anything should divert their thoughts from our present anxiety.

Harold proposed they should accompany him below on a visit of inspection, and they all tripped cheerfully down the narrow staircase. They came back, still excited, and asked me if I knew there was an old oak chest down there, with one or two yellow papers in it.

I told them I had looked round pretty thoroughly when first I found out about the spring, only a fortnight before my accident, meaning always to pay another visit one day. On telling our father of my discovery, he had advised our keeping it to ourselves, in case of troublous times arising, when we might be glad to hide our valuables away.

We both felt sure our old great-uncle had left instructions with his servant to pass on his secret, and understood why, in dying, his dim eyes had so wistfully sought the dog's face.

Harold asked me if there was any way of opening the door from below, but this I did not know; only I had discovered by pressing the dog's left eye, the panelled door would shut.

"Well, if I am to be there for hours, I would just like you to shut me down first for half-an-hour, that I mayn't feel quite so queer," said Harold, "and there is no time like the present."

Armed with the lamp, and Elsie's company, he descended again; and Tom pressed the left eye hard, and so shut the panel, when we judged they had reached the hidden room.

Then we waited half-an-jour, and opened the panelled door for them to return. They seemed in no hurry, and at last Madeline went down to see what they were up to.

By this time I knew I was in for one of the dreadful spasms of agony any extra exertion always gave me, but I trusted it would not overpower me until danger to Harold was past. It seemed ages before quick steps up the staircase announced the explorers' return, and when I saw their white, excited faces, I felt sure they had discovered something fresh. They were very dusty and quite breathless.

On going down Harold and Elsie had just reached the hidden room when a loud click sounded near them—the spring of the panel shutting, Harold said, but Elsie declared it came form the chest.

They lifted the lid, to find the bottom had slid up against one of the sides, and another set of steps lay below.

Down this, of course, Harold with his lamp must go, and, rather than be left alone, Elsie followed close.

The steps wound round and round, until Harold had counted forty, when they ended in a passage like the one above, leading into another well-ventilated room, with a tiny barred door.

This was so fast set and stiff, it took Harold some time to move the rusty bolts, but at last he pulled it open, to find a thick wall of ivy, through which he made out the door opened on the wilderness part of the garden, quite hidden from any window.

They shut the door again, and looked about the room.

A small table, on which stood a brass-bound box, stood in the middle, with an old chair alongside, and all round the room were various-sized carved chests.

Opening the box, they saw a bag of gold, and an exact copy of the staircase above, drawn on paper, with the springs shewn, and also plans of the dungeons, with the hidden rooms blacked in. On the wall was a carved panel of the dog, with the same deep-set carven eyes.

"Depend upon it," said Harold, "this is the counter spring, and opens and shuts the doors from below."

They decided not to try them then, or to open any of the chests, but to bring me up all the papers; and shutting the box again, hurried up above, only just getting through the chest door before another loud click closed the bottom down, and opened the panelled door above.

Here Madeline met them, and they got talking, so no wonder it seemed ages to me before they returned.

"I must say," observed Harold, "I feel happier in mind to think I can get into the open from the lower room; suppose the springs snapped up here, how pleasant it would be if one could not!"

"It is easy to see, Frank, why you only knew half, because you see you were up here shutting the panel. My boy! How bad you look."

"Please Nurse, give me my draught, and don't mind my not talking much."

So silence fell around, Nurse and my sisters being used to these occasional fits of agony, which, as a rule, did not last long.

The hours passed quietly on, and, at last, I was able to talk and write again, and we had just settled cosily together to look at the old yellow papers, when Tom came swiftly in, and said, quietly: "The men will be here in ten minutes, and they look like mischief."

     *   *   *   *   *   *

Written by Elsie

Frank then asked Harold to go below, I worked the springs, and assisted to pull my brother's couch across the movable panel, then we sat down quietly and waited.

The tramp of many feet and the hoarse murmur of angry voices came rapidly closer, and then a furious peal of the bell. Tom had had his orders, and immediately opened wide the great entrance door.

I turned sick and faint for a minute, when I saw what a crowd of evil faces looked menacingly at us.

Calm, and quiet, Frank lay; with a most peaceful look, one I had often noticed on his face, after his awful pain was over. A hoarse unintelligible murmur from the men, and then his low, clear tones, "My friends, what do you require?"

"The Papist! the foreigner! Him with the black mark!" Louder and louder grew their tones, and many shook their fists savagely.

"What do you want with him?"

"Never you mind," was the rough answer, and then one man stepped forward, and waved to his comrades for silence.

"See, young sir," he said, "this is the matter in dispute. We have sworn to drive all Papists from this place; we mean *you* no harm, all we require is for you to tell us where to find the man saved from the wreck last night, then we will depart orderly, and quietly."

"The man you ask for is my long absent brother, known beyond doubt by that cross some of you noticed on his arm. To give him up, as you call it, is impossible, I am sure you will all agree."

Frank could hardly finish for the storm of oaths and execrations that arose in deafening clamour when the men heard who the foreigner was.

Half mad with fury, they uttered any and every threat they could think of, and, suddenly losing all command over themselves, they rushed up the staircase, along the passages, down to the dungeons; here, there, and everywhere, making the most hideous noise.

We women shook and shivered, and drew close to Frank, fearing, dreading every moment they would return and, by some evil fortune, find out our secret!

"It is all right dears," Frank faintly said, as he saw how frightened we were. "At the sound of the spring working, without a call from us, Harold, who is in the lower room, is to go through the door into the ivy, where Tom is waiting to guide him to another safe place, a hollow tree, which he will have reached long before these poor creatures have found out the double spring, if they ever find any."

We waited what seemed ages, presently all sounds of uproar died away, and then Tom came back, and said all had left the Caste, and gone back to their quarries, and he should have sure word, before they returned.

Nurse went and got some food ready, and we released Harold from his hiding-place.

The old hall looked very comfortable with the curtains drawn, and the warm firelight playing all about, and we did not have lamps for some time.

Frank seemed so drowsy, that, when we had had our meal, we sat in silence for a long, long while; and then, hearing Frank sigh, I fetched a light in case he wanted anything.

Ah! nevermore, my brother.

At first we thought him still asleep, but there was something about him that startled us, and then we saw God's finger had most softly touched him, and he slept.

We sank on our knees beside that quiet sleeper, with his peaceful look; surely the angels had been very near us.

For long we had known how frail his life was, but all the same it came suddenly at the last.

There was a quick footstep in the hall, and Tom stood beside us, the eager words on his lips dying soundlessly away, as he saw what had happened.

It might have been five or even ten minutes later, when again that hoarse hum of angry voices approached. Almost as in a dream I heard the angry battering at the door, even stones flung sharply against it, whilst strong arms tried to shake old bolts and bars.

I suppose Harold, who was now standing at Frank's head, signed to Tom what to do, for he went quietly forward and undid the massive door.

A savage shout, a great burst of furious men, and the hall filled with an angry riotous crowd.

With a dead stop, so to say, on an instant every sound was hushed; as the fierce, famished eyes of quarrymen and fishers fell on the motionless form they loved so well, then another silent pause, and the hall was empty, except for us.

Poor misguided creatures! all bitterness against them died away then and for ever, as we saw the look of despair and grief that fell on every face as they saw what had happened. The forlorn way in which they vanished away, pleaded better for them than any speechifying could have done.

Next day my father returned; a sad home-coming for him, though he did not fail in all his sorrow to give Harold a most warm and loving welcome.

A few days more, and again a large crowd had assembled at the Castle door.

Welsh folk always pay the last respect possible to their dead by attending them to their graves, but I think it must have been centuries since such a concourse was seen as that which followed Frank to our quiet little mountain churchyard.

A deputation came up to my father on his return home, and most humbly prayed they might be allowed to act as bearers.

"We carried him once before, sir," urged one man eagerly, "it would make us feel happier like, to do summat for him."

"There *is* something else you can do," said my father, firmly, "remember, I have another son, whose life must not be made miserable by your ignorant prejudices."

So they carried him carefully along, and many a sob resounded as the beautiful service was read.

It was touching to see how even the poorest in that great crowd had put on some mark of mourning.

Then the home life had to be resumed with a great blank in the middle.

We have had no strikes since, and we heard the agitators of that time had had such a rough handling from those they had for a time misled, it would be long before any more disturbances troubled our parts.

We looked over the age-worn papers one winter's night, and found, besides most carefully explained plans of the hidden rooms and springs, a short explanation from our old ancestor himself.

He said he had found these old rooms with trap-door communications bolted down, soon after he came into possession.

They were then in a very dilapidated condition, and he was afraid, from various relics he found, that they had been used for cruel and wicked purposes.

On entering the lower room, he thought he saw a dark crouching figure in the corner (where afterwards he had opened, or rather made, a small door), but it seemed suddenly to melt, and when he reached the spot, only a heap of dust and a few bones were to be seen; a rusty chain on the wall still holding one poor bone in its grasp.

On the wall were several words scraped deeply. "God help me," was quite clear, and then another one with only the "Duw" readable.

An old chest with some money in it was all the furniture then in the lower room.

With the then rector's cordial consent and assistance, he and Michael had carefully buried the bones and heap of dust from the lower room, one dark night, in the churchyard; and handed over to the clergyman all the money from the dungeon, to be spent as he deemed best for the good of the poor.

Who could say that perhaps now the doom on the family might be expiated?

He decided to restore and improve these chambers, for their use as a safe hiding-place might yet be invaluable. It had been a pleasure to him to carry out the alterations as ingeniously as he could, the day might come when his labours would be of use; indeed, for many years before he wrote this explanation, he had removed there all the family heirlooms, jewels, silver, etc., and placed them in chests, also all his money, of which he had never had any lack.

That there should be no mystery about the matter, besides drawing two different sets of plans (one of which he placed in each of the hidden rooms), he had left with Michael full and complete instructions to pass on his secret to his successor on his taking possession of the Castle.

With a parting charge to all who succeeded him to keep the rooms in order, the old man signed his name.

The miser's secret was at an end!

ONLY A SMUDGE!

Belgravia, Volume 81, August 1893.

T HE darkness of a winter's night was falling fast around an old gabled house in the beautiful Lake District. Already the jagged peaks of Langdale Pikes had become indistinct, and soon they would vanish as completely as their brethren, while, except for the bitter wail of the wind and the creak and strain of the swaying trees, no sounds broke the silence of the lonely hills.

The old house possessed numberless queer tales concerned with its thick walls and winding passages, and for many a long year now had been haunted by the sins of the past—whose dreaded headless shapes were believed in, and shunned by most about.

The present master was well on in years, and, though still hale and hearty, in all human probability would not live many more years, and then—who was there but a slip of a girl, his orphan grandchild, to inherit alike his wealth and lands and all the traditions of the family?

Some said, but few believed them now, that the old man had no moral right to the place at all, for *his* father had been a younger son, whose elder brother, hot-headed, passionate, rash, had been disinherited for marrying a penniless girl, and on the day they married, the father, in unbridles rage, had willed all his possessions to the younger son, who took after him in many ways—certainly in being careful of his money—and far from persuading his father to alter his mind, had carefully fanned his wrath against the rightful heir, of whom but little was heard afterwards. That his young wife had died in a few years, and that he had gone abroad, was the sum total of intelligence that reached the old gabled house.

On the night young Mrs. Dane passed away, her old father-in-law had an awful dream, and after that he just shrivelled up and died, and the unjust will placed, beyond the power of alterations, all the possessions in the hands of the younger son who, though at the time he had diligently scoffed and pooh-poohed his father's dream, yet lived to learn it was surely a message from the spirit-land.

*   *   *   *   *   *

The library was a cosy room, one much used by old Mr. Dane and his granddaughter, and now with a roaring fire and several lamps, with thick curtains closely drawn, they were chatting comfortably together. The old man seemed very restless, he could not sit still five minutes at a time, so that the answers to Olive's questions were rather jerky, but so interesting were the subjects to her, that sometimes she rose and joined him in his tramp about the room.

"What is that old rhyme you keep on muttering, grandfather, I never heard it before?"

"Likely not, likely not, and I don't now why it has got so into my head to-night. I can't keep it off my tongue—but there, child, there, it's nothing to do with you. Pray God it never may be anything," he whispered to himself.

Seeing he would not tell her, Olive began afresh:

"When will you give me the key of the ghost's passage? I want to see her myself, and you always said when I was grown up you'd let me try."

"*Want* to see her, oh! Good Lord, good Lord! what will she say next, and as for its being a *her*, why many say it is a man, no two ever say the same, except they are always headless, poor creatures.

"Oh, grandfather, won't you tell me the story?"

"No, child, no. I feel very tired to-night, talking of these old tales would only excite you and trouble me. I wish I had done what Carter asked me to do last time he came—but there. it's not too late now. Give me a sheet of paper, and call in Barton and Mrs. Phipps."

How the old man's hands shook as he tried the nib of his quill pen against his thumb nail, and in what a scrawl were the few words penned written, then his signature was duly witnessed by the two old faithful servants, and, with a satisfied sigh, Robert Dane leant back in his chair.

"There child, I can't write more, dry it for me."

Before Olive could take it from his shaking hands, the sheet with the undried writing fell on the floor, and in haste she picked it up and passed the blotting paper quickly over it, and then by her grandfather's direction locked it up in his desk.

The servants had left the room, and when she turned from the side-table where the desk always stood, she saw the old man had fallen asleep, and so deep was his slumber, that the dinner-gong failed to arouse him, and Barton in alarm came to see what was the matter."

"Best let him have his sleep out, Miss Olive, my dear," said rosy-faced Mrs. Phipps. "Come you, and have your dinner while it's hot. Master mayn't wake for hours, and we'll soon get some soup hot when he does."

So Olive ate her dinner, chatting between whiles to old Barton, and commenting on the storm that was rising in angry clamour outside.

Still the old man slumbered on, and when Olive again bent over him, she called out in horror, for his face was all drawn down on one side, and his breathing was loud and hurried. With the coachman's help, they carried him to his bed, and put strong mustard to his feet and neck, but nothing roused him, and long before a doctor could be procured, still in the same deep stupor, as the clocks were striking eleven, the old man passed away.

*   *   *   *   *   *

"Dear! dear! to think he should go first, why I thought he'd outlive me by many a year."

Mr. Carter's face was very lined and troubled, and he kept pacing up and down the library, the day after the funeral.

"Now, Olive, my dear, we must think of you, you can't live here all alone, you know, I wonder what we'd better do. Did your grandfather tell you his wishes?"

"Oh, yes, godfather, often. He said if I had Mrs. Phipps and Barton with me, I should come to no harm, and he hadn't a relation in the world that he knew of to look after me, but *you* were better than a whole tribe of connections would be. Oh! and he signed a paper too, just before he fell asleep, have you seen it?"

"Thank God! Many and many a time have I been at him to make it straight in black and white. What was on it?"

" 'I leave all I die possessed of to Olive Dane,' that was all, with his signature, for I was close beside him, and he didn't mind me seeing; he has told me again and again what I was to do about the property; the old servants, whose leases on the farms could be renewed, and all sorts of things."

The girl's voice trembled, but quietly she opened the desk and handed the lawyer the sheet of note-paper.

In one moment his face had changed, the satisfied expression, so lately visible, died away in a great shock of surprise, and dismay stood out in every line and wrinkle; with a start he walked over to the window, and read and re-read the few words of straggling inky writing.

Olive's gaze seemed fascinated by his face, her eyes grew large and troubled as she noted the knitted brows and puzzled frown with which he pored over the few short words. What could be wrong with them? she wondered. A silence fell on the room, broken only by the coals in the fire dropping apart; then with a long sigh the old man faced about.

"Who put this paper in the desk, Olive, and when?"

"I did, directly I had dried it as grandfather told me. Why, what is the matter?"

"Wait a second, child. Did you lock it up? Think a minute, didn't you leave it on the table and forget it for a while?"

"Grandfather held it out to me to dry directly Barton had put his name. I remember distinctly, it fell on the floor from his hand, and I rubbed the blotting paper over it, and locked it up in the desk at once, and when I turned round grandfather was asleep!"

"Now child read this:

" 'I leave all I die possessed of to *Oliver* Dane.' "

Again a silence fell as both stared fixedly at the altered name, altered how and when? But a half stroke to Olive's name, and instead of a wealthy heiress she stood a destitute girl!

"The one hope, the one chance for us is that there should be *no* Oliver Dane alive, and then perhaps if we can make it plain that you are the great-great-grandchild of old Oliver Dane, we may set it all right, but it is a sad pity that it is, and I had urged him so to leave it all clear for you!"

Mr. Carter ruffled up his hair in perplexity, and tramped about the room.

"Grandfather always wrote my name with a little dash at the end, but I know he only put Olive, not Oliver; what am I to do?

"Do! Why stay quietly here, of course; we've got first to find an

Oliver, prey God we never may. We'll take no steps for proving that bit of paper until we know one way or the other, and I don't despair things 'll be all right yet."

*   *   *   *   *   *

Far away, 150 miles from Natal, two or three white tents stood conspicuously out on the green Veldt; outside, round a fire, a group of Kaffirs squatted, enjoying their favourite snuff. For three days now they had been encamped here, whilst a fierce battle for life or death went on, unheeded by them, in one of the white tents.

Now the fight was nearly over, the strength quite exhausted, and to the tired eyes of the watcher beside that dying man, the end seemed very near.

"God bless you, Dane, for all you've been to me," had been the last conscious remark made by the poor swollen lips days ago, whilst still the little party were struggling bravely to reach Natal; then, as the disease made its rapid strides, it seemed cruel to move the poor fellow from his bed to the hastily improvised litter, and Oliver Dane had ordered a halt, and nursed his friend with untiring patience.

A doctor by profession, he had known for days what the end of the struggle would be, but from the weight of his own head, and the pain in his limbs, feared greatly that *he* should succumb before his friend actually died. He never troubled himself to fancy what would happen *then*, or who would care for him, and indeed, for many hours now the effort to think at all was beyond him, and he could but struggle still to fight off the stupefying drowsiness that was yet winning in the end. A week before, they had been passing through a native Kraal late in the day, when an awful storm came on, and the Kaffirs refused to proceed further that night. It was not until the mid-day halt next day, that Dane gathered from the men's gossip that small-pox was simply raging in the encampment of last night, and two days afterwards his friend and comrade sickened, and now lay dying. His eyelids closed in spite of the resistance of his will, then opened with a jerk and shut again in deep, overpowering slumber.

Swiftly the daylight faded, the shadows of night fell around, and the stars of God in countless brilliance looked down in peaceful calm on the pitiful earth-scene below, but one of how many visible to their bright radiance!

*   *   *   *   *   *

Olive found the old home very dreary in spite of all Mrs. Phipps' endeavours, and fretted sorely for her grandfather and his loving care. From room to room she roamed with an ever-increasing fear upon her, that after all the home she valued so greatly, and the dear familiar objects all about, would know her soon no more. The old woman told her many a quaint tale of the past, and, amongst other things, of the vivid dream that had impressed her great-great-grandfather so much, and of the old rhyme that had remained in his mind as a warning.

> The number *three* shall always be
> Sign of dread and woe to thee,
> Sorrows deep and shadows long
> Who shall break the magic song?
> Until in darkness comes a third,
> Rightful heir by blood and word.

Olive read for herself in church, how *always* since that far past time the number three had come in for the various deaths, and now there was yet another to be added to the list, for her grandfather had himself died on the 3rd of December, 1883.

Mrs. Phipps said there had been many and many a trouble and sorrow to bear besides—that had somehow always arisen, either on the 3rd, 13th, 23rd, 30th or 31st day of the month, and when the year itself held a 3, then nothing ever went well for long.

As for the headless ghost, she said that had appeared from the night when Oliver Dane had left his home for ever. In passionate anger at his father's threats, he had rushed wildly to his room and packed in desperate haste, then his door slammed with a loud and startling bang that sounded all over the quiet house, and before anyone knew what had passed between father and son, he had gone, never to return again.

That night, as the old man walked to his room, a headless figure, misty, indistinct, came slowly from the opposite end of the long, narrow passage, and then it was gone!

The master changed his room, but the story grew, and at last it was found advisable to close the wing and lock the door, and no one had been in that part now for years.

Olive took in the old stories with eager interest, and resolved in her own mind that some time she would try for herself.

One cold night in January, she sat and thought of recent events until she felt restless and excited. The days of her happy childhood came vividly before her, then the close companionship with her grandfather, and the sudden shock of his death, with all the sad details. Again and again in fancy, she went over the writing of the paper, wondered if a loose hair or thread in the carpet could have altered the name, or if she had used a worn-out bit of blotting paper in her haste. That no one had tampered with it she felt certain, for who but herself knew where it had been placed?

Several times had Mr. Carter questioned her on the subject, but the mystery remained unsolved.

Of a sudden her desire to visit the ghost passage flashed into her mind, there was no time like the present—she would go at once.

The house was vey silent for it was late, long after eleven, in her musings she had quite forgotten the flight of time.

Armed with a candle, matches, and the key which hung as usual on her grandfather's bunch, she went upstairs, turned the key in the closed door, pushed it open with some difficulty, and passed through, holding her candle high above her head. Dust was everywhere on the floor and walls and hanging in long cobwebs from the vaulted ceiling above. The passage was very narrow and of great length, the air was heavy and oppressive, and a damp, mouldy smell made her feel sick and faint.

Surely *that* is a figure coming slowly along with a light shining round her in the deep gloom of the gallery; hesitatingly and yet steadily nearer the figure approaches, headless as she had been warned so often the apparitions were! A cold chill ran over her from head to foot, and just as *something* went squash under her trembling steps, and she almost screamed with fright, the heavy door swung to behind her, and the sudden draught extinguished her candle.

With hands stiff from fright she struck or tried to strike a match, but her fingers either shook too much, or in her hurry she tried the wrong side of the box and she could not light one. Instinctively she backed from the dread Presence that might by now be so near her, fearing in another minute a clammy hand might grasp her, or a weird sigh sound in her ears, stumbled against the door, which was a swing one, and was safe on the other side, her curiosity more than satisfied, and with not the shadow of a wish remaining ever to behold that misty moving form again, come what might! In haste she turned the key and shaking in every limb descended the stairs, with many a backward glance; quicker and quicker went her feet, urged by that nameless dread, and not until she had shut the library door, and sunk into one of the deep old chairs, did her fluttering heart grow quiet, and her mind begin to reason on what she had really seen.

A misty, moving figure slowly coming towards her, illuminated by an unearthly light that only lasted a few minutes.

Oh! coward, coward, why had she not waited calmly it approach?

*   *   *   *   *   *

February 12th.

Dear Olive,

At last I can send you some news, but first let me state, I have shown the paper to several of the cleverest lawyers of the day, and asked them how they read it. One and all, quite laughed at me, they said the "Oliver" was so plain.

There are therefore two courses open to you, to contest the will, go into court yourself and fight for the possession, or for you to resign all claim once and for ever, and come and be another daughter to me.

Most probably you would gain your suit, though all the long-buried past would have to be dug out, and the disinheriting business gone into—very unpleasant publicity for a girl of nineteen.

Then there *is* an Oliver Dane, the great-great-grandson of that hot-tempered old man who justly or unjustly deprived his eldest son of his birthright. *The* Oliver is an orphan and a doctor, said to be a clever man, and is at present travelling for his health somewhere in S. Africa. That branch of the family seem to have had hard times, but in spite of all, they bear a good name, and have always been respected.

On hearing your decision I will write again; should you come to us, I must let this fellow know.

Your affectionate godfather,

W. CARTER.

This was the letter that greeted Olive one fine morning as she sat at her lonely breakfast. Over and over again she read it, feeling as if to leave the old home would almost break her heart, and as if death itself would be preferable to giving up for ever the place and things she so dearly loved.

It was her grandfather's intention she should inherit after him. A stranger would have no interest in anything—what cruel fate had come upon her?

Ah! that was it—Fate—or should we not rather say in a higher, truer sense, the finger of God in His Almighty Providence setting a cruel wrong right.

In a minute, as the conviction flashed upon the girl that for her to resist and rebel was useless, *she*, a mere atom in the universe, clear as it had appeared before that old, old man, his vivid dream took shape and form! A bright, weird light filled all that quiet room of long ago, and close beside the sleeping form a white-robed figure stood, with warning gesture and impressive power, and the echo of the quaint old doggerel, she now knew to heart, floated all around:

> The number *three* shall always be
> Sign of dread and woe to thee,
> Sorrows deep and shadows long
> Who shall break the magic song?
> Until in darkness comes a third,
> Rightful heir by blood and word.

*   *   *   *   *   *

February 18th.

Dear Child,

Your decision is a right one, I believe, about the property, but I am sorry you are so determined to be independent; however, young people will go their own way, now-a-days, and it happens oddly enough I know of a really nice old lady who wants a travelling companion—liberal terms and light duties—and I have arranged for you to have an interview with her next week, so please come here on Monday. I have advertised at once for Oliver Dane, for no one knows quite where he may be. Mrs. Phipps and Barton must take charge of the house until we know the new owner's wishes. I am writing them full instructions. All join me in love.

Your affectionate godfather,

W. CARTER.

*   *   *   *   *   *

" 'Dane'—did you say 'Oliver Dane' was advertised for?—pardon my interrupting you, but the name caught my ear."

"Don't mention it—we were but saying what a time this notice has been inserted for. Week after week, and month after month."

"Allow me," and the tall man who had risen so quickly from the comfortable chair in the club room, read the sentence for himself.

"Will Oliver Dame send his present address to W. Carter, Middle Temple, at once. Important news."

"A friend of yours? hazarded one of the trio beside him.

"Ay, about the best fellow I know, poor chap. I'll go and see Mr. Carter at once. Good evening, gentlemen."

*   *   *   *   *   *

"You say you found him quite unconscious beside his dead friend, and that it was touch and go he pulled through himself?"

"Yes, I shall never forget that evening, it was the saddest thing I've ever seen. I learnt afterwards that it was only by the greatest self-denial Dane was able to pay all the fees of his profession, and then his mother, whom he almost idolized, fell into a lingering illness that only ended with death. Then the long strain on an over-taxed frame would no longer be ignored, and he was ordered complete change of scene and rest. His friend, young Allen, a wealthy man, had a fancy for big game, and they had been quite a year travelling about when I came across them in their sad plight.

"When Oliver pulled round a bit, we had a lot of chat, and one night he told me that long ago his ancestors had been wealthy people, but his great-great-grandfather had married against his father's will, and been disinherited. That the disliked daughter-in-law only lived a few years and then died, but that waking suddenly on the night she passed away, after some hours' sleep, she told her husband that in her dream she had visited his old home, and delivered a message to his father; she could not remember all the lines, but one was to the effect that in darkness an heir should come, and the wrong be righted."

"Strange, strange how things come about in the little lives of men, against the Almighty's will. I thank you very much for your help, Mr. Austen, we are on the right track now."

*   *   *   *   *   *

The crowded through-train was rushing on. Brussels was left leagues behind, Basle was the next important halt, when all of a sudden the brakes were sharply applied, stopping the train with a jolt and a jar felt severely by many of the passengers, and the conviction of something amiss grew apace.

Olive Dane sat quiet in her corner, waiting for the next move, and wondered again as she had done over and over in the last few hours why her opposite neighbour sat so motionless, with his large eyes gazing dreamily out of the window, apparently lost in a world of the past.

Most men would have had their heads and as much of their bodies also as possible out of the window ages ago, when first the brakes were applied, but not even an air of curiosity appeared on his plain face—plain—well, *any* face with such swollen features would look plain, but there *had* been a time when no one would have used that word to describe her fellow passenger.

A guard flung wide the door, and ordered them all to alight at once, then hurried on to another carriage.

Olive and her old lady, who had been sound asleep when the train stopped, were out of the carriage in no time, though as a rule, Mrs. Chirp took a good while ascending or descending from a compartment. A feeling of anger and contempt filled the girl's mind as she noticed their fellow-passenger did not offer to assist them in any way, and it was an awkward step to the level of ground.

"Bear," muttered Olive under her breath, as she saw her *vis-à-vis* stand up, and begin feeling for something in the rack; then in the confusion she forgot him for a bit.

The bearings of one of the wheels had got over-heated, and the carriage caught fire, which had spread with awful rapidity, several carriages were already alight, the one they had left being quite the worst, for dense smoke was coming up between the boards of the floor, and bright little flames were shooting out in all directions.

"All out, of course," one Englishman remarked to another, "and none too soon either."

A dreadful doubt flashed over Olive's mind. In haste, she turned, and pushed her way to the door of their compartment; a dark figure standing as she had left him, quickened her fears.

"Make haste, sir," she called, "don't you see the flames? what madness to linger?"

"I am blind, and I can't find the door—I but tried to feel a small bag of importance and then could discover no opening, perhaps the smoke bewildered me."

"For God's sake, give me your hand and hurry. All the people are busy trying to prevent the fire spreading, and emptying the luggage cans; now then, three short steps, and one long one, and you will be on the ground."

The smoke was stifling, and it seemed hours to Olive before she got her helpless charge safe out of reach of the flames, which darted eagerly at him as if hungry for their prey.

"I cannot thank you—to whom do I owe my life? I must seem very stupid to you, but I have not been blind long enough to be independent."

"My name is Olive Dane."

"Dane! why that *is* queer—mine is Oliver Dane. It was my mother's likeness I tried to save. Well, most things go from me, I seem to have been born under an unlucky star."

"Found at last!" exclaimed Olive. "Mr. Carter *will* be glad; why, we are cousins!"

      *   *   *   *   *   *

The sunset splendour of a summer's sun was gilding Langdale Pikes with a lovely light, so beautiful that two pedestrians stood still in their steady tramp to watch the golden glory fade.

"Yes," continued the elder man, pointing to an old, old house, "I little thought to see such good come out of apparent evil when my old friend died so suddenly, it seemed such a mess all round."

"Well, you found Dane all I told you, and more, didn't you?"

"He *is* a good fellow, and a happier couple you'd go far to find, a power for good all about. When you think how at one time trouble after trouble fell upon him—mother, health, friend, sight, profession, all taken from him, that he should have come out of it all so perfectly happy and contented, speaks well for the sterling worth of the man. And Olive has had her trials too, poor child, but there!—I get prosy. Did you ever hear the end of the ghost?"

"No, I left England again after the cousins' marriage and no news has reached me since."

"Well, you know all about the train being on fire, but perhaps you never heard that Olive wouldn't tell Oliver of his new possessions, said she wanted to know him better, and I was the proper person. When I arrived on the scene, the two were great friends, and he refused absolutely to usurp Olive's rights, for he said her grandfather had intended her to have the place, and so she should.

"There is no saying how the matter would have been settled if, in turning over some old papers, I had not come upon the will of the first Oliver Dane, who built the house, etc., and I found there it was left absolutely, and for ever, to heirs male, daughters could not inherit. A portion, and an ample one, was to be their dower. This settled the affair once and for all, but then I got a hint from Mrs. Chirp to bide a bit, and hold my tongue, and soon after came Dane's letter to me, saying *both* were going to take possession. The first night they came down here they went together to the Ghost's passage, and, rendered brave by her husband's presence, Olive ventured along the narrow vaulted corridor.

Two misty figures came to greet them, but as they went further down the passage the ghosts suddenly disappeared, and when they reached the poor son's room, right at the end, the mystery was plain, and very simple.

An old convex glass hung loosely from the wall above the door with a three-cornered piece cracked and gone right down the middle, and the ghosts of the wing were reflections only of those who visited the gallery; the violent slam of the disinherited son's door had not only broken the glass, but shaken it roughly from its proper place, and freed it from a thick curtain of dust that for ages past had covered it over in its exalted perch. The floor was a moving mass of black beetles.

And so the ghost was laid, the old doggerel played out, and all is well.

Dane not only came in darkness, but is the third to inherit since his great-grandfather's time, and though Olive dislikes the number "3" in any form, no harm has happened since to keep up the old superstition.

> The number three shall always be
> Sign of dread and woe to thee,
> Sorrows deep and shadows long
> Who shall break the magic song?
> Until in darkness comes a third,
> Rightful heir by blood and word.

IMPOSTORS?

Belgravia, Volume 83, April 1894.

P EALS of ringing laughter filled all the room, such laughter
as comes only from hearts without a care; and when from
sheer exhaustion it died away, Elizabeth Vaughan tried to make
herself heard.

"Girls *do* listen; the week is up to-day, and I must send our
answer to Mr. Hinton; what am I to say?"

"I know I shall never be able to do it, Bessie; I had better give it
up at once. Aunt Maria must have been crazy to think of such a
thing! what do you say, Phil?"

"I am not sure it is right for us to try, but I am *sick* of
being poor."

"Aunt Maria tells us the reason for her stipulation, and you
must remember she had a perfect right to leave her money as she
chose; if you two don't wish to fulfil the condition, why, we shall be
no worse off than we were before, obliged to count every penny,
and the Grants will have the chance given to them."

"Horrid creatures? They have more than they know what to
do with already! Read over that bit again, Betty, there's a dear."

"When I was quite young, very nice-looking, and a wealthy
heiress, I became engaged to ——, several years older than myself,
and apparently of independent means. All went well until one
day Furton's Bank failed, in whose shares most of my money had
been put. Almost as soon as the news appeared in the papers I had
a letter from ——, full of hypocrisy and palaver, but plainly letting
me see it was my money that was desired, not myself. Of course,

I at once gave him his freedom, and then he had the pleasure of hearing that owing to timely warning all my shares had been realized, and the money invested safely again before the smash came. Then he *cringed*—no other word will do—and this is why I want to save you three orphan girls from the same sad experience, and I hope you will humour an old maid's whim, which, after all, is only to last six short months.

"You may safely trust Mr. Hinton, and your own old servant; otherwise, the secret must be kept to yourselves."

"Well, girls?"

"We shall have to try, I suppose, but I draw the line at false teeth, so I tell you! Write your letter, Lizzie, and then we'll settle the programme of as wild a scheme as I ever heard tell of. I'll go and take a turn with Mr. Leslie to pass away the time; he's only just below."

"Well, don't you tell him, Cicely, mind."

* * * * * *

"Old Miss Hayton's house is being cleaned up ma'am; new blinds, fresh curtains, and two gardeners hard at work, and the postman says the ladies are expected to-night. After being empty all these months it will be pleasant like to have neighbours again. How many nieces would there be now, m'am, should you say?"

"Indeed, Hannah, I've no idea; Miss Hayton always kept her concerns to herself; time will show! Perhaps Mrs. Arnold will know— I'm to have tea there to-day."

"Mr, Hugh rode by an hour ago; he does look bothered, and I hear he and Deacon marked a lot more trees Saturday. It seems a pity."

"A rich wife would be his best chance, Hannah; perhaps one of the Miss Haytons may suit."

The evening shadows were falling long that June afternoon, when a heavily-laden fly left the station of Rushleigh and crawled slowly out of the little town on the direct road to old Miss Hayton's comfortable home. The luggage was marked with many foreign labels, and was rather a medley. Many curious glances fell on the slowly-creeping vehicle, but beyond the fact that four females and a parrot took up the inside, the gossipmongers were disappointed. At last, after many a jolt and a jar, the old machine drew up with as imposing an air as it could manage before Hope House; the steps were let down, and the ladies descended.

The first to alight was tall and dignified-looking, with snowy hair and spectacles, the second had her hair in rolls on either side of her face; she used a stick in walking, on which she leant heavily; the third wore a front, openly and unmistakably, and all three had dark shadows under their eyes, and lines and wrinkles on their faces.

An old servant, who seemed more lively and energetic than any of her mistresses, hopped briskly above here, there, and everywhere, ordering the women-servants about with right good will. On arrival they went early to their rooms, and none of them appeared until twelve o'clock next day, when they went over the house, and interviewed the servants, and for the next few days busied themselves in re-arranging the rooms.

Then came an afternoon, when with their lace caps and mittens on they sat in the carefully-shaded drawing-room ready for visitors.

The parrot seemed a great pet; he was placed in a very conspicuous position close to Miss Hayton's low chair. Some half-done knitting lay in her lap, under which an open book peeped out.

Miss Philippa seemed lost in the paper, and Miss Cicely was trying various pens on a bit of paper.

"I have done it at last; if I use an etching pen my great sprawling fist looks quite Italian, else I really should have had to give up letters for the present. Oh, Elizabeth my dear, you look quite angelic! There!!! I heard a bell, I do believe."

The visitors came in constant succession; all the folks in the neighbourhood flocked to welcome the rich Miss Hayton's nieces. Some drove in from long distances, and waited whilst their horses rested; others living close by stayed to make the most of the occasion, and it was not until dinner-time that the last visitor departed.

The ladies looked quite flushed as they sat over their dessert, and, free from the servants' watchful eyes, talked over the afternoon.

"Mrs. Arnold *has* a good face, and she spoke so nicely of Aunt Maria. She said she had lost such a kind friend, and she hoped we would let her help us in any way she could. But my dears! she's years younger than we are. Do you think we could adopt her son? —he was Aunt Maria's godson—quite a child now, only twenty-five! It seems to me it would be very suitable, and rather amusing."

"Cicely, how you do run on! I sat on thorns when you began to chatter so fast to that shy young clergyman. Once you actually laughed, and I saw how surprised old Miss Evans looked. Do be careful, I beg."

"I like you talking like that, E-l-i-z-a-b-e-t-h, my dear, *you* were nearly caught when Mr. Cookson asked where we had lived before. Zermatt is not *quite* the place for elderly ladies to reside for any time."

"Cicely, did you hear that mannish young person telling me that a Mr. Arthur Leslie was coming to them next week. What if it should be your friend?"

"Oh! good gracious! I never thought of that! What shall I do?"

"Don't worry yourself. You can't play tennis or golf, and as for riding, give it up with a good grace. Tea-parties will be our line, you'll see."

"Well, I always thought a little play-acing would be rather fun, but this passes a joke."

"Aunt Maria knew all the people about thoroughly, and she must have had some very good reason for making such a point of our residing here all the six months."

"The visitors I liked least were Sir John Godsell and his two sons. How loud they talked, and they looked so bold and insolent, and not one good word had they for man or woman."

*   *   *   *   *   *

Hugh Arnold leant in a brown study on the back of an old chair, gazing out over the wide park-lands that stretched away in front of the flower-decked terrace below. The timber must once have been very fine, but of late the woodman's axe had caused many a blank in the clumps dotted all about.

Inside, the furniture was quaint and faded, an old-world air over all; but that careful hands had bestowed the goods and chattels to the best advantage was very evident.

Mrs. Arnold's soft hand on his shoulder roused her son from his dream. "Any fresh bother, Hugh?"

"Only a continuation of the old, little mother. Deacon wants me to sell the Home Farm. We can hear of no likely tenant—he thinks he can get a fair price for it, and we can't cut down any more timber without spoiling the place."

"I wish you'd take some of my jewels. The ceaseless trouble about money is making you an old man before your time!"

"Never mind, mother, no one could tell that that American Company would go smash, just as we were getting clear, too. But there—talking won't mend matters. We must live somewhere, and, thanks to you, we could hardly do it more cheaply than this last year, though I hate to think of all you have had to go without."

"It has only been a pleasure to *me*, and that you know well."

"What do you think of our new neighbours? A nice wife for me, eh! with money bags too. Ah!" as a conscious look stole over Mrs. Arnold's face, "didn't I know it just? Which one is it to be, mother? and is she dark—fair—or nondescript?"

"I was rather surprised to find them quite elderly; but they are well preserved, and their complexions look quite soft and young, and they were all three beautifully dressed. I hardly recognised the drawing-room, it was so tastefully arranged. Still I had thought to find them quite girls."

"Ah! ah! so I thought, you old match-maker. But what would you think of me if I had gone in for one of the heiresses, just for the sake of those same money-bags?"

"I know you couldn't have done such a thing if you had not cared for her as well, but there's no chance for you now."

  *   *   *   *   *   *

Time passed on—the limits of this story will not allow space to mention how often and often the sisters nearly betrayed themselves; how irksome and tedious their daily getting up became, the severe task it proved to them, to act up to their apparent years, and the daily—nay, more truly hourly, watchful, ceaseless guard required alike on words and actions.

  *   *   *   *   *   *

"Cicely, what ails you? In bed at eight o'clock?"

"I can't help it, Bessie, and so there. It's all that horrid girl. Why, I hardly spoke to Mr. Leslie, and you know what friends we were."

"*Were*, dear, yes! as Cicely Vaughan, but not as Cicely Hayton, remember. Tell me what has vexed you so."

"Well, you know how dull we all find these afternoon parties, where *we* are expected to sit glued to our chairs and thankfully accept tea and cakes from elderly men too old to play, and far too toothless to talk. I was just walking a few yards with Mr. Leslie, who, old though I may be, does not seem to find it quite such a bore as some do, to talk for a few minutes, when up came with a rush that hateful girl. "*Do* take a seat, dear Miss Hayton, you must be *so* tired. Mr. Leslie, will you play with me?" And then again, when their match was over, and he offered to get me some claret-cup, she interferes again, and sends him tearing to fetch her sunshade, or her racquet, or some rubbish, horrid creature!"

"Cicely, you don't deserve to be told that I heard him talking of his foreign trip with Mrs. Anstruther, and he said he had liked Zermatt best of all, for he had made friends with some nice English girls whom he hoped to meet again! Now go to sleep and don't worry over Gertrude Clayton."

"What did Mrs. Arnold say that made you smile so, Betty?"

"She said she and her son felt so greatly obliged to us for renting the Home Farm from them on such liberal terms, as they had been afraid their only chance was to sell it. Now, Cicely, we are going to dine there to-morrow, mind you get yourself up all right." . . . . . .

"Miss Cicely is very feverish this morning, Miss Elizabeth, I think it must be influenza."

"Oh, Nannie, don't mention the word, whatever should we do? It never entered my head that we should want a doctor! Can't we cosset her up between us?"

"Well, Miss, we can *try*, but her skin is like a hot coal, and her head is dreadful, I don't like the looks at all."

By evening Cicely was so bad that sending for a doctor was a matter of necessity, for she was quite light-headed and very restless.

Dr. Burton was away, but his *locum tenens* was soon on the scene, and he said positively it was influenza of a severe type.

In a close-frilled night-cap, with shaded lights all about, Cicely looked very small and fragile, but the doctor did not stay more than a few minuted, as he said he had a very urgent case on hand, and nursing was really what Miss Hayton needed.

The weather set in very wet and chilly, for it was now well on in October, and it seemed as if Cicely's example was to be generally followed, for case after case rapidly occurred, until whole families were laid low; then, as Cicely recovered, the villagers got very well accustomed to the two elder sisters' gentle presence. Very sisters of mercy did they prove themselves in the sad time that followed when the dark angel's shadow fell on many a neighbour's home.

Those who had made most fun of the old ladies, and openly calculated how they would leave their money,—now—in their hour of need were thankful for the beautiful fruit and the good soup, and most of all for the personal sympathy bestowed on them, and when the epidemic had died out, the sisters seemed to be trusted and loved by all.

Then somehow a rumour began to spread—who started it first no one knew—that there was something wrong.

Soon it got about that a lady visitor on opening an album at Hope House came on some photos bearing the Christian names of the heiresses, taken only last year; presently it was openly stated that the Miss Haytons were impostors, and, angry and disgusted, the neighbourhood sent them to Coventry, whilst sinister hints of proceedings to be taken against them became common talk.

In vain Mrs. Arnold tried to stop the gossip, and her son stood up for the ladies fearlessly and frequently;—the fraud had been found out, said the wiseacres, and *now* they must bear the consequences.

The sisters felt this trouble very much. Sometimes they thought they must give in—lose their fortunes and depart; but November was half over—one month more, and the story could be told.

One day the second post brought them quite a budget. Elizabeth received a letter from the lawyer, telling them for the first time how Miss Hayton had wished their disguise abandoned, and suggesting that, if all went well, Christmas Eve should be selected for this grand event.

It was a nice letter, saying how sure he was that humouring the old lady's whim had been no light matter for them; indeed, when first he made their acquaintance, he had doubted much if it was possible for them so to forget their youth for what he knew they must have found six *long* months.

"I knew from my old client herself how much she hoped you three would earn her money; and again and again I begged her to think of some other stipulation; but she said that what with property being willed to heirs only as long as the testator's body remained above ground, or valuable lands left only as long as the inheritor daily drove certain horses, it was impossible for her to think of anything more original, and what was more, she *would* not. If her nieces did not care to have her property as she chose, then they had only to leave it. All arrangements for Christmas Eve I must of course make with you, and I shall hope to be your guest on that occasion, and have the pleasure of seeing you all in your proper persons, so to say."

Philippa had a letter from Mrs. Anstruther, who had taken a house at the seaside for a few months, and when she could speak for laughing she read out the contents.

"The house is a nice one in many ways, but our sitting-rooms are very small, also our bedrooms; but this matters less, as the kitchens and the bedrooms I have given the servants are very large, light and airy. *Our* beds are dreadful, but the maids said, unless they had feather beds or springs, they could not possibly think of staying; so what could I do but give up ours? There are none to be hired in Shawlford.

"We always dine early here, as the servants objected to washing up in the evening, when they wished to get the benefit of the sea air; and for the same reason we are rather late in the morning. Our meals are *very* plain—just roast and boiled—I wonder Frederick puts up with them; but whatever I order, something much plainer appears, always with excellent excuses for the alterations as sauce. But there! I must not bore you further, etc., etc."

Cicely got very red over her letter, and then threw it on the floor in a passion. It was from her pet aversion, Gertrude Clayton, who announced her engagement to Mr. Leslie, concluding her scrawl with saying how sorry she felt for her *old* friends, to have had such a nasty letter in the local paper about them.

It was quite evident that the writer was simply enchanted to be able to have such a fling at them, for else the acquaintanceship was so slight there was not the faintest need for her to have written at all.

The sisters were horrified to think they should be mentioned, even in such a little third-rate paper as the *Rushleigh Organ*, and seizing the unopened sheets, hunted till they found the paragraph alluded to, under the title of

"THE LOCAL MYSTERY.
UNVEILING A FRAUD!"

By hints and innuendoes it was implied that impostors were about—householders were warned to be careful—the mischief might be wide-spread, etc., etc.

Then underneath came the notice of a grand concert, to be held at the end of the week, at which two of the suspected parties had promised to assist, little knowing, said the paper, how largely this fact had helped the sale of the tickets. A little mystery went such a long way.

Who likes anonymous letters in any shape or form? Printed or written, they have a power of their own to rankle and fester almost unequalled, and though true dignity of course consists in taking no notice, human nature is very weak, and the sting remains.

At first, Elizabeth and Cicely said *nothing* should induce them to play their duet, or shew themselves at all at the concert. Then they saw the paper had been posted to them, directed in Gertrude Clayton's writing, else it was one they never saw; so their pride came to their rescue, and they agreed to fulfil their engagement. Indeed, at such short notice it would have been almost hopeless to find a substitute, as both were such first-rate musicians.

*   *   *   *   *   *

The concert-room was very hot, and greatly overcrowded, and when the sisters stepped on the small stage, a perfect sea of faces swam before them. They had timed their arrival well, so as only to have a few minutes in the waiting-room beforehand.

In the instant of coming forward and bowing, Cicely saw a man sitting beside Gertrude Clayton and bending over her in a most devoted style, whilst Arthur Leslie sat quite away, near the Arnolds, who were almost in the front. Their presence comforted Elizabeth much, as they were now great friends, and thus, both feeling happier and more cheerful than they had expected, they took their places and began.

The most impatient person must have listened to such music; it was not often Rushleigh Hall heard the like, and there was a minute's silence when the last chord was struck; then Hugh Arnold began to clap, and in one minute the hall seemed filled up to the very roof with hisses—hisses like serpents that curled and twisted, and began again and again—hisses that drowned the cries of "Shame—Shame!" Hisses from folks they had counted friends, from those they had tried to help—nay, even from those they had nursed!

One minute spell-bound the ladies stood alone, then with a swift rush and spring, Hugh Arnold, Arthur Leslie, and Dr. Lennox had gained the platform and offered their arms to the ladies. None too soon either, Cicely was shaking like an aspen leaf, and Elizabeth, after tottering slightly, fell right into Hugh's arms as he stood beside her; but in a minute she was on the sofa in the waiting-room, and he was back on the platform, and facing the people with a very determined expression, only uttered clearly and distinctly the one word "Cowards!" and was gone. The sisters were so upset that night, they could not even talk the matter over, and retired to bed very sad.

Next day they consulted over it, and counted up the days that yet remained till Christmas.

If they went away *now* at almost the end of their penance, the inheritance was lost; yet it needed the vivid memory of their struggling days, when their great endeavour had been to keep out of debt, by denying themselves in every way, to give them strength to persevere.

"Now I feel there was really a grain of sense, the first I ever could see in Aunt Maria's plan; for certainly else we should never have found out the true from the false," said Cicely tearfully, "but I always said I didn't know if the disguise was right, and now I doubt it more than ever."

"Cicely, did you notice that my wig was all askew when I came home, and some of the grease-paint had trickled down my face, from the water some one sprinkled over me?"

"Oh, my good creature, no one had time or inclination to think of such a trifle, don't worry over *that*. My greatest comfort lies in the thought that in a fortnight more, we may shake off the dust of Rushleigh from our feet, and never return unless we like! At present I feel as if *that* date would be far distant. And now let us set our minds to play out the last scene well!"

"Well, Nannie, what do *you* want?"

"I thought you ladies might not have heard that several of Mr. Arnold's ricks were fired last night, and some men were heard to say as they left the Town Hall last night, *they'd* teach him to call them '*cowards*' again."

*   *   *   *   *   *

The spirit of evil and mischief had a busy time during the next fortnight, and in every way that was possible the idle men of the place made Hugh Arnold pay for his championship of the ladies by acts of petty spite quite beneath notice, and yet none the less annoying.

One night he was driving home late from the station, when, as he passed the last public-house in the High Street, a band of tipsy rollicking men came out, and seeing by the gas-light who occupied the dog-cart, began singing in loud and mocking tones the last verse of "The Three Old Maids of Lee." Louder and louder waxed the voices, then something whizzed through the air with a whistling sound, struck sharp on the horse's flank; one instant the creature

216

stopped dead, then with ears laid flat, and bit well between his teeth, was off over the clattering stones, in headlong, heedless flight.

The night was dark, the road was rough, how it all happened was never quite made out, but when some scattered bystanders after hard running at last came up with the runaway dog-cart, a dark heap of man—horse—and broken cart lay right in the hedge. The groom must have fallen out first, for he did not make one of the tragic group.

The horse was dead, he had staked himself, poor beast, and at first all thought his master was so too, but when at length they got him free from under the debris that half stifled him they found he was still breathing, though badly injured.

*   *   *   *   *   *

Hope House was illuminated from top to bottom, outside and in, and crowds of guests kept pouring in from all quarters.

The people of Rushleigh were there in great numbers—shame for their behaviour to the ladies had not obliged *their* consciences to decline seeing the theatricals that evening.

That a London company had been secured and no expense spared, had leaked out long ago; and now whilst a military band played old familiar airs, the audience waited in expectation of what was to follow.

Mr. Hinton showed all the people to their seats, and in a temporary gallery put up on purpose the tradespeople and villagers found ample accommodation.

Mrs. Arnold came in alone, her sad, gentle face reminding all of the peril her only son had so recently been in.

When the short play began, everyone's attention was rivetted on the stage, and very shortly all grasped the fact that a real life story, part only of which was known to them, was being played out there—in dumb show indeed, but every gesture and action full of speech and power.

Then the interest became so keen, that the silence seemed intense, the very air full of sympathetic mystery.

Tears rolled down several faces unchecked as one or two of the pathetic bits of the young sisters' struggling life was skilfully introduced; in spirit they followed them in their resolution to win their aunt's money—saw them having lessons in Paris how to get themselves suitably up—felt what a weariness the day's toilette must have been—how irksome and fidgetting to young spirits the long pretence of age and staidness had become.

Mr. Hinton had tried to get the sisters to allow the concert-room scene introduced, but they would not hear of it; so after their first reception at Hope House, there was a long and impressive pause. Then an illuminated calendar suddenly marched in, and when July, August, September, October, November had slowly glided away with fading lights, December suddenly divided in half, and as the rightful heiresses of Miss Hayton's wealth, the three sisters—visible for the first time on the stage, and also for the first time to their neighbours without any wigs or wrinkles—stood forth in the sight of all, holding a long glittering motto—"A Happy Christmas to all."

One minute thus they stood, and then the curtain dropped, the play was over. Cheers long and loud filled the room, the very lips that had so lately joined in hisses, now helped to swell the shouts and hurrahs that rang to the very echo, drowning the band as they struck up the National Anthem.

Mr. Hinton had wished to make a few scathing remarks, but he kept his tongue between his teeth, feeling in his own heart convinced that the humiliation of some and the disgust of others were better punishments than his angry words could produce; but he let it clearly be understood that the ladies were going abroad almost at once, and it would probably be long ere they returned.

The light of a great surprise shone over Arthur Leslie's face as he grasped Cecily's hand in his, and he could only repeat:

"To think I never guessed, dolt that I was, and I've been trying to track you down again and again."

A puzzled look from Cicely made him pause in his eager words—"Surely Miss Clayton expects you?"

"Me!—Herbert you mean, poor wretch! his fetters are clanking already; what he could see in the girl I can't think, selfish creature!"

Elizabeth's last words were all for Mrs. Arnold, who seemed so excited that it might have been a personal cause of gratification to her; and late though it was, when at last she reached home, she could not sleep till she had told Hugh, whose surprise was as great as her own; and as he said, *the* one who had gone nearest the truth was poor Dr. Lennox, who still blamed himself sadly for having caused innocently enough some of the late unpleasantness by laughingly remarking at the time of the influenza, that Miss Cicely Hayton had surely made a mistake in the certificate of her birth.

"But," added Hugh gravely, "I think, little mother, we have all cause for thankfulness that we did *not* find out the truth before those poor girls had finished their strange and trying penance."

"Hugh, I have promised Elizabeth to pay them a little visit abroad as soon as you are well again, and her last message was that a welcome awaited you also."

*   *   *   *   *   *

The Christmas bells rang out in the clear frosty air, and while the sisters knelt in the old church of Rushleigh, bitterness and enmity were far from their thoughts, as they remembered in thankfulness the penance ended, and the grim wolf Want driven for ever from throwing his haunting shadow over them.

As Mr. Hinton watched the three young faces he saw how heavy the strain had proved, what an anxious, guarded look had become habitual to them all, how unstrung and nervous they seemed, and he wondered more than ever at the courage and perseverance they had displayed in persisting to the end.

Friends for life they had most certainly made, and unless he prophesied wrongly, a happy future lay before them.

THE SECRET OF THE DEAD

Belgravia, Volume 87, August 1895.

O'er all there hung the shadow of a fear,
A sense of mystery the spirit daunted,
And said, as plain as whisper in the air,
The place is Haunted!

—T. Hood.

"WHEN I get to the next stile I shall rest," I assured myself, for I had been on the tramp all day through the hills and dales of Derbyshire, and now, tired, hot, and dusty, felt disinclined for much more walking.

My pitching on this Midland county for my holiday tour had been rather a sudden fancy, but, on spreading out my much-used map, I found amidst all the red-marked patches of acquaintanceship one Midland county shone out in simple white, and though there were many other spaces yet to fill up, this Derbyshire land persistently asserted itself in such an aggressive fashion that, turn away from it as much as I could, it would not be ignored.

At last, with rather a strong expression, I threw all my guide books in a heap, packed a knapsack with necessaries and a valise with extras, and took the night mail for Derby.

This was ten days ago, and now my furlough was nearly over. In one week's time I should be on my way to India and work, and it would probably be many years before I could visit old England again.

Of farewells I had none to say, the few relations I possessed were scattered to the four quarters of the world, and my friends were far too numerous for me to go the round of them, neither would they expect it from previous experience of their old comrade the Rover.

The flies were very teasing, utterly useless to shake one's head nearly off, wave them with a hat and hands—hum—buzz—sting, they were on one again, nipping and pinching at their very good pleasure.

At last that hoped-for stile appeared beside me, and with a satisfied yawn I threw myself upon it.

Then just below me, nestled against the hill-side, I saw a little greystone church. Inside, should the door be open, it would at least be shady, and I felt nearly broiled.

So down I went.

A quaint old Norman arch with stone seats was the nearest entrance, and such a delicious coolness filled the tiny building that with a great feeling of contentment I thankfully sank down on one of the open seats, and stretched out my tired limbs.

Surely in former holidays I had done much more with less fatigue, maybe the long hot years spent in India had weakened my muscles and tried my sinews.

You will remember of old, a more matter-of-fact fellow than myself didn't breathe. Jokes were always an abhorrence to me. I never could see the point of them, and as for light literature so called, one novel was all I ever managed in that line, and I fell asleep over *that* more times than I care to say—all this by the way.

Presently I glanced round the simple building, and soon found, from the various monuments around, it was far older than I had fancied at first.

One old tomb struck me much, it was so very carefully carved, and though Time's touches had long since softened the sharp edges and crumbled the figures and letters more than a little, it yet had a power and life of its own that would never be lost.

Only the old favourite style of its generation. The father and one son kneeling on one side of an oaken coffer, the mother and four daughters facing them on the other side.

The wife must have been a handsome woman if she resembled her stony likeness, and it was no doll prettiness, but a woman of will and power, whose effigy with tightly clasped hands knelt there. Her husband it was plain had been of rougher, ruder mould, a bluff old English gentleman. I got up from my seat and went nearer to look closer at the group and inscription. All the names and dates were filled in, with the exception that no date came after the son's name—the blank space remained.

I went back to my former position and sat down for yet a few more minutes' rest, and then a strange thing happened—the kneeling lady rose swiftly from beside the coffer, and fell almost prostrate at my feet with thin hands raised in piteous prayer, and heavy tears trickling down the saddest face I ever saw. I rubbed my eyes to clear my vision, and with a start jumped up from what I suppose *you* will call a doze. *I* think otherwise, but that matters not.

The lady in stone looked quite a fixture on the tomb again, as my last glance fell on her, and finding by the lengthening shadows my rest must have been longer than I had thought, I put on a spurt, and tramped onwards to my next sleeping place, an old-fashioned inn.

Over my bread and cheese I asked the landlady about the quaint carved tomb I had so lately seen.

She told me that long ago the family had been of some importance, and that the old Squire had himself carved the tomb, and filled in all the names, leaving only the dates of death to be added.

The family heritage was an awful temper—"passionate" would not describe it—it was a fierce unbridled rage, dreadful to witness.

When first the Squire's wife came to the Manor her grief and fright had been so apparent, that for love of her, her husband *did* try to curb his fearful temper, but of what use then? As well try to check the mountain torrent on its rapid downward rush, as in full-grown manhood after the whole habit of a life-time.

Soon the restraint was forgotten, and though custom and use never became second nature to the poor lady, doubtless she soon knew that whilst the fierce rage lasted, she was powerless to interfere.

Two of the daughters died as children, the others fought and quarrelled from childhood into youth, and then another black drop filled poor Madam's cup—husband and son disputed so fiercely together that often they came to blows, and once or twice indeed, it was said, that but for the poor mother throwing herself between them in their mad fury, bloodshed would have resulted.

The one night there was an awful uproar, and when it at last died away, father and son rode off from the old manor, and the mother was left weeping on her knees.

Days passed, and when with a heavy frown, and in a savage humour, Squire Malcolm returned alone, the servants began to whisper they had but gone away to finish the quarrel elsewhere—doubtless Master Hugh had been silenced, perhaps for ever, and none would know where his poor bones had been hidden secretly away.

My landlady paused to notice if I appeared to take a proper interest in her bygone tale, and finding I waited for more she went on.

Shortly after Hugh Malcolm departed, the tomb in the church was put up, the Squire carefully choosing a suitable place, not too high up, he said, for folks to admire his work; and though one or two suggested it was a creepy notion to have it put up when he was alive, he utterly pooh-pooh'd the idea, and said all family stones and tablets had spaces left on them for the survivors, and the names being properly filled in would hasten no one's death.

The two surviving daughters married and left the old place. Time passed on, the parents were getting well on in years, when one day the old squire broke his neck in the hunting field, and the shock of seeing him brought home lifeless was too much for Dame Anne, she fell senseless to the ground, and the doctors said, though she might probably live some years, she would never speak or walk again.

Over and over she tried to ask for something, and pointed always in the direction of the church. One day, when she seemed rather better, they carried her down into the building and harder than ever the poor soul tried with her helpless fingers to shew them what she wanted.

The disappointment of failure brought on a second and worse attack, and before a week ended, she passed away from this earth. The daughters could throw no light on the son's whereabouts— they almost inclined to the popular idea that he had come by his end unfairly.

For the time being the property was divided amongst them, though neither cared to reside in the old home, which was accordingly shut up as it still remained, Mrs. Lennox said, up to the present time, and was now known far and wide as the Haunted House.

At the present time a descendant of one of the daughters was the sole owner, and said to be in a bad state of health.

The old house was going to rack and ruin and there were many that declared they had seen a white figure glide swiftly down to the church and pass into the old building; some said even, that on entering in the quiet evening a kneeling form with upraised hands caught their gaze just where Madam's chair had rested on her last sad visit.

No news of the absent son's life or death had ever been received.

The longest lane has a turn, and so the queerest tale sometimes ends, and stifling a yawn, I thanked Mrs. Lennox for her entertainment and went out for a smoke.

It was a frying night, quite impossible to sleep, and if I dozed off for a minute, kneeling figures in long processions passed and repassed in countless numbers.

Wishing to goodness I had never rested in that queer old church, and caring very little I fear for what remained untold of that unfinished tale, in despair at last I dressed and went out for an early stroll, and on my return decided I could fill my foreign letter well to you, Alexander, with all this rubbish, then it will be off my mind, and I'll post it at Derby before Thursday. Heigh-ho! how the time goes, my holiday is all but over.

*   *   *   *   *   *

In other lands for many years I toiled away, and now again I am on the eve of departure once and for ever from India's burning suns.

I have come in for a legacy too—supplementing my retiring pension; not much in the way of money, the lawyer says, but an old house and a good bit of land, splendidly situated in a most healthy part. I think the letter said Staffordshire, but I can't find it anywhere, and haven't time to hunt round.

On my return I shall go and have a good prowl by myself, without any blue-bags dancing attendance.[17]

*   *   *   *   *   *

---

[17] Blue-bag: solicitor.

What a bore it should have come on wet, to be sure, just when I wish to admire my new property; old Wigs did look surprised when I marched in on him this morning and asked for particulars of my rural cottage.

"A *mansion*, my dear sir, and on a large scale, and the land all round very rich."

"Then I suppose it brings in a good bit, as I conclude it is let, or did my very distant cousin live there herself?"

"No one lived there for ages, and then a farmer consented to on condition of paying really a peppercorn rent, and having all the land at eight shillings an acre, instead of the proper rate, £2. He uses some of the rooms, but the whole place is in the last stage of decay. However, my dear sir, you'll soon see for yourself."

"Supposing I wish to live there, will there be any bother?"

A queer smile showed for a minute on the learned gentleman's face, as he gravely assured me should I wish to take up my residence at Wynadotte Hall, no one should hinder me.

I certainly forgot to ask him *why* my valuable property had got into such evil repute, but that I can soon find out, and here we are, I do believe.

    *   *   *   *   *   *

Five hours later!

Well, this is a rum start; let me just get it down straight, for I seem plumped into a dream of the past.

When I left the station that old Chips told me was the nearest to Wynadotte Hall, I found of course nothing in the shape of a conveyance going my way, but as the rain was only then a drizzle I started off quite cheerfully. The first check I got was on asking my road to the Hall.

The fellow looked at me, took off his hat, scratched his head to awaken his brain, and at last directed me to the Haunted House. No one knew it by any other name, said he with a fine air of scorn.

At last the outbuildings came into view, extensive, solid, and in good repair, and then the house itself, standing back from the road, with a large courtyard in front, and handsome wrought-iron gates. The courtyard was nothing but an expanse of common rank grass, the gates were broken and rusted, with railings missing all along.

Then the house itself gave me an unpleasant shock, with windows blocked up everywhere, and woodwork on doors and frames equally innocent of paint.

I entered by an unlatched door in the lower part of the house, at the side, and saw at once that lawyer fellow was right, when he said it was indeed a mansion.

A wide elm staircase with slender spiral supports went right up to the top of the house, with large landings and archways on each floor. An iron pillar propped the much worn steps, dark with age. The banqueting hall opened straight to the great door leading I presume down to some steps into the overgrown courtyard.

Many of the rooms were in twilight from the darkened windows, and only one here and there out of the whole fifty-two let in heaven's light and air.

Old faded tapestry in tatters and strips hung still in some of the rooms, but holes in the floors, great gaps in the walls, weather stains in all directions, told a mournful tale of their own. One beautifully worked four-post bedstead took up a good part of one of the rooms, and over all hung that strange sad air of desolation. The upper floors had gone and the whole looked almost unsafe.

I saw the dark shadow of a tall man thrown strongly on the wall of an inner room, but when I reached the spot 'twas but the reflection of a battered can piled on top of some old chairs.

The air was heavy with stale odours, and, depressed not a little by this private view, I left the house and neglected grounds, and tumbling almost over a fine old man made enquiries about my nearest way to the "Hare and Hounds."

He told me of a short cut down the valley easy to find.

I rummaged in my pockets for matches, but could only find a rumpled sheet or two of foreign paper, which on smoothing out I found was a faded letter written to a cousin and never posted. It was dated from the "Hare and Hounds," Derbyshire. Strange that I was now on my way to its namesake.

And there above me stood a little old church; as I live, the very identical building of long ago. Why, dimly I still remembered some queer old dream connected with that church. Curiosity alone would have obliged me to look round it again, and I found it little altered. It is true there were candles and flowers on the alter, and the place looked more cared for than of old.

The old carved Malcolm tomb stood unchanged, and as I paused in front and read again the sunken lettering, "Of Wynadotte Hall," caught and held my attention. Why, *that* was my new possession. What was the story that old house could tell?

With a feeling of kinship I went closer to the inscription and read it carefully to the end. The top of the coffer was highly finished off, and the lid itself looked so realistic that involuntarily I put up my hand to lift it, and to my surprise it opened at once, and a cloud of dust flew right in my face. My first impulse, with smarting eyes, was to drop the lid immediately, then I saw the inside was really hollow, so plunged my arm down to the bottom, and fished up in triumph a small bundle of old yellow papers tied with a blue silk ribbon.

To put them in my pockets, and close the lid was but the work of a minute, but even in that glance I saw they were likely to prove of interest to me.

I found the same "Hare and Hounds" I remembered, but Mrs. Lennox was getting old and did not recollect me.

My solitary mean did not take long, and I was soon at the papers.

Well, truly the sins of the father are indeed visited on the children to the third or fourth generation.

The papers were mostly written in a fine pointed Italian hand and here is the story I read:

"I, Anne Cranley, married John Malcolm against the wishes of my parents, and, indeed, only a few days before the wedding, my poor mother called me into her own room, and pleaded earnestly yet again that even now I would give John up. She told me that the awful temper that all the family shared had again and again broken bonds, and crimes numberless had been the result. Certainly one in each generation died a violent death, little accounted of in those lawless times, when most families had their favourite skeletons, only occasionally aired by the light of day.

"Still I refused to yield, and then my mother told me that if I married John I should need indeed a brave heart and true, for the curse *must* lie on him and his children, though maybe by no fault of his own.

"His father had had his full share of that evil spirit of old— two sons and a daughter had lived at home, and the mother was virtually a nonentity. Quarrels with four hot-tempered people were matters of everyday occurrence, but one wild, stormy winter's night a fierce row began.

"The men, at least, had taken more than enough even for those hard-drinking times, and soon a regular stand-up fight began, when blows rained thick and fast and bitter oaths filled the air.

"What part in the quarrel Miss Laura took did not transpire, but certainly she was present. When the fierce gestures and threatening words led to cuffs and knocks, and the father's hand struck a violent blow at the younger son's head, sending him staggering down, striking his temple against a corner of the old carved table, her cruel words were silenced. Sobered instantly by the sight of the motionless form on the floor—finding their efforts unavailing to revive him—Laura Malcolm rushed wildly out in the darkness of the night, saddled herself her own white horse and rode off at a reckless rate in search of the aid that yet could not avail. She was a good rider across country, but in the darkness the path was hard to find—the horse got fidgetty and frightened, and stumbling into an unseen rabbit-hole just as they entered a small wood, fell heavily to the ground, breaking his neck against a bank, and though Laura had been thrown off in his stumble, one of his hoofs in his dying agony came with a horrid dull crash on her head, an with little more than half-an-hour between them, two of the wild, reckless band were summoned to the Unknown Land.

"At the Hall itself the night was one never to be forgotten; the father was simply not responsible for his actions, and it fell on John Malcolm to make all arrangements, but when, in the early morning, the sister's body was carried home, it was sad to see the brother's grief, and one would have thought the lesson strong enough to last a lifetime; but after a while, however, when the shock had worn off, quarrelling began again.

"Here my mother made a long pause, and glanced appealingly at me. Heredity was an awful thing, and rather would she see me in my coffin than married to John Malcolm.

"As well whistle to the winds!

"That day week, as Anne Malcolm, on a pillion behind my husband, I left my dear old home, and I lived to learn that every word my mother spoke came true.

"I thought in my pride of ignorance *I* could manage so well there should be no quarrels. Mother was old and timorous, John would do anything for me!

"I had the house pretty much to myself in those days, and somehow the gloom that hung over the fine old rooms, the footsteps on the stairs that yet never entered, and that John declared was only the elm creaking as all old wood might, the stories servants told me of the place being haunted, and that the sound of angry voices issuing from the banqueting hall, and a white horse and its rider, galloping wildly along, were of frequent occurrence, etc., etc. It took some years to break my spirit down, but the mills of God grind surely if they grind exceedingly slow.

"How my heart sank down when Baby Hugh went into a storm of temper. It was so dreadful to witness. I expected the child to go into convulsions any moment, and the way he threw things about with tiny fists, and kicked and plunged like mad—frightened me. What would the future hold for him? God knows I tried my best, and poor John prayed me to persevere, but *he* never took in when he was having what he called a 'flare up,' that the work of months and years was undone in five minutes of such rage.

" 'Father does so and so,' the children were sharp enough to notice, 'so of course *we* can.'

"When my little twin daughters died of the fever, I felt sadly thankful that though this was no doubt part of the Visitation of God that certainly sooner or later would fall on us, they at least were innocent. Soon after, I lost my parents, and only then I realised how sensibly my mother had always helped me in every way and cheered me when nothing else could. She never told me I had myself to thank, but pointed me steadily on my rugged path to where the light shone clear at the end.

"My husband spent hours sculpturing, and the whim seized him to chisel a family tomb. Anything that kept him occupied and shortened the time spent over the endless meals was a boon to me, and with my wheel humming busily along, many a quiet hour was passed.

"Hugh also was very anxious to copy his father and carve, and one sad day, after a long pillion ride to a distant cousin, we came in to find a great ugly hole made in the top of the old coffer that my husband had nearly finished.

"There was a terrible storm of course, and the boy was severely punished, but afterwards I found his idea was to make a money-box of it 'for Hugh,' he said.

"The notion tickled my husband's fancy, and he said he would follow it out, so he made a fresh top with a split in it that could be easily lifted up.

"As the tomb was nearly finished, and this addition would take a little longer, I encouraged the idea, and my husband took pains to carry it out well.

"Indeed, Hugh's pocket money gradually came to be always kept under the coffer lid, and many other little valuables belonging to him. Naturally, *the* charm of the thing was the slight mystery about it, Hugh begging the secret of his money-box might be kept.

"Ah! those were peaceful days—the lull before the storm.

"Time passed on, and the shadows came closer! Father and son quarrelled bitterly, generally about money, and one day, or night rather, that old evil spirit entered into them both, and they came to fierce blows.

"I thought my heart would break, for surely *this* was the Visitation again.

"I parted them somehow, and sullen and ashamed both looked, and I saw they would soon begin afresh, when something snapped suddenly in my brain, and I fell senseless to the ground. Thank God for his mercy in coming to my aid! for, seeing me fall, brought back to John's memory that long-ago night of tragedy, when his brother fell—never to rise again!

"My hair was damp with water, and wine was at my lips, when at last, with a shuddering sigh, I came back to earth's troubles, and my husband, with shaking lips and trembling hands (he had thought me dead), promised solemnly the next time he and Hugh quarrelled should be the last, for he would send the boy away, but surely after such another awful fright, there would not be another time!

"I would not discourage him, but from that day I began to save, and coin after coin found their way into Hugh's coffer.

"My daughters took more after me than their father, I am thankful to say, and helped me much, especially as about this time I became very subject to long fainting fits.

"With a dread on me that nothing ever lifted, I wrote to a cousin of mine settled in a quaint old Dutch town, and asked him if we found it advisable to send Hugh abroad, if he would give an eye to the lad, and help him on a bit, and a great load seemed lifted from me, when at last an answer came saying the boy should at any time be welcome, and come when he might, he should have a second home with him, for the sake of his cousin Nan!

"Carefully I placed this letter with my cousin's name and address in Hugh's favourite hiding place.

"Then one night a dispute began about a village youth who, John declared, spent his nights poaching, and should be made an

234

example of. Hugh defended him vehemently, and protested his innocence—louder and louder rose the angry voices with bitter sarcasms, cruel taunts, fierce oaths and threatening gestures, and then they came to blows.

"Hugh was slight and wiry, John ponderous and powerful, and at first it seemed hopeless to stop them, then I seized a great caraffe of water from the sideboard, and threw the whole contents of the ice-cold water into their faces.

"The shock and surprise made a minute's pause, and gave me my chance. Seizing an arm of each with all my force I prayed them for the love of Heaven to remember their solemn oath, and part before bloodshed came of it!

"The water was falling in pools on the floor and trickling in streams down their necks. I ordered Huh from the room—to pack his clothes at once—never mind the wild night—and then I had a sad scene with poor John.

"Of that I shall not write here. For weal or woe I won my way at last. And when the tide of despairing remorse had fully set in, I began to hurry Hugh's preparations. In vain John begged me to let them try again—next time I might fail to check them, and then that awful doom would fall. *No*, twice *no*. I had rather never see my boy's face again, than think that the curse of Cain was on one of the two I loved so well.

"The money in the little coffer made quite a good sum, and John gave also all he could, and then when the dawn of another day began, in the chill of a winter's morn, father and son—now in peace and love, thank God! rode forth together, and I knew I had seen the last of my boy.

"Kneeling, I watched them go, and kneeling I prayed for courage never to recall Hugh in his father's time, come what might.

"It is by my husband's wish I have written out this long account, the third that I have made, but the others coming in John's way when angry and unreasonable, he tore them into atoms. So this copy I shall place away in Hugh's hiding place, it will be safe there, and when he returns he will surely know where to look.

*   *   *   *   *   *

"I came home from paying a sick friend a few days' visit, to find John had had the tomb taken down to the church and put up, and though somehow I had never thought of my papers going there, where could they be safer than in God's own keeping? so now I have only to walk quietly down, and put this last sheet with the rest.

"Neither my husband or daughters are aware where Hugh has gone, indeed the latter have never mentioned his name to me, since that sorrowful morning when I told them, for reasons known only to their father and myself, he had gone abroad for years.

"In all human likelihood, John will long out-live me, for I am ageing fast, and should anything happen to *me*, what more natural than that Hugh should be sent for? and then the pain and the sorrow of the wearied years of absence from my only son, would all go for nothing, for well I know, alas! by now, that John will carry his fierce temper to the grave, poor soul, and in the quarrels that would surely come, the curse might afresh begin.

"And neither can I leave even a sealed letter behind, for fear of some evil chance. The papers rest in God's own house, and so shall the secret of the boy's whereabouts. Some day—somehow—when the time has come and God's solemn curse is removed, and the dark shadow of the Visitation lifted, perhaps there will be happy times in this old haunted house. 'Haunted,' ay! truly and indeed, but by man's own wrong-doing.   "ANNE MALCOLM."

*   *   *   *   *   *

So my castle is indeed in ruins about my ears, in more senses than one, for if that wanderer married abroad, his children are the rightful heirs, and rather than claim unfairly that sorrowful heritage, I would let it lapse to the Crown. Now I must make enquiries abroad, and never did anyone part with a legacy with less regret than I shall, if only I can find a Malcolm living.

That poor brave woman has set me a lesson to learn, and an example to follow. I should indeed be proud to count kinship with her.

*   *   *   *   *   *

The clue has not been easy to find, the threads of the tangled skein had got so mixed and knotted. The first big tangle of course had been that all believed so stubbornly in Hugh's death at his father's hands.

Step by step, thread by thread, I at length wound the frayed and broken hank out straight, and all is plain sailing now.

Hugh had married a gentle Dutch girl, whose very limited knowledge of English perhaps, helped to keep the peace when the Malcolm rage broke forth. Then his days of idleness were over, and in hard labour, if it *was* voluntary; several years were passed.

Three little children and their mother depended on him for their daily bread, when one day in passing along a narrow street, where the high projecting houses overhead almost seemed to touch, a quaint, heavy old sign fell suddenly on him, hitting him just on *the* fatal place on his temple, killing him on the instant.

His wife knew little of his English home, though of his parents and his sisters he had often talked.

The kind old cousin would have known with whom to communicate, and what to advise, but he had left his business in Hugh's hands and gone, it was thought, to England.

The children grew up somehow, but they proved a heavy handful. The little girl was deformed from an accidental fall down some stone stairs when left in her brothers' charge, and from that day she had possessed such an influence over the lads that her word was indeed law to them.

One boy went to sea, and in the rough life of those times on board ship did fairly well, but he never came home again, as he was washed overboard in a heavy storm. The other son did his utmost to support his mother and sister in comfort, but every now and then times were very bad, and then short commons prevailed.

It fortunately never entered his head to think of marrying until rather late in life, but when his mother and sister were both dead, he missed a woman in his house so much that after years of friendship he suddenly married good Burgher Kant's youngest daughter, and *her* temper being very fiery, instead of having everything his own way, he found for peace and quiet's sake it was expedient that Vrow Gretchen should have hers.

Their only child, a boy, was three years old, when in a cholera outbreak both parents died, the home was pillaged of everything of any value, and the little fellow sent to the poor house.

And here I found the child.

I liked his looks, and the officials spoke well of him as an honest, likely lad, so I have made up my mind to look after him, do guardian in short, give him a decent education and a chance in life, and then if he turns out well, when he comes of age he shall have that old land handed over to him. The house will most likely have tumbled down completely long before then, for this poor, destitute, friendless child is only eight.

In the meantime the property is *mine* to all intents and purposes, and as I have puzzled out the thing unaided, and consulted no one, there is little fear of the lad's hearing about his forebears' sins, about the worst thing for his future welfare that could happen to him, in my opinion. Should he prove free from that awful taint, then there is before him a useful, and I hope a happy life, as an English gentleman.

*   *   *   *   *   *

L'ENVOI.

The boy is now sixteen, and I have not seen him lose his temper yet, so I am very hopeful for the future, and I have bit to add that my Derbyshire agent in reporting on farming matters and local gossip, said in passing, that for eight years now no one has seen anything of a ghostly nature at Wynadotte Farm, as it now seems generally called, and though still known as the Haunted House, I can live in comfort, believing that good Dame Anne will rest in peace. The dark stain has been wiped out from the Malcolm family, never, pray God, to fall on them again.

AUTUMN CLOUDS

Belgravia, Volume 88, October 1895.

T HE cloud angel sighed as the order reached her to let the grey clouds go free! It was always a trial to her gentle nature to see the wild havoc they wrought, when with the fierce wind as coachman they swept in swift flight along—for four-and-twenty hours, and then the sky was to be dressed in blue, with tiny flecks of white.

Out they came, in size and colour varying according to age, and carefully the angel examined their water reservoirs, and saw all the syringes were in working order. Right in the middle of the powerful dark grey masses moved the thunder-car, and when disputes arose around as to their speed or height, these heavy bodies flew at each other to such purpose that out flashed the bright, wild lightning's flame, and the angry roar of the tempest's voice.

With what a rush and spring they bounded forward, rejoicing in their much-prized liberty. They had not had a good race for so many a long day; indeed they had only been exercised once or twice for nearly six weeks, and it was no pleasure to the stormy greys just to be driven wildly forward and round home again, without pause or rest. No! what *they* enjoyed was the angry clamour of an awful storm, when they had dropped so low they hung like a great pall over the earth beneath and drenched the land from end to end with their great squirts; watching with keen pleasure the oceans rise to meet them, with crested waves and thundering surf, and all the forms of life below, animate or inanimate, bowing in dread and fear. Often and often when so engaged in real sport and pleasure to them, the recall had sounded most unwelcomely, and very, very reluctantly had they ceased their pleasant game, and in disjointed groups mounted slowly and lingeringly to their home above, meeting half way their white-robed brethren, with their edges tipped with sunlight, carrying warmth and hope to the drenched land below.

So on this glad day to them, out they came, passing the angel in splendid order, with all their torn edges mended, and their colours smooth and unblotched. The last to sally forth was a tiny soft grey, who bowed joyously to the sad-faced angel. "You said I should go to-day, dear friend; I have been looking forward to my trip for so long."

"Remember you keep the sun on your edges as long as you can, and never do any needless harm! You are very young to go on such an errand. I shall keep an eye upon you, and in four-and-twenty hours the recall will sound!"

"Am I to have any peep-holes?" said the sun as the clouds swept over his face. "Let me know when a rainbow is required."

"Part in sunder, kind friends, now and then, that I may touch up your sharp edges for you; the effect will be all the greater, and I hate being out of the fun," whispered the sleepy moon. On, on in mad joy raced the storm's messengers; and then the wind relaxed the reins, and down lower and lower they dropped. The little cloud felt giddy and breathless at first, and got left a trifle behind. "Now I must leave you," whispered the last sunbeam. "You have your work to do. Farewell."

Slower and slower the rate became, and the ranks began closing up in a hurry; the little cloud caught hold of a friend, and waited for what would happen.

Below lay a large and populous town, whose streets were full of evil smells, and where water had long run short. The poor and the feeble had suffered greatly; the rich could still buy their water, and the strong fetch it from afar, but in the poor courts and rookeries, fever was raging terribly, and in the last few days an awful whisper had spread that dread pestilence in the shape of cholera had broken out!

Strikes were everywhere about, want and misery frequent household guests.

In the church of "All Saints" day after day the prayer had gone up for blessed rain, and only this morning as he went his round old Mr. Fortescue had scanned the blue ether above, and his brave heart had sunk in fear as he watched that Italian sky, as to what would befall if the drought lasted much longer. To him his people looked for help for body and soul, and all honour be to him!—so far they had never looked in vain, but at what a cost God and himself only knew!

His only daughter lay ill—dying—they said of the awful fever, and as she tossed from side to side, and moaned in her weakness and pain, the father's heart felt broken, for money was very scarce, he could not provide her with the comforts she really needed most.

The room was hot and stifling, and yet if the window was opened the smells from the ill-drained streets adjacent were so offensive they dared not run the risk.

On a stipend of £150 and no private means the margin in case of need could but be small, and of late, with starvation around, the reserve, and more, had long been exceeded. There was not much of luxury in the home, and the larder was painfully bare.

"I shall not be in for lunch," said the vicar as he left his home. "Miss Irene will like a little soup; can you manage it?"

"Certainly, sir, we had a sheep's head yesterday, and I can taste it up nicely for her, never fear. How bad your cough is; must you go out?"

"Indeed I must, old Granny Hughes is passing fast, and they have just sent from the Smiths' to say the poor baby is dying for want of nourishment."

"Sir, would it be any sin to use a bottle of the communion wine? We have but a wine-glass of brandy left. I *must* keep that for Miss Irene."

"No sin in dire need, Jane, perhaps, but unless absolutely compelled, I must not fo it; there, my good soul, don't fret, with you to nurse her, Miss Irene is well off."

His hand was on the latch when again Jane stopped him:

"For the love of heaven, don't go fasting into the Friar's Court; they have fires at each end now, and a black flag flying— for Miss Irene's sake."

"Jane, I am *surprised* at you—would you have me turn coward? Nay, nay," as he saw the worn face quiver. "I am as safe in Friar's Court as here! *I* will sit up to-night, you are tired out!"

"Dr. Hunt said he expected the crisis to-night, sir, I meant to tell you."

"Fetch me a crust of bread, pray, if it will make you happier."

Out into the street passed the old man with shabby coat and frayed linen indeed, but a heart as brave and true as ever beat in human frame.

With a start he saw the clouds were gathering up—nearer and nearer they came—surely the rain was coming. Into his church he stepped as he passed the ever open door, and there at the altar rail, asked for help in this hour of need.

Then down that poor narrow court, with policemen on guard at each end. Not him would they dare to stop, as they touched their helmets in salute, and watched his unfaltering steps.

"It is a spasm of the heart, I fear, sir," said heart-broken Mrs. Smith; "if I had but a drop of brandy, I think I could save her yet."

Was it the tempter's voice that sounded so loud in his

ears? "You have but the one wine glass—keep *that* for your daughter's need."

Five minutes later, Constable Burns of the "A" division handed Jane a small folded paper, and then in another five, a grateful mother looked up in her vicar's face and blessed him for the life preserved!

*   *   *   *   *   *

"You are the youngest—begin." The whisper travelled along until it stopped at the little grey cloud. "Yours can be only summer rain; we will back you up well—make haste."

Gently the soft drops fell, hardly touching the old man's coat, as he went farther down the court, and in a very few minutes, jugs, basins, pots, kettled and cans—chipped, ugly and old, were put out from every door and window to catch the pure drops as they fell. Lower and lower dropped the clouds, as one by one their fountains began to play on the sun-baked earth below.

"It may save us yet," the doctor said, "if only it lasts long enough—a week's rain would be the thing!"

"A week," whispered the tiny cloud, "dear, dear, I must take a message back when we go home, and pray to return again."

His neighbour gave him a slight jostle.

"Hadn't you better wait and see?—these mortals can't judge for themselves, and in the meantime, your spray wants seeing to; you had better hold firmly on to me when we move on, or you'll get yourself badly torn."

"Move on—oh, mayn't I stay here and help these poor creatures?"

"What nonsense you talk, to be sure! Don't you know we go on expanding and spreading until we hear the recall from above, when we drop quickly apart, and hasten above as fast as the wind permits?—*what* a baby it is, to be sure."

The poor cattle below were licking the damp grass with hungry pleasure, and the mist was now so thick, it was difficult to see anything clearly. Presently it lifted a little, and the young cloud saw they were playing over a vast stretch of country right in a hop-growing county. . . . . Crouching under a dripping hedge, a wretched and miserable group of hop-pickers paused on their weary tramp till the worst of the storm should be over. What dirty, depraved-looking creatures the *best* of them were, and the *worst* looked of the very lowest scum of the people—coarse, ignorant, friendless, homeless—tramping from day to day in search of their daily bread, sleeping at night in unions and shelters, and often out in the open.

Is it their fault they grow up brutal and ignorant? Have they had their chance of better things?

"It's going to rain all night; come, father, we must push on for Worcester at once. We have none too much time already."

"My limbs ache so sadly, I shan't get far," moaned the wretched old shivering creature, "best let me stay behind."

"A likely tale *that*, to be sure, at this time of day, there's my arm to help you and a stout stick to lean on, and as we are now all soaked, it's safer to move along."

"How is Tom to-night, Susan?" she asked, as the poor draggled group began to start. A sad look answered her, and the shivering young mother opened a fold of her shawl to shew the ashen white face of a child of five, who might have been only three from his tiny size and light weight. "He has done nothing but talk about his Robin dinner last Christmas, he will have it he's going to one to-night."

A low, hacking cough interrupted her, and she pressed her hand hard on her side.

"I think I have done my last hopping, I feel quite worn out and so weary. What a noise our boots make, now they are soaking wet!"

"Boots," thought the little cloud, as he looked at the shapeless bits of sodden leather, gaping wide in the front, and bulging in holes at the sides, only however in keeping with the rest of the garments of rags . . . . "Is there no one to help the poor hoppers, to give them a meal and a shelter and to wash the dirt off the roads? Why, the gipsies are rich compared with them, for *they* have their caravans! Can't we stop raining now?—see, we are drowning those poor souls."

"How inconsistent you are," scoffed his friendly comrade, "did I not tell you to wait? Dear, dear, what *is* the matter?" as a dull sullen roar began.

"It's only a dispute on the road, I felt we should soon come to blows!"

Out flashed the weird lightning's flame, zig-zagging in all directions—crash!—bang!—came the thunder's answer, and the shock was so strong and long, the little cloud felt dazed and had quite a job to hold on to his neighbour; and now the fierce whistling wind caught up his reins again, and urged on his willing steeds, at a very rapid rate. And the wild ocean's voice, thundering on shore and rocks, joined in the din of the storm—higher and higher rose the dashing crested waves tossing in gleeful play the cockle shell boats of men up on to the top of the billow, and blown in the trough beneath.

Curiosity made our young friend peer close through the gloom below, and he saw the poor fishers' wives in crowds on the stormy beach, straining their eyes into the grey distance and watching the boats struggle in.

Then in the shades of evening a rocket's wild gleam went up, and he saw on the cruel rocks a vessel fast going to bits. But with a rush and a cheer out sprang the life-boat, her crew firm lashed to their seats, and with their lives at their brothers' call. And the cheer from a hundred hearts brought hope to the drowning crew.

"Room for one more," was shouted hoarsely, "we'll soon be back for the rest."

The captain turned from the bridge, and signed to a man standing near with grizzled hair, and furrowed face, "Now, Mike, your turn."

"I'd rather stop with you, sir."

Too late for either, the chance was gone, the boat was well on her homeward way—would she return in time?

Only a few stood on the sloping deck, and the grinding, grating noise of the poor ship on the rocks, warned them their time was short. The captain did his best, the belts were served out, and the men lashed to floating planks, and then they could do no more, but peer with their eyes into the darkness and strain their ears for the life-boat's cheer.

Captain Fortescue's heart was heavy, as he thought of his much-loved home, his father's voice of welcome sounded so near at hand and he felt the warmth of his sister Irene's arms around his neck? A sob rose up in his throat as he knew he should see them no more! Never repay his father's care, and all his self-denial!

Close home on Old England's shores, the Master's call had come; in the simple discharge of his duty, he should pass to the Land of Rest—thanks to his father's teaching in humble faith and fear.

Higher and higher rose the mighty crested waves, lifting the ship like a child in their arms, and throwing her down broken and smashed on the cruel rocks beneath.

The little cloud felt so sad, he tried to stop off his rain and dropping his comrades's side, pressed his damp edges together; for one minute there was a lull, and in the small rift thus made the moon sent her silvery beam right through to flash on the scene below.

Only a swirl of water bubbling and circling round in a whirlpool marked the grave of the gallant ship, whilst here and there tossed about the helpless form of a man. Above rose the beetling cliffs, below, the jagged rocks, far in the distance a speck struggled across the huge waves, the life-boat again to the rescue.

"Catch hold of me, you stupid, and don't play such a prank again," hissed an angry murmur around; gone was the silvery light lost in the deepening gloom.

All of a sudden a great hush fell—the like of which can only be felt—and a silence that could in the darkness almost be seen, when the tumult's wild rage was still and the powers of the air hung waiting.

Frightened at the awful scene, the baby cloud gave a grip to his friend, "What is the matter now?"

"HUSH!" came the answer back, "the angels of Life and Death are passing through us to the earth, to gather the golden grain."

"May I not see them pass, and who will they fetch to-night?"

"Only the Good God knows, you can ask when we get home. Now we're off again, and there comes the morning light—dear me, what a mess you're in, pull yourself well together, and overlap some of your edges; how did you tear yourself so?"

"I am sure I don't know,: sighed the cloud, "I feel very much knocked about, and I don't like the work at all—must I always remain a storm cloud?"

"Yes, if you've any constitution you must; it's only the weakly one, the wadding clouds, as we call them, that get off the ranks of the storm masses—then when you are old and weary, in the sunset's golden army a niche will be found for you, and robed in beautiful purple, you'll watch the angels dressing and painting the heavens. Do leave off sighing, child; our work is by no means done."

"Shan't we soon go home?—I do feel so very sad."

"No, our time is extended for some hours, but the wind has altered his course and is driving us now from the opposite quarter, so we really are on our homeward way, and I must to work again."

All day long they rained, spreading a covering of grey, whilst from the earth beneath heart-felt thanksgiving rose on its heaven-ward way.

Then the clouds lifted a trifle and eagerly peered the little cloud, through its soaking mantle of grey, to see any familiar faces below, but at first he looked in vain, all seemed strangers to him.

He saw in the colliery districts the starving women and children, whilst groups of stalwart men lounged and smoked the day away, standing out for a better wage, and a fairer share in the profits.

Were they right or wrong?—the little cloud wondered. He tried to linger to see some more, but the others would not wait, and off he had to go. His body was feeling so light he felt sure the cisterns must be low, and he noticed it was a steady downpour that fell from his comrades around; the fierce storm and bluster was over, gone with the light of the day.

The sun was sinking fast, as they passed over the fishermen's cove, the shore was thick with wreckage, boxes, and barrels. A group of men bent over a lifeless form just thrown up by the tide. All the earth lines were gone from the face, sealed with the peace of God and a smile on the silent lips.

The sailors who stood around drew their hands across their faces, as they told in disjointed whispers, what a friend he had been to them, in helping them all to do right. And then as the question came, why *his* was the only life lost, old Mike in faltering tones explained that the lifeboat's crew could have picked the captain up one of the first, but he would not have it so; he refused to be taken in until all the crew were safe, as he said there was not room, and just as again they neared him, with all the others aboard, a plank was dashed by a mighty wave against his head, and to their regret and sorrow, he had sunk like a stone at once in the powerful swirl of the sea.

In vain they waited about, till the danger for all was so great, overcrowded as they were, they were obliged to give up the search and make for the shore.

The old man lifted the curly hair, and showed a long purple scar, that told its own tale to all.

"We can't rain any more without a fresh supply of water," said the little cloud's friend. "See, the big blacks have parted asunder, and the moon is lighting them up; now look out for our orders, our flight is nearly over."

The clouds paused in their steady pace, and the silvery light of the moon fell like a ladder to earth, making a path for the angels' feet.

Vainly the little cloud peered, in hopes of getting a sight of them, only the light shone clear on land and sea below. Illuminating for a minute's space a large infirmary ward, where in a clean white bed, a poor young mother lay, whose sands of life were so low, the sun would find her gone—gone up the silver track, helped by the angels' hands. Beside her sat watching a friend, who yet in her heart of hearts, could not wish for the struggle to last.

"My child," came faintly from the white lips, and the pitiful eyes were wide open, "who will take care of him?"

"You won't have to part from him," sobbed poor kindly Susan, "he's only a little ahead, and you'll soon overtake him, poor lamb! He's gone to his Robin dinner to-night, as he always said he should."

Oh! what a look of peace fell on the dying face.

"Thank God for his great goodness, he knew what was best for us, and if he had lived to grow up, he might have been like the others."

Again an upward flight, and now to the cloudlet's pleasure, through a wide open window he looked in on Irene's face. Sleeping like a little child, she lay, with the flush of fever gone, and very close beside her, her father knelt in prayer.

God in his Infinite Mercy had spared him the light of his home.

A poke in the tiny cloud's shoulder startled him from his pitying gaze. Across the great vault of Heaven, a shooting star was rushing, leaving a trail of glory, as his message he carried afar.

It was the clouds' recall—they must hasten at once to obey, now they were in the way when the sky was required clear—so up jerked the wind his reins in a hurry, and away higher and higher mounted the clouds; the little one was so light he went up just like a bird, straining his eyes to the ground, all the time with an eager, wistful gaze, but now in his rapid race he could not distinguish clearly and needed his breath to keep steady, and clear of the beautiful stars.

"You didn't give *me* much room," grumbled the moon as he kissed her. "I have had a dull time of it behind your backs, and now I'm going to bed."

The cloud angel stood waiting the return of her regiment with a smile on her patient face, and as she held out a hand to steady the baby cloud as he reached the clouds' great home, wondered to see such a shadow on the fleecy robe of grey.

"What is the matter, my child, are you quite worn out with your journey?"

"My heart is so very sad with the woes of the earth beneath and the unfinished lives of men."

"Only our own Great Master even sees the whole life; it is but a few stray bits that shew to the world at large, each works out a portion of the design, that forms in the end a perfect whole. Now hurry to rest, the others are close behind. Be content, my child, you see such a little way. Remember the Lord of All holds the clouds and the winds in the hollow of His hand, and He doeth all things well!"

ON THE SPUR OF THE MOMENT

A Tale of a Rhine City

Heart and Hand, Volume 91, November 1896.

> "So, if unprejudic'd you scan
> The goings of this clock-work man;
> You find a hundred movements made
> By fine devices in his head."
>
> —Prior.

I T was very hot in Coblentz and Ehrenbreitstein—86° in the shade day after day—whilst in the sun the heat was almost unbearable, and unless obliged to venture forth on business, or other imperative claims, most of the well-to-do folk reserved themselves for the cool of the evening, and the favourite promenade of the well-known Bridge of Boats. The streets in such heat were none too savoury, and the pavements struck hot to the feet of the tired pedestrians. The flies buzzed languidly in the vapour mists that hung over the old town; dogs with hanging tongues and panting sides occupied the few shady corners.

Crossing the Platz one evening as the clocks were striking six came a slender girl, who threaded her way almost mechanically, so little heed did she appear to give to her steps. Indeed, more than once she jostled against a passer-by, simply by forgetting abroad she should pass on the left side instead of the English right.

At last she reached the poorer part of the town, and stopping at one of the tall, dismal-looking houses—all of which, in this neighbourhood, looked shabby and dull—made her way slowly up the dirty, common staircase. Flight after flight she passed by, until at last she reached the attic story, with its sloping, high-pitched gables: these outside, with their picturesque red tiles, all weather-stained and tinted, did their utmost to enliven the street, but inside, the rooms they covered were dark, and owing to this, and the sloping roofs, the rents of these top attics were very moderate, not to say cheap.

Only three small rooms all told, but clean and tidy as soap and brush could make them. Opening the middle door of the three, Ethel Charlton advanced gently into the tiny salon—workshop, kitchen, all combined—that represented home for her and her brother Arthur, who, when she entered, was lying asleep on a chintz-covered couch close to the open window. The sister was thin and delicate-looking, but beside the brother she appeared strong and robust.

Tears filled her eyes as she noted his fragile, worn aspect; then as her glance travelled round the room, and fell on the tokens of his daily work, she clenched her hands tight and muttered, "I hate the thing, *that* I do!" and she shot an angry glance at a tall clock case that took up a very large space of the room. Strewn about on a rough table in the window were springs of various kinds and sizes, coils of wire, chains, cylinders, wheels and weights.

The temper died out from the girl's face as suddenly as it had flared up; she sat wearily down on a low seat close to her brother's couch, and thought of the past and present, and the unknown future. Ethel and Arthur Charlton were the children of a well-known banker, senior in an old-established firm. The father died in the assurance that his motherless children were well provided for, since, though the son's health forbade his taking an active share in the business of the bank, by the terms of his father's will he came in for considerable profits as a sleeping partner. Asthma, that insidious foe, held him in her cruel grasp, but medical authorities on the subject held firmly to the belief that, given certain favourable conditions, in the course of years the probability was great that he would outlive his distressing ailment, yet for some years he was positively forbidden to winter in England.

The father died suddenly, early in October, and before November was a week old the brother and sister had taken up their winter quarters at St. Moritz, in the Engadine.

Mr. Charlton's papers were quite in order, leaving by will all he possessed, with the exception of a few legacies, between his children. Failing them, the money passed away to the orphan son of a distant cousin, a ward of Mr. Charlton's, who had been brought up with his own children, and whose greatest wish was to become the son in reality that he had practically been ever since he could remember.

Before he sailed for India to fill the post in a well-known bank that had been considered a good opening for him, Carl Melville had spoken to Mr. Charlton, and was sadly upset when the old man shook his head, and said it would not do.

"It is but a boy and girl fancy; such things rarely answer. Go out into the world and forget the child. You have your way to make. I feel no doubt you will climb well up life's ladder; at present remember you are only on the bottom rung. Ethel will have ample means; she is barely seventeen, too young to know her own mind. In the years to come, if you feel the same, and she is free, come back and ask her again. Believe me when I say I would rather give her to you than to any one else."

The young man had grown very grave as his guardian spoke, but he accepted the decision as final, and simply saying, "No other wife will I have," went off to finish his packing, and make the last the last arrangements required for a lengthy absence abroad.

He sailed away to the golden East with youth and hope beside him, and a dream of a happy future that kept him safe from evil and vice, and spurred him on, ever on, up the steep steps of the ladder of life.

Five years later came Mr. Charlton's death. Up to that date news from Carl had come regularly, after that the intervals between letters grew longer, and now eight years had passed since young Melville had gone abroad, and no tidings had reached his friends for over eighteen months. They hardly knew what to think or believe, though still clinging to the hope that the letters had been lost owing to their frequent wanderings.

*　　　*　　　*　　　*　　　*　　　*

The executors had barely finished winding up the last of Mr. Charlton's business, when one day a whisper, faint and low, began to circulate in the City. Men spoke it with cautious gestures and watchful eyes, and presently all the whispers joined together in an ever-increasing murmur that spread wider and wider, like circles caused by a stone thrown into calm water. The bolt fell with sudden, awful force on those beyond the circles' reach, at home and abroad.

The Spindle Bank had stopped payment! One of the partners had been speculating, and *here* was the result.

The smash was complete: one halfpenny in the pound was all that the creditors ever saw of their money again.

Of all on whom the blow fell, none were more concerned than Arthur and Ethel Charlton; all they possessed was gone, and gone for ever!

The sun was shining gaily when the tidings reached them, and in that sudden dislike to a place where trouble and sorrow have fallen on us so many feel, they left St. Moritz that very day for a cheaper, less well-known resort, where they could think out the problem of the future, and face the puzzle of ways and means. The money they had with them represented all their capital; neither could bear to be dependent on other folk's charity. Relations, they had none, except poor ones; their father had always been considered *the* rich man of the family. It was very hard for Arthur Charlton to be obliged to allow his sister to go out teaching, whilst he remained inactive at home; but by turning his skilful fingers to work on mechanical toys, little figures, musical clocks, worked with springs, he soon became so dextrous and clever with his puppets that they found a ready sale at the foreign toy shops. After the percentage was paid his profits were not large, still he gave his full share towards the current expenses, and in spite of constant attacks of his old foe, had never yet been a drag upon his sister.

A drag! What was he not to her! How could she have faced the weary life she led without the memory of that patient man waiting always for her return with a smile of greeting on the lips that grew whiter every day?

Two years ago she had been offered a better post as English teacher in one of the many schools that flourish at Coblentz, and leaving, not without regret, the little village of Campfer, they had moved into their present quarters. Hardly had they been established a week when one day going home a huge placard caught Ethel's eye; she soon mastered its contents. It was a proclamation from the Burgomaster of Niedrichstein offering a handsome prize in money for the best mechanical clock suitable for their town hall.

The design must be original; ample time was given: the clocks would be judged in the Saal at Coblentz the last day of July, 18—, that day two years.

The successful candidate would have rooms apportioned him close to the clock tower of Niedrichstein for the rest of his life, or as long as he cared to occupy them, and receive a fixed salary for keeping the clock in perfect order.

It was a long-felt want in this old town on the Moselle, and fired by ambition the townspeople were determined to have something quite out of the common.

The competition was open to any one. The judges would be carefully selected and quite uninterested.

Ethel's feet carried her swiftly home, hot though the day was; she was so breathless when she arrived in the tiny salon speech was impossible. When at last in jerks she got out her tidings, Arthur's excitement fully kept hers in countenance; nothing would serve but that he must read the poster for himself. So off they set, and when they returned Arthur's mind was fully made up to compete for the clock prize. As it would be the largest piece of mechanical work he had tried, he was very diffident about succeeding. Plans were drawn that night—his head seemed full of designs—and neither brother nor sister could think of anything else.

At that time there was only one clock-maker of any repute in Coblentz, and between him and Arthur a certain coolness had sprung up, for this reason—several of Charlton's mechanical effects in carved clocks and such like had been most unscrupulously pirated by the man Schmidt, to whom, on first coming to Coblentz, Arthur had been in the habit of mentioning his new designs. It was an unpleasant shock to him to find these ideas boldly carried out in a rough-and-ready style and offered for sale in the clock-maker's window before *he* had elaborated and delicately worked out his plans to the finish he considered necessary to do them justice. It was not, therefore, to be wondered at that on entering for the clock competition, both brother and sister decided on being close as wax to *all* outsiders.

It was noticeable about this time how frequently Schmidt found it convenient to appear suddenly in the Charltons' quarters, always with some question to be referred to Arthur, whilst his beady black eyes were here—there—everywhere, trying to see more than was apparent. These visits got so frequent at length, and Arthur so fidgeted by them, that at last he hit upon the expedient of saying he could only receive visitors between 5 and 6 p.m., this being his resting hour. Schmidt was furious, and it was an open secret that he owed the young Englishman a heavy grudge, which he had vowed to pay, sooner or later.

The evening our story opens on was two days before the trial of the clocks. Next day, all were to take their places in the Saal for the private inspection.

*   *   *   *   *   *

Tired of her own thoughts Ethel took up a book from a table, and was deep in its contents when her brother opened his eyes.

"What have you got there? You seem quite absorbed."

"Only that old piece, 'Curfew shall not ring to-night';[18] how could that girl do it! Why, I should have turned giddy and fallen at once, or died of fright before I reached the clapper! Do you think she did do it, Arthur?"

"I suppose so; stranger things have been done before to-day. Desperation makes timid folks brave when their hearts are concerned; anyway, the idea is beautiful."

"I know that *I* could never do anything grand like that, not even for you. Do you feel fit for a stroll to-night, Arthur? The clock is done"—a cloud fell over her face—"and *at last* you can think of me!"

The jealous words would out; they gave a key to the bitter feelings with which for many a long month Ethel had regarded her

---

[18] The poem by Rose Hartwick Thorpe (set in the 17th century). Bessie's lover has been sentenced to die when the curfew bell rings, so she climbs the bell tower, risking her life, to stop the bell from ringing.

brother's work. At first her interest had been so keen, the little help she could render gladly given, and then as she saw her brother absorbed more and more in working out his ideas, toiling far beyond his slight strength, a feeling akin to hatred grew and strengthened day by day against the unoffending clock.

"Child, you are never last—right well you know it. But for your sake should I have cared to compete at all? You are tired with the heat; we will go on the Bridge, and then you'll get cool and rested again. To-night you know you are to see the grand work as a complete whole!"

After tea the pair strolled down to the old Bridge of Boats, and watched the dusk creeping up, the railway bridge in the distance, over which the trains like fiery serpents swept frequently with a very weird effect, the stars coming out, and the lights in the town shining forth. Small wonder that all who could made their way down to the Bridge!

The ripples of the Rhine as it slipped swiftly along, the coloured lights from the boats reflected in dazzling pathways over he glittering water, the frowning fortress right above, the silver sounds of bells and clocks carried forth on the still air, the soft strains of music from crowded casinos, the gentle kiss of the passing breeze, the quick step of smart soldiers in their well-fitting uniforms, all made a whole, soothing and refreshing alike to mind and body. The Charltons sat long in silence till an ominous gasp from Arthur aroused Ethel's fears, and made them turn homewards.

Arthur looked so ill and breathed so heavily before they reached their attic that Ethel's heart misgave her; he was in for another attack on the very eve of the competition! He cheered up, however, after a little rest, and had all the candles they possessed lighted to show off his treasured work. The door was locked, the machinery set in motion, and Ethel saw for the first time as a perfect whole what she had seen him busy at in bits for all those months.

"She was to judge as a stranger," he laughingly said, "and be sure she was not partial."

The top part of the clock represented an old latticed window with a sloping red-tiled roof and great projecting eaves. A weather-cock adorned the top; below the window came a quaint old dial with clear-cut numerals. The bottom part was carved to represent a tower in unstained linden wood, with little slits through which bits of the machinery could be faintly seen. A door at the back, fastening with a spring, permitted a full inspection of all the interior.

Tick—tock, tick—tock, the wheels revolve, the pendulum swings, the hands indicate twelve; and, at the first sound of a silver bell sounding in the roof above, the lattice window opens softly, the head and shoulders of a girl in costume appears, a hand drops over the window-ledge as if in signal, and down fly twelve snow-white pigeons to a given ledge on the tower beneath, above which apparently grow four strong trails of passion flowers—the first in leaf, the second in bud, the third in flower, and the fourth in fruit. Then figure, hand, birds, and creepers vanish again as the twelve bells above end their triumphant peal.

The finish of the whole looked perfect—at all events, in Ethel's eyes. The wire wheels on which the birds appeared were so slight they were almost invisible, though there were so many of them; the number of pigeons that flew down being regulated by the hour, as were the bells, and, of course, the length of time the head and hand remained, before the window closed. The machinery of each part was quite independent of the rest, Arthur explained, so that if one set got out of gear the remainder would go on without.

"It is the first time I have worked on this plan," he said. "Before, in my attempts, if one spring snapped, or slipped, *everything* came to a standstill; here at pleasure the figure can be removed, the birds suspended, or the bells unhung, without the least damage to the clock. Come and stand at the back, Ethel, and see hoe simple it is."

Arthur detached the figure's spring to show her. "You seem all her weights are at the base, and I have made her just your weight. I won't lift her off the platform now, for I don't feel up to putting her back again. There is a lot of spare room in the bottom of the tower, only a little occupied by the birds in the four slits, who come out to mark the quarters with the creepers. You notice them? They each appear in turn, and then, as a perfect whole, fall below the shelf when the hour strikes. You have seen it all; do you approve?"

"It is beautiful; it *must* take the prize, Arthur! I heard by accident Emilie Schmidt talking of her father's clock to-day, and I am sure she said something about Noah's Ark. Surely he has not copied your toy?"

A flush rose on Arthur's thin face. "If he has, Ethel, mine was not arranged for a clock; though, now you mention it, the idea would work out well."

"It would be *yours*, not his!"

"Mine as a toy only, not as a clock; I couldn't object, and if I could I wouldn't. See how careful I am; I have two keys—if I lose one, it matters not, there is yet another. The locks are so old they'd be a job to pick, and they will *only* unlock from the outside; they shut with a spring."

Next day the clocks were set up in their positions in the Saal for the judges to examine the works privately. One pass was given to each of the competitors, who were allowed entrance as often as they chose, to wind up their respective clocks—and all was ready.

Arthur managed to walk to the fine old room, where all the clocks stood ranged in order on a platform roped off from the body of the Saal. He was one amongst twenty qualified competitors, some of them well-known mechanicians. No names were allowed to be put on the clocks themselves, that the judges might be quite unbiased; but a list of those competing was suspended on the wall, and Arthur saw he was down as the only Englishman on the list.

Schmidt's clock was easily distinguishable, even if his sister had not given him the clue; he saw enough outside to convince him his rival had kept as close to the working of his own toy as he possibly could to fit in with the clock works.

As he went out into the street again his sister joined him on her way home, which they had nearly reached when Schmidt passed them hurriedly, with surely a smirk of triumph on his face. Was he so sure of winning already?

Arthur sank into a seat exhausted, with a choking fit upon him, directly they reached their own rooms, but his eye noted first the *second clock key* was gone!

One was in his pocket, the other—where?

He was almost too ill to think, but of what use to throw suspicion *now* upon any one? Make a fuss, foreigner as he was, and most likely his name would be erased from the list at once, and with his other key he was safe.

Before night came he was in the grasp of one of his worst attacks; the suffering was so distressing, Ethel was quite frightened. He had fought it down for days, now it took revenge. In vain the usual remedies were tried, no relief was gained until the last, when the light of another day lit up the dark old rooms, under their high-tiled roofs, he had fallen into an uneasy dose. Slowly the clock ticked round, the hours sped on, and when ten clear strokes cut through the hot, still air outside, Arthur awoke with a start, and stared dreamily round him.

"Shall I ask Schmidt to wind up your clock for you, Arthur? The judges begin at eleven."

"Not Schmidt," he gasped out; "you do it, Ethel, yourself. Take my pass and key, turn it seven times, mind, and you need not say I am ill. Don't hurry back again; stay and see the clocks until your school hour. I shall sleep, and want nothing for hours. Good-bye, dear; you don't mind doing it for me, Ethel? I can't trust any one else."

"Except for leaving you," she answered. "I am glad to do it. I know I have been very nasty about the clock, and I am sorry."

"Hurry, dear; there goes the quarter-past; you won't be there any too soon."

Ethel was quickly off, with the key clutched tight in her hand. When she arrived at the Saal the place was empty, and all the clocks ticking away at a quarter to eleven.

All! except *the* one that mattered so much to them.

An old man lifted the barrier for her on her showing the pass—the proper doorkeeper was putting on his best coat, and would be back in a minute. She hurried up the long room, mounted the platform, and with trembling fingers inserted the key in the quaint old lock, and pulled the door open. The same key wound the clock up.

Ethel started in dismay when she saw the figure had been disconnected and lifted down from its platform, and now lay a dead weight in the bottom of the tower.

What could *she* do?

There was no time to fetch any one to replace the figure, even if she had understood the springs sufficiently, which she did not, to connect them again. Only ten minutes and the judges would arrive!

*   *   *   *   *   *

The committee entered the room, and took up their position in the front row of seats facing the platform, at a good distance back from the clocks, the better to judge of their several effects. The time for the decision had been carefully selected: to begin at 11 a.m., and last till past 12 noon, to give all the mechanism fair play. It would take too long to enumerate the performances, some with figures, animals, ships, flowers, and all sorts of devices.

There was a great shout of admiration when the latticed window sprang open, the figure appeared, the pigeons flew down and up again, the beautiful creeper laden now with its lovely flowers sank down behind the ledge into the tower again.

Then a loud roar of laughter filled the room from end to end, caused by the procession of Noah's Ark, struggling bravely up their inclined plane into the Ark above. There was an unsteadiness about some of the little animals that hardly looked as if they would stand another march at 12 o'clock without getting disorganized. That time alone would prove. The judges made copious notes; the buzz got louder and louder.

Just before 12 struck out, Schmidt took up his position right facing Arthur's clock, shoulder to shoulder with a tall, fair-haired Englishman, who had accompanied the judges into the room, but had been so busy talking to a friend at the bottom of the room, he had paid little heed to the performances taking place. Both men started in surprise when the window opened, and the figure showed once more. Oh, the burst of applause that rang around on the flight of the white-plumed birds!

Schmidt jumped so violently, he shook his companion, who

265

was gazing, as if petrified, at the face in the window. Glancing in surprise at the man, he saw such a look of baffled rage on his face, he felt surprised, though in his haste to question his neighbour on the clockmaker's name, he forgot until afterwards the man's sinister look.

"How can *I* tell you," he growled; "he's no friend of mine; mayhap he hails from Köln: some two years ago, there was a clever chap lived there who made toys."

The light of intense pleasure shone in the stranger's face. "What is his name; where is a list?"

He spoke too late; the black-browed man moved away, unaware that from a hole in his pocket an old-looking key had dropped just at his questioner's feet. Naturally the Englishman looked round for the man, and not seeing him, pocketed the key for the present. The crowd in the room were too absorbed to notice that a man with beady black eyes edged quietly up to the list and wrote "Köln" after Arthur's name, "Coblentz" after his own.

Shouts of derisive laughter now arose as the poor animals of Noah's Ark struggled bravely to keep their balance down their sloping plane; the upward march was beyond them. Slower and slower the springs worked in jerks, and finally failed altogether, leaving the giraffes with astonished air, lions and tigers in silent rage, outside the Ark of refuge.

"Gimcrack!"[19] hissed the crowd; "*we* want something better than *that*, indeed. Why, the thing's only half made!"

The judges retired to consider their verdict together, carefully weighing the merits of the various clocks. A loud bell was rung, and the crier announced in his strident voice that the judges considered

---

[19] Cheap, shoddy.

the clock representing "The Evening Meal" had fairly earned the prize, both for originality of design and careful workmanship. The maker would shortly be communicated with. Loud acclamations filled the Saal for some minutes, and then the crowds melted away, as they always do, and, except for the ticking of twenty clocks, silence prevailed.

* * * * * *

Arthur Charlton spent a lonely day; at first he expected his sister back shortly after twelve; but when she did not appear, he concluded she had gone straight to her school; the examinations were imminent, he knew, and at these times she was often kept until late in the evening; and going off in such a bustle in the morning, she had probably forgotten to tell him she would be detained. Propped high by pillows, he dozed again and again, and it was quite 8 p.m. before he roused up fully, and began to listen for Ethel's footstep. At last the stairs creaked, but it was a man's voice that asked for admittance outside, and a man's tall form with sparkling eyes and outstretched hand that shortly stood beside his boyhood's friend.

"Arthur!"—"Carl!"—came simultaneously, and the hands joined in a long, close clasp! Then in brief sentences each learnt the story of the vanished years—how prosperity and esteem followed the absentee, whilst dark clouds of sorrow and trouble had fallen on the other's fragile shoulders.

Carl had written frequently with no replies, and in his various moves he could but conclude that his letters had been lost. The last news he had received after the tidings of his guardian's death was in a letter from Arthur, in which he mentioned some musical toys he was busy over—for amusement, Melville supposed. Uneasy beyond measure at last, at the long silence, he had applied for his carefully hoarded leave, and come back to hunt his cousins out.

It was no easy matter, but at last he found a clue that led him to Germany. He arrived at an uncle's at Bonn, his mother's brother-in-law, the day before the clock trial, and as his uncle was a judge in the competition, had accompanied him to Coblentz, where the trail seemed very hot when *Ethel's* face looked out at him from the clock's latticed window. In vain he questioned right and left; either he pronounced the name differently to the German, or he had made inquiries of strangers, like himself. The hint about "Köln" was the best he could gather. First assuring himself that neither brother nor sister was presently in the crowd, he started immediately for Köln, and after a weary hunt was directed back again to the Elisabeten Strasse at Coblentz. In a local paper in the train he read Arthur's name as prize-winner, and a notice that the clocks would remain locked up until the early morning of the second day, when, the Saal being required for a concert, the workmen who were entrusted with the moving of all would commence their labour.

Arthur started up in surprise and pleasure, with flushed face and sparkling eyes, when he heard he had won the prize.

"Thank God!" he murmured; "that will be something if my ill health gets worse. We have often had short commons, old fellow; but now, if I never do another day's work, we shall not want. How late Ethel is; I wonder if she knows?"

"Ethel out alone at this hour? Why, Arthur, it's long after nine! Can't I fetch her? Where is she?"

"Oh! kept at her school in the Charlotten Strasse, No. 40. You'll meet her half-way."

Mme Ibach herself came down to speak to the impatient young Englishman, who *would* stick to his belief that Fraüline Charlton was in her house. She had to repeat several times that she was at Rudisheim before she could half convince him.

"I sent a note round to her at 10 a.m. to tell her that little Else had been taken dangerously ill, and did nothing but call for her. The parents are half distracted, and I begged Fraüline to go at once, and remain all night. There is no train now until the morning; as she is not at home, of course she has kindly stayed; indeed, it is such a serious case, I doubt her being there for days, but of course she will write to her brother." Carl returned and told his friend.

"I wonder she did not tell me," said Arthur, as he turned uneasily on his pillows. "But there was only a minute before she had to fly to wind the clock: perhaps it slipped her memory, or she may have sent back a message by some untrustworthy person—Schmidt, perhaps. Anyhow, we'll hear to-morrow."

"I can look after you, Arthur, and the couch in the salon will make me a better bed than I've often had, I can tell you."

No letter next morning puzzled both men, and Carl would have taken the train at once for Rudisheim, only Arthur was so ill he feared to leave him, and it was not until late in the evening that Carl consented to go as far as the Saal, and disconnect the springs of the clock in readiness for its journey to Niedrichstein.

"There are little catches at the sides to hold them firm; they would get bent if left hung as they are, and please give this note to the porter in charge; he will see to the moving for me."

"All right, give me your key."

"I can't," said Arthur, "I never thought of that; Ethel has it, and the Saal will shut in an hour!"

"I picked up this, yesterday," said Carl, fishing a quaint old key up from his pocket. "Perhaps it will serve your turn?"

"Why! it's my marked duplicate! Hurry, Carl, and I'll tell you about it on your return."

An old woman admitted Carl to the Staal, on his showing the pass, but nothing would induce her to hold him a light.

"Not she indeed; them sort of puppets were none too canny. When it came to their speaking——Well! she for one was not going to stay and listen. A candle he should have, and welcome, but he'd have to manage by himself."

Carl smiled at the old dame's queer fancy, and whistling softly, unlocked Arthur's clock case.

What is THIS that makes him start back in sudden fright, whilst a thick stream of grease runs gaily down his coat!

A white, motionless figure of a living woman, leaning unconscious against the clock case, and *that* woman the one in all the world for him! Shocked and startled, he lifted the slight figure out of her strange prison, and laid her gently down on the platform. Great was his relief when in a few minutes the eyes slowly opened, and he saw her wondering glance around, and heard his own name spoken in a faint whisper. It was no time to explain matters; lifting her again in his strong arms, he carried her straight out to a passing fly, and in a very few minutes she was lying on the old couch in the little salon, while Arthur and he waited on her anxiously. The sound of the heavy steps on the stairs had brought Arthur out to meet them, and neither would allow her to speak until she had taken some of the strong broth which had been sent in for Arthur from a neighbouring restaurant.

Leaving the brother and sister together, Carl hurried back to the Saal, to unhang the springs and relock the clock. On his return Ethel was able to explain how she got shut inside the clock case. When finding she had no time to have the proper figure replaced, she had decided on taking its place, quite aware if she did so she would be obliged to remain a prisoner at all events for many hours.

She remembered the trick of keeping her eyes from winking, but found holding her breath long enough for the performance a difficult matter; however, the fear of failure made her brave. At dusk, on the last evening, she had spoken to the old woman and asked for some water, but the frightened creature had fled in a hurry, and no one had been in that day, to her knowledge, until Carl came.

"I slept a long time," she said; "the place was so hot, and all the buzzing about of the machinery made me drowsy. If it had not been for worrying about Arthur, the time would not have seemed so long; and, as by accident, I had a new box of his jujubes in my pocket,[20] the thirst was not unbearable. To think that Arthur really has the prize, and that Carl has come home again!"

*   *   *   *   *   *

L'ENVOI

There are several little children in a happy English home who, crowding round their Uncle Arthur on a winter's evening, love to hear his oft-told tale—how long ago he won a beautiful clock prize—how mother had pretended to be a machine, and how father found her inside the clock case when he came to unfasten the springs.

---

[20] A gummy candy drop.

IN THE DAYS OF THE CAGOTS

Belgravia, Volume 91, November 1896.

"MARGOT"

"Henri, my friend, what can I do for you?"

"Is not the child home yet? I like not her being out so late; see how the mists are sweeping down the mountain's sides and the wail in the wind tells of storms at hand."

"Nay, nay, good man, it is unlike you to feel nervous; any moment the child may come. Very likely François will see her home; she had a message for his mother from me, you remember."

The old man gave a long, tired sigh, whilst his once keen eyes peered from under his shaggy brows out through the cottage door to the sloping hillside beyond, and the hamlet down in the valley growing faint and dim in the twilight shades.

Very lonely would folks have thought that low, weather-beaten home perched on one of the steep slopes of the Hautes Pyrénées. Ah! but what toil and patience, time and self-denial had gone to build the rough, thick walls, how perfect had the building seemed when in the long ago of youth's hey-day, that feeble old man had led, with springing step and dancing eyes, his wife of but a day into their new joint home. With what pride had been displayed all his grand contrivances, *here* a cleared potato patch, *there* a brood of chickens! How bright the living-room looked with its red-tiled floor and whitened walls, whilst from the ceiling's hooks hung quite a supply of bacon and ham, with dried herbs and onions, presents in kind from many friends. The blue smoke curled picturesquely heaven-wards, and the kettle sang its song of welcome, as one thing after another came before the proud mistress's eyes!

"Who are our nearest neighbours?" asked she, and the bright eyes only looked amused when Henri answered:

" 'The Cagots' for aught I know;[21] thou art sure it will not be too lonely for thee?"

"With *you*, my friend, nay, nay, name it not." That was in the long ago, how stands the picture of to-day?

A gentle-faced old woman, with her red hood worn over her snowy cap, and her brown, wrinkled hands busy with her distaff. Except for the wear and tear of Time, the cottage was little altered, spotlessly clean as of yore, but with no signs of luxury anywhere. How could there be when it needed steady, constant labour on the two women's part to keep the wolf from the door?

When the son of the house had set up for himself twenty years agone, the father was only in his prime, a trusted labourer on a comfortable farm. All went well in the light of prosperity until one awful night, when in the wild uproar a baby girl first saw the light at the cost of the mother's life!

Out from his happy home rushed forth the heartbroken husband and father, not to be stopped or stayed by any device of man. Alone with his God on the mountains, in the hour of his greatest need; for, when two days later, his father and friends at last found him, he had fallen asleep in the snow, kneeling as if in prayer. That sight broke Henri down, worn out, as he was, with the suspense and agony of trying to find him sooner, baffled again and again by the mists and fine falling snow. He had wandered so far away, with his blood at fiery heat and his head quite dazed by grief, it was a wonder indeed they found him at all before the spring.

---

21 A class of French outcasts who lived in the West Pyrenees.

Utterly crippled by rheumatism, from that day forward poor Henri Duclos had to sit aside and see the burden of life fall with all its weight on his wife's shoulders alone. Her spinning was now their mainstay, where before she had done it just in her leisure, or when some extra call arose. For long his trial had seemed more than his manhood could bear, but at last, in the long quiet evenings, in the lisping voice of the child he learnt of the Great Father's care, who chooses for each his cross. The tears ran unchecked down his furrowed face as he called to Margot to come near, and begged her with all his strength to forgive him the extra burden he had laid on her by his constant and bitter grumbles. Woman-like, she tried to stop him, whilst the child's soft little hands patted the twisted fingers, and the baby voice whispered low, "Grandpère is werry sorry he was coss; kiss him and make him well!"

So by long and slow degrees Henri fought his fight, and tried to bear the cruel grinding pain that often never ceased day or night without one bitter word, though ever and again poor Nature wrung a low moan from his that made his wife's heart ache. She never left him for long together, just once a year going down to the sheltered hamlet below, where in a quiet corner two low mounds of earth held sacred for her!

The Curé was very kind,[22] and paid them frequent visits, but now *he* was getting old, and his failing steps found the steep zig-zags that wound and wound up the slopes to their door, a difficult walk for him, and his calls could be but seldom. Marie herself was reckoned the village beauty, with her curling raven hair and snowy skin, and proud indeed was François, the cobbler's son, when he could proclaim aloud, the Mountain Maid was his!

---

[22] The parish priest.

"If the Cagots leave her for you," laughed a thoughtless youth, and indeed of late this outlawed tribe had become very troublesome. Sweeping down from their mountain fastnesses, they carried all before them, robbing the lonely traveller, raiding the peaceful cattle, trampling down the grain here, there, and everywhere, of late the pirate band grew dreaded. In many and many a part, darker crimes hung round their path, so that the name alone was a household word for terror!

The little old church in the hamlet had on its southern side an old arched-doorway with its holy water stoop, built in the far back ages when the tradition of leprosy clung to the Cagot race. Never in the memory of the oldest inhabitant had that rusty lock been turned, or the creaking, straining wood yielded to the outlaw's hand.

*   *   *   *   *   *

At last cheerful voices sounded on the listening ears, and out from the gathering mist Marie and François came gaily in, hand in hand.

Very far would anyone search before they found a fairer face than the girl's, as François fully recognised as she told of her expedition and showed her purchases.

"What do you think, grandmère, François' nose is quite out of joint, he is very jealous already! I was just passing the opening of the Vigneron Pass, when I heard such a clatter behind me I jumped up a bank by the path, and by me like a flash rode at full speed four men—one, the leader I suppose, bent low on his horse's neck the better to see my face, and kept his head turned over his shoulder even after he passed, till his comrades roared with laughter, and made some joke or other. 'So I will,' was his answer back—all I could understand, and they were out of sight. Such a handsome fellow too, with a long gold chain slung round him and a scarlet cloak thrown back. François' mother looked so grave when I told her my fine tale, that she said of her own accord just for this once,

François must see me home, and all the way up when breath would permit, I have been praising that good-looking man to him!"

François laughed, not *quite* light-heartedly, but then had his news to give!

A stranger passing through the hamlet a few days back had given so large an order to the young man's employer, with promises of further commissions to come, that he had been given his expected rise in wages at once, and now came emboldened to ask if he and Marie might not be permitted to marry immediately; they had only been waiting for his promotion, and he could not bear to think of them, in their long, cold winter's evenings, all alone on the mountain side, without a strong man near!

So they weighed the pros and cons, and before François left them, to run down with light heart the winding way, it was settled in three weeks' time, a quiet wedding should take place in the hamlet below, and the young couple begin their married life in the weather-beaten hut above.

François was considered quite a proficient on the flageolet,[23] in great requisition at all merry-makings, and Marie would not allow him to say "Adieu" until he had treated them as usual to her favourite air "Sauve Marie."

Busy indeed had the women now to be, but never too busy for Marie to have long quiet chats with her grandfather in the glow of the cheerful fire, and as his loving gaze rested long on her face, he thanked God in his heart that the child could still be a part of his home—not wander far away, as many a village lass must when she marries out of her clan, so to say.

*   *   *   *   *   *

---

[23] A wind instrument related to the recorder.

Up in the rocky fastness where the Cagots had fixed their temporary home, all was noise and revelry. Disorder reigned supreme, rich stuffs thrown here and there, soiled and dragged underfoot, broken glasses in plenty lying on the dirty floor—weapons of every device strewn heedlessly round, made up a total of discomfort hardly describable.

Down in the loathsome dungeons were several of the plundered travellers, waiting their tyrants' pleasure, in fear and dread of their lives.

Of the women who moved about, in kindness we will say that, rough and degraded though their lot, yet some few amongst them were not yet actually brutalized, though well on that same high-road.

The chiefs of the little band had lingered long over their wine, bragging of feats performed, and boasting of others to come, then in pure malice they laughed and joked with the captain on the time he took for his frolic, for it was an open secret that he had vowed solemnly on his sword that ere the moon should change the Mountain Maid should be his!

The red flush mounted higher on the young man's dark face, as he listened to all the jibes, and then when his fevered blood could brook no further word, he banged his fist on the wooden table, until the glasses rang again, and vowed to keep his oath or die!

Sadly the moon in her last quarter looked in on the noisy scene— naught but vengeance, strife and sin, and every man's hand against his brother. A reckless and desperate band, on whom no laws of God or man were binding.

*   *   *   *   *   *

Marie was hurrying home later than she wished to be, but everything had conspired to hinder her, and she had so much to do, it was hopeless to think she could save time to come down again now before her marriage only a few days off. Everyone was so kind that even when her errands were done, friendly greetings stopped her on all sides, and only when she was free of the village did she realise how late she was, and how fast the evening was closing in. Misty too, for the peaks of the mountains were already dim, and white vapours rising from the ground. Suddenly, she started in fright, for out of the earth as it seemed a dark figure rose, and a whistle, clear and shrill, went echoing up the heights.

All in a minute something thick and soft was wrapped over her head and form, she was swung clear from the ground, and held in a man's strong arm whilst, from the motion beneath her, she knew she was on a horse, urged to its utmost speed. In vain to scream for aid, or try to free her arms, that thick muffling wrap choked the first, and prevented the second, whilst the vice-like clasp of the arm round her, might have been a bar of iron, for all the feel to her.

Thoughts of her home, grand-parents and François, swept in a wave over her heart, the fear and dread of the present swallowing all else up. Perhaps it was the rapid pace as much as anything that finally overcame her, for when at last in a lather from the speed at which he had struggled upwards, the horse reached the end of the journey, and with a shout of triumph the brigand chief called on all to see how *he* had kept his word, the maiden was quite insensible when they freed her from the muffling wrap.

The *one* pure thing in all that haunt of evil, how out of place she looked. With the fierce, cruel faces round, and the signs of unholy living on every side.

Her swoon was long and deep, and when all had tried to bring her to and failed, one of the older women said she must be put to bed at once that stronger measures might be used.

Far up in a turret chamber her captor laid her down, and ordered the women to bestir themselves, for should she not recover, on them would he wreak his vengeance.

A little soft cloudlet, only a baby thing, floated close to the window just in the moon's bright track and full on the maiden's face rested the heavenly light. With a quivering sigh and a shudder the eye-lids gently opened, and Marie gazed around!

Oh! the coarse bad look of the women about her, their clothes untidy, dirty, torn, their brutal language, their breath smelling of powerful spirits as they scoffed and jeered at the girl as only such creatures can.

Almost frightened to death, she watched them as if fascinated when suddenly up from below an awful clamour arose. Men with their evil passions let loose, snatched up the handiest weapon, and bloodshed of course ensued. Down from the turret chamber the women hurried, above all things anxious not to miss their share of venting their private grievances, and paying off old scores.

Left to herself at length, Marie grew somewhat calmer, and the cold touch of the night wind, blowing in from the open casement, soothed her fevered brain. The mists had cleared off wonderfully, and in the light of the moon, though her immediate surroundings were unknown to her, the sleeping faces on the higher mountains that guarded her own dear valley, spoke in their quiet grandeur of the Great Creator's power, and the watchful Eye of God that never slumbers nor sleeps!

*   *   *   *   *   *

In the cottage home in the valley, grief and dismay reigned supreme when the darkness fell around and no Marie crossed the threshold. What had become of the child, was ever the constant word. In vain they tried to cheat themselves into believing that the mists had prevented her starting homewards; never had such a thing occurred before, and they knew not what to make of it. The old woman could not leave poor Henri, and neighbours they had none! Never had a night seemed so endless, as sleepless and watchful beside the peat fire, they counted the hours strike.

As soon as it grew light Margot dressed up warmly, and taking her husband's stick, with slow and careful steps made her toilsome way down the mountain side. With aching limbs, and a heavy heart she reached the curé's house and asked if he knew aught of Marie? Quickly the tidings flew that the Mountain Maid was missing.

François was half beside himself, whilst anxious questions as to when and where she had last been seen, spread from tongue to tongue.

Then all in a minute someone breathed the word *Cagots!* and of a sudden the rumour took hold and grew that of a very truth they had carried off the girl. It seemed the only possible solution, and alas! one that filled all with horror!

"I would rather know her dead than up in that stronghold of vice," faltered poor François forth, and there was none to say him nay; all felt indeed it had been better so.

Snow was falling fast when a sturdy band of willing men stood ready to start on their quest, and François took his flageolet, for he said the high wild notes carried well, and it would be comfort untold to Marie to know that friends were night. Not a trace could they find to give them even the right direction.

Three great passes led from their peaceful valley—which should they try the first?

Some of the older greybeards shook their heads sadly; it was folly and worse to try at all, with a snow-storm coming on, but the hot blood of youth, on fire with righteous wrath, was neither to be stopped or frighted, and with steady even footsteps they began the rugged ascent.

Off and on all day long the fine thick snow fell, and every hour the men found it more and more difficult to steer their way by their own rude landmarks, and when darkness began to steal around them, and not the faintest clue had they found, either of the missing maiden, or the Cagots' evil stronghold, all with the exception of François agreed there was only one thing possible to be done, namely, to retrace their steps, and with the light of another day search in a fresh direction.

François was very loth to turn backwards, but alone he was utterly powerless either to rescue his love, or punish the brigands, and so he also stumbled sadly along, noting how the snow was drifting, and what a heavy fall it had been.

Slowly and not without difficulty they gained their own valley in the darkness, and even then François went on up to the Duclos' hut to tell them of the fruitless quest.

The door was on the latch, and as his weary footstep crossed the threshold two pairs of eager eyes sought first his face, and then peered keenly into the gloom behind to catch, it might be, a glimpse of Marie's young slight figure!

Alas! alas, she was not there!

In wordless grief poor Margot rocked herself backwards and forwards, whilst her knotted, wrinkled hands trembled as if with the palsy. The old man had tried his best to keep brave through the hours of that endless day, but never had his helplessness so galled him, when his one great longing was to be searching—hunting— on the wild mountain's sides. He knew Marie so well, there were a hundred little tricks the child had, he *must* have found a clue. Lost— of course she was lost, nothing so very odd in *that*, after all, and as for anything worse, he would not even think of it, it was too black a thought. She would be in any minute now, and how he should scold her for the fright she had given them all!

"Margot! Margot! don't you hear her singing? Good child! I knew she'd come."

Once or twice did Margot and François rush wildly to the door, believing the old man's fancy that footsteps were drawing near, and then with the tears of age trickling slowly and painfully down her withered face, the poor woman realised Henri was not himself, and took to soothing him softly, as you would a factious child.

All the next day a storm raged; thunder, lightning, and snow preventing any search whatever, and the close of the week only found it possible for the men to get up the third and last pass, with very little hope of success to cheer them on their path.

The second pass had proved so very steep and difficult that no one riding could possibly have gone that way; it was a case of clambering over boulders and stones all the time, with excellent chances for breaking legs or having nasty falls. They had all objected to wasting their energy going up it, but François pleaded that what seemed to them so difficult, to a mad Cagot would be nothing, and looking in his thin, flushed face, and noting his miserable eyes, in silence at last the good fellows had given way, and against their better judgement toiled up over the rugged rocks.

The third pass was the usual one for leaving their peaceful valley, too easy and simple a way surely for robbers to patronise.

The snow still lay in drifts, and the ground glistened as if strewn with diamonds as the sun came out from the clouds and cheered the hearts of the searchers. It did something else also, for when in doubt and perplexity they gained the head of the pass, one of the men's quick eyes noticed a queer-looking black thing sticking up, left bare by the melting snow.

It was *the* clue they wanted; now they were on the road, for that was a clog of Marie's, of that they had no doubt. So the men straightened their doublets a bit, buckled their belts anew, and looked to their various weapons.

In spite of the clue, however, they must have wandered greatly out of the direct route by which Marie had been taken, for the sun had just said farewell, and the waiting sunset clouds were spreading their crimson and gold across the evening sky, when they came in sight of the great rough Cagot stronghold.

Nearer and nearer they marched to the wailing sound of the flageolet, but no one tried to stop them, the silence was unbroken. Was it a trick to catch them?—what could the meaning be?

*   *   *   *   *   *

Marie stood by her window gazing out on the mountains around; she had not an idea where she was, for not a familiar peak could she see; she might be close at home, or miles and miles away. Often her grandfather had told her when she was talking of the mountains near, that seen from the other side, she would not recognise one.

Day after day had dragged along with terror for the girl, for though in his daily visits she had so far made the Cagot captain keep the length of the room between them by saying if he approached her nearer with his hateful words or love, out of the window she would jump, and that on the very instant, how long she should keep him at bay she did not know, not for more than a few days, her heart told her, and then——? She was but a weak woman, but God would give her strength to do right—into the arms of His mercy, she should spring her dizzy height.

Dizzy indeed it was, on the edge of a steep ravine, but if it was her only path to Heaven, it must be the way for her. Day after day she stood by the casement with her hand clutching the frame, afraid to wander from it, for fear she should be surprised, and not have that one loophole of escape to fall back on. The women who came to visit her told her tales that made her blush with shame that man in his Maker's image could ever have fallen so low.

One curious fancy she had which grew stronger and stronger each day, that a soft little baby cloud, hovering close by her window, was her own Guardian Angel, sent by the God above to keep her from black despair and worse.

In the silence of the winter's night she stretched out her arms in the darkness and prayed to the Virgin Mother for aid, and to the cloud to keep close. "I shall jump into you then, dear friend, and you will take care of me."

Certain it is the cloud never left, it might indeed have been an angel guest sent to cheer her fainting soul, and it crept closer and closer to the girl and spread larger arms around.

All day long, sounds of unusual bustle and noise, and there always was a good bit, had reached poor Marie's ears, but now all was silent, not a whisper stirred the air. She knew quite well what had happened, for some of the women had gossipped.

The brigands were on the move to another lonely fortress; they had made this one too hot to hold them, avengers were on their back from many a valley near, and their wisest course was flight. The captain had given his orders; all were to be off at noon. He should remain until sunset, and then overtake them all.

Alone? Nay! Never!!! Adieu for the present; they should meet anon!

       *   *   *   *   *   *

Marie strained her ears—were her senses leaving her *now* in this awful hour?—Oh! Holy Mother of God, have mercy, keep her clear.

Surely it was *no* fancy that distant, soft wailing music, playing her favourite air; nearer, and clearer it sounded, but her straining eyes could see no moving forms, naught but the shrill high notes coming evidently nearer! Was it the angels harping, or life and hope for her? A heavy stumbling step on the stairs, a fall, a muttered oath, and Marie knew the worst——

He was drunk, hopelessly drunk, one glance at his bloodshot eyes revealed, and reckless and cruel beyond measure. In vain she cried to him to stop, or she would jump at once—he told her she had cried "wolf!" too often. *Now* was his hour of triumph, he lunged heavily towards her, his hand almost seized her shoulder, when there was a flash of something white springing into space, a waiting cloud closed round her, and Marie was safe for ever!

*   *   *   *   *   *

Up to the entrance gate the brave little band made their way unmolested, entered the hall, and searched through the rooms below. They stumbled over one man lying face downwards, at the foot of the stairs, with his neck broken by the fall, and all his sins upon his head.

Not a soul else in the place living or dead, but in a turret chamber a warm knitted hood, and a red peasant cloak François could have sworn to anywhere.

The cold wind blew in at the open casement, and tried to tell its tale, and when they looked from the window, with the sunset tints still lingering, they saw something white below in the ravine, that sent them rushing downwards like mad, and out to the steep decline.

But a little way down, lying on a sofa bed of moss, was the form of the girl they sought. Asleep for ever in God's good care, with her peaceful face turned to the heavens.

It needed great care to reach her, so precariously the sides of the ravine went down, but somehow they all gained her side, and on the mossy platform knelt down by her lifeless form!